EMISSARY

MELISSA MCSHANE

Night Harbor Publishing
Salt Lake City, UT

Chapter One

Zerafine had only a moment's warning before the ghost was upon her. A shout, a flicker of movement, and it enveloped her like a chilly whirlwind. *Seicorum* pebbles the size of large, rough marbles pelted her from all directions, stinging where they struck the bare skin of her hands and face, sheering away where they brushed her red robe. It was fortunate for everyone on the road that the ghost wasn't powerful enough to make more of the strange ore that gave a kind of physical form to its insubstantial body, but even more fortunate for them that Zerafine was there to draw its attention. Gerrard shouted something made unintelligible by the roar of the unearthly wind, but she pulled the heavy crimson hood over her head and all sounds faded to a hum. She felt surprise, but no fear; it was nothing she hadn't faced hundreds of times before.

From within the shielding folds of her hood she closed her eyes and drew three deep, cleansing breaths, felt her shoulders relax and her center of balance shift downward. She opened her heart's eye and saw the ghost in its true form, not as a violent hail of stone, but as a collection of memories emerging like shattered glass that now glowed with the white-blue light of a discorporate spirit. She called out to one, and it unfolded before her —

an infant, swaddled close and breathing a milk-scented sigh of contentment —

and golden symbols rose up within Zerafine and danced behind her eyelids; she chose one that spoke of home and hearth and traced it with her heart's eye. Then she spoke to the ghost in quiet tones like water over stone, reminding it of that soft bundle, of children running, of motherhood in all its stages, and as she spoke more memories came whirling in to connect to the first.

She pieced together the woman's life, soothing her, reminding her of who she had been. Mitela, her name was, and her final memories were of fire and agony so profound that her spirit lost the way to Atenas's court of judgment. Zerafine's efforts would help

1

her find it. More symbols, this time ones of release and relief from pain. She chose two and drew them in her mind: the crossed sticks of Ormus, god of travel, for safe journey; and the triple arch, for the gates to Atenas's realm.

With a final gust of wind, Mitela's ghost vanished. *Seicorum* ore rained down around Zerafine like hailstones, no longer propelled by the whirlwind of the ghost's desperate need to create a new body. She tried to stand, and stumbled before she realized she was already standing. Gerrard's huge hand wrapped around her upper arm, supporting her. "Steady on," he said, his voice muffled as if he were speaking from a great distance.

With the ghost's cold presence gone, Zerafine felt suddenly very warm. She swept her hood back with her free hand and shook her dark hair loose of its folds. She dashed away the tears she never remembered crying during a consolation. The afternoon sun beat down on her unprotected head, but a warm breeze stirred the air enough to cool her sweat-damp forehead.

All traffic on the dusty road had stopped. Two women had their hands full trying to control a horse that screamed and arched its back against its harness. Almost all the pedestrians had backed off the road into the tall summer-scorched grass, well away from Zerafine, though they appeared too fascinated to actually flee. Three men and one woman stood nearby, as still as trees rooted to the spot. One of the men balanced a rusty metal box, about three feet long and one foot deep, on his shoulder. Its outer door hung open, revealing the inner mesh too fine to allow *seicorum* to pass through. A ghost trap. And four hunters. They wouldn't be happy at being deprived of their catch, but Zerafine wasn't very happy either.

"I would love to hear your excuse," she said, her words acid-etched, "for driving a ghost into the middle of a populated area with no better way of controlling it than an antique ghost trap and—I'm just guessing here—blind greed."

The woman's eyes went narrow, and she opened her mouth to say something that Zerafine knew would be too offensive for the god's curse to ignore, but the oldest of the men, dark-haired and with lines creasing the corners of his eyes and mouth, stepped hard on her foot and her words came out a cry of pain instead. "Forgive us, *thelis*," he said, removing his wide-brimmed hat. "It got away from us in the woods and we've been tracking it for over a mile. We were somewhat lost, ourselves, and didn't know we were on the highway until we were...on the highway...."

Zerafine glared at him. "That would no doubt have been a great comfort to anyone it attacked." The man cringed. She turned her glare on each of the others in turn, fury building in her like a bonfire; all, even the woman, turned away rather than meet her gaze. *Ghost hunters*, she thought. *Atenas preserve me.*

With ritual slowness, she raised her hood until it settled above her forehead, leaving her face uncovered. "Get out of my sight," she said, "and may Atenas have mercy on you." It was not a blessing.

The four turned and ran for it, the tall man staggering under the awkward burden of the ghost trap. Zerafine maintained a stony mask as she watched them flee into the shelter of the twisted olive trees beyond the dry grass, but inside she sighed. She saw them more often these days, toting those metal boxes, capturing ghosts so they could harvest their *seicorum*, then letting them loose far from civilization. Lucrative, if it didn't kill you first. She despised their kind, but where else were the people to turn when the *theloi* of Atenas weren't around to provide a more permanent solution?

The small crowd of travelers still hadn't moved. They seemed enthralled by the spectacle Zerafine had just enacted. She sighed again, this time out loud, and stepped to one side so Gerrard could collect the *seicorum* that lay around her feet. It would bring them a decent pile of coin to help support them in the coming days, but Zerafine, moved by inspiration, whispered "Give each of them a nugget" to Gerrard. He made an irritated face, but obediently went to each bystander to give away their windfall. Atenas, god of Death, could use all the goodwill Zerafine could manufacture, and they had plenty of *seicorum* already.

Gerrard still had five or six *seicorum* pebbles when he'd finished distributing the rest. He reclaimed his longstaff, which he had probably dropped when the ghost appeared, and they continued down the road, her sandals and his boots scuffing up tiny puffs of dust with each step. None of the bystanders moved. No one wanted to walk the road with a *thelis* of Atenas. His *theloi* were sometimes respected, always feared, but never loved and certainly not desired as traveling companions. After forty feet or so Zerafine and Gerrard had the wide, dusty highway to themselves.

"Will we make Portena by nightfall?" Zerafine asked. Behind them, she could hear the movement of two dozen people trying not to catch up to them.

"I hope so," Gerrard said. He held his longstaff ready in his left hand, though Zerafine doubted they'd meet anyone he'd need to use it against. "Portena's legendary for its maze of streets and almost as well-known for the crime rate in its lower city. We might have trouble finding the shrine after dark."

"Just let me know when I can lie down and sleep, that's all I ask."

"Don't tell me that consolation exhausted you? Little thing like that?" He took his helmet off and scratched his head, blond hair turned dark with sweat.

Zerafine pushed her hood back again and gathered her dark brown hair into a horse's tail high on her head. "No, just the little thing of having walked for six days in the brutal heat of Ailausor, sleeping rough and unable to bathe like a civilized person. We're so close to our destination, I feel impatient." She tied off her hair with a long piece of leather cord and, bending her head, made it twitch exactly like a horse tail sweeping away flies. The breeze it generated felt wonderful on her bare neck.

"My people believe bathing weakens you," Gerrard said. "But my people are well known to be uncivilized."

"Your people don't believe in drinking coffee. That's a fair definition of uncivilized."

Their solitary occupation of the road didn't last long. After about a mile they began to overtake other traffic, oxcarts taking up most of the road, riders and pedestrians jostling for what space the carts left. The stink of unwashed bodies and animal waste filled Zerafine's nostrils, occasionally wafted away by a hot breeze. She wasn't used to being so closely surrounded by strangers, though her robe and Gerrard's tall presence at her side kept the other travelers from approaching too closely. The dust kicked up by all the travelers and their livestock became nearly unbearable, and Zerafine had to pull her cowl over her nose and mouth despite how much hotter this made her. Gerrard, his head nearly a foot higher than hers, had no such problem. Zerafine eyed the twisted olive trees that lined the road, just far enough from the verge so as not to afford any shade to those moving along it, with a rueful sigh. Only a few more hours, and their journey would be over.

They reached the city before sunset. The famous wall of Portena stood thirty feet high and was nearly that thick, the biggest manmade construction Zerafine had ever seen. It curved out of sight in both directions, its huge tan limestone blocks, each wider than Gerrard was tall, taking on a pinkish cast in the light of the setting sun. Above the wall, in the distance, Zerafine saw two of the five hills of the city-state, green and lush in defiance of the summer sun, white buildings flashing in the late afternoon light. Just the sight of them made Zerafine feel weary.

She saw no one atop the wall, watching the gate. Instead, two tiny booths flanked both sides of the road about fifty feet in front of the wall, each one containing a guard who seemed too large for his post. The guards waved the oxcarts to one side, but allowed everyone else through without comment, though the young guard on the right stiffened and wouldn't meet Zerafine's eyes when she glanced his way. The gate was more like a tunnel, blessedly cool and dim, and Zerafine breathed a sigh of contentment, then coughed on the dust lingering in the air.

Beyond the gate, booths and stalls occupied every possible

space, leaving barely enough room for the road to meander its way through, sprouting tiny streets and paths as it went. Though evening was closing in, the market was still full of people buying, selling, bartering, making a noise like geese chattering on their way north for the summer. Zerafine tried not to gawk like a provincial, but it was hard for her not to be a little overwhelmed at the size of the oldest city in the known world. Still, she saw far too many unoccupied booths. Portena had suffered greatly from plague fifty years ago, and it had yet to return to its pre-disaster population.

Though Zerafine was eager to get to the shrine and, after that, to a bed, she couldn't help slowing to watch the dozens, maybe hundreds of transactions being made. Whole streets were devoted to just one kind of merchandise: in one place, thousands of shoes sat out for inspection; on a different street, all kinds of brass and copper pots lay on the ground or hung from booths. The smaller, lighter ones turned in the evening breeze and sang out, bell-like, above the honks and clamor of human conversation.

"Wait—that's wrong," Gerrard said. He didn't point, but took Zerafine's chin and gently turned her head so she was looking in the right direction. Ahead, at an empty stall whose signage proclaimed that fine brass pots had once been available for sale, a young woman stood with her head bowed as if inspecting the merchandise that wasn't there. Her fingers dipped into a purse hanging by her side--

"She shouldn't carry her purse in the open like that, you mean?"

"No, *look* at her...or actually—" But in that moment Zerafine figured it out. The woman's hand raised as if to give coins to a nonexistent shopkeeper, and pale light filtered through her arm. Now she realized the woman was entirely translucent, just solid-seeming enough not to draw attention to herself. Her body was becoming increasingly filmy, though, and Zerafine shook free of Gerrard's hand and ran across the street, dodging the thinning crowd. The woman turned and began to walk away, but Zerafine caught up with her, reached to take her by the shoulder, and felt her hand slip through—nothing. No cold, no dust, nothing. The woman had vanished.

"Do *not* go running off like that in this city," Gerrard growled behind her. "She wasn't a ghost, was she."

Zerafine shook her head. "She was not," she said, "but I couldn't tell you what she was. Maybe you and I both had the same bad pork at dinner. Maybe she was some kind of illusion."

"I know that's not what you believe."

Zerafine sighed. "I don't have enough information to know what I believe. Anything else will have to wait until we speak to the Council. Did you get directions to the shrine?"

Gerrard made a sour face. "You don't get directions in Portena, you get a direction-finder." He led the way toward a large booth, walled on three sides, that was still doing a brisk business when many of the other shopkeepers were beginning to close for the night. A board hung in the front, with prices chalked on it. Boys and girls lounged around it, laughing and talking, but the noise petered out as one by one they registered who their new clients were. Gerrard dug in his pouch for a brass coin. "Shrine of Atenas," he said. "Another if you get us there before nightfall."

The young guides shared glances of fear and cupidity. One disappeared inside and returned with a much older woman, her face creased and brown with sun. Her lean hand plucked the coin from Gerrard's and spun it in the air. "Nacalia," she said, her voice as brown as her face, "take these good people where they aim to go." A girl leaped up from where she'd been sitting cross-legged and lit a small lantern from the coals in a brazier by the door. She seemed motivated more by excitement than fear, Zerafine thought, and she nimbly threaded her way through the crowd that parted more quickly for the red-hooded *thelis*.

As dusk fell, Zerafine saw acolytes of Kandra lighting much larger lamps all along the wide road, so she guessed the girl's tiny lamp was more symbolic than utilitarian. They soon passed out of the marketplace and into an area where houses loomed over the street, wooden structures four and five stories tall. Their dark windows flickered with dim lights; no large fires for the inhabitants of these rickety structures.

Nacalia turned around and jogged backward for a few steps. "This way, *thelis*," she said. She turned off the main road to the left and led them along a narrower road lined with more of the tall houses, which leaned just enough to give the illusion that they were walking through a manmade forest with branches interlocking to block out the sun or, in this case, the half-moon that rose over the city. Gradually the buildings gave way to single-story homes built of concrete or stone—limestone, perhaps?—sharing a single wall fronting the street, their slate or tin roofs bumping up against each other. Through iron gates, spaced well apart and marked on each doorpost with gods' symbols, Zerafine glimpsed small courtyards, white marble benches, a fountain or two. From here she could see another of the five hills of Portena, its top still gleaming gold from the last light of the setting sun.

"That's Telerion Hide," Nacalia called out over her shoulder, pointing back in the direction of the warren of homes, "and this is just a nest of the new-come's houses. That hill's Rodennos, and the other's Talarannos—" she pointed as she trotted ahead. Zerafine thought Nacalia the tour guide was determined to earn her bonus, both in speed and in the quality of the trip.

Nacalia now led the way through a maze of narrow streets in which Zerafine would have become hopelessly lost—*was* hopelessly lost, as she'd been trying to keep track of the turns Nacalia made. But in only a few minutes they emerged onto another broad street, not as wide as the main road, but wide enough that Gerrard, who disliked narrow places, breathed out heavily as though he'd been holding his breath the whole time.

This neighborhood was identical with the last except that the homes were larger, the courtyards bigger, the stone finer. The road led past these homes and terminated at a building that looked very much like all the rest, except that it was faced with black marble and did not bear the symbols every other front door was marked with. Death had no symbol, for it was everywhere.

Gerrard dug into his pouch again and came up with another brass siclo. Nacalia took it eagerly, but instead of pelting off in the direction they'd come, said, "I never met a *thelis* of Atenas before. Thought you was all ten feet tall and gug-ugly."

Zerafine laughed. "I'm so grateful you don't think I'm gug-ugly," she said.

"Not even. Nor even ten feet tall. *He* might be." Nacalia seemed a little disappointed. Gerrard straightened to his full six-foot-four height.

On a whim, Zerafine asked, "How much of that do you get to keep?"

Nacalia considered the coin in her somewhat grubby hand. "Maybe 20 soldi." That would mean Nacalia got around a third of the total sum. She added, with a sly look upward through her lashes, "Plus half the tips." Zerafine raised her eyebrow at Gerrard, who went fishing for another siclo. Nacalia's eyes went wide when she saw it. "Thanks so much, master guardsman!"

"But your boss won't know how much we paid you," Zerafine said. "Don't you think about keeping it all?"

"She knows anyhow. Got a luck-eye blessed by a Sintha *thelis* can see into our souls, or some such. Can't keep nothing like from her."

"Do you do other things than guide? Run errands and so forth?"

Nacalia beamed. "Sure I'd like to," she said, "if old Karra says yes. She owns my contract next few years. Can't cross her."

"Then tell Karra I'll be back in the morning to negotiate with her. Now, hurry back!"

Nacalia turned and bolted back the way they'd come. Gerrard said, "How whimsical of you."

"Oh, shut up. It was hardly whimsical. She'll be a perfect

runner."

"You barely know the girl. What makes you so sure?"

Zerafine stared in the direction in which the girl had vanished. "She wasn't afraid of me. That counts for a lot."

"Really? How were you going to find her again?"

Zerafine's mouth opened, then shut. "Oh," she said.

"Oh, exactly," Gerrard said. "Fortunately for you, I *did* memorize the route. A few more trips and you won't need to hire a guide."

"But I *will* need someone who knows this city and how to find anywhere or anything, and I believe Nacalia is that someone. And that's not something you can do for me."

Gerrard shook his head. "I wonder if they're expecting us so early. We're at least a day's journey ahead of schedule."

"Expecting us or not, we're here, and there's no point putting this off any longer." Zerafine adjusted her hood so that her face was in full view, then pushed open the door to the shrine of Atenas.

Chapter Two

The black marble of the building turned out to be a façade; the interior of the shrine was white marble that gleamed gold in the light of a dozen torches affixed to the four walls. They flickered in a slight breeze that appeared to come from near the high ceiling. Other than the torches, the room was empty. An open door in the far wall led to a second room, also torch-lit, but with rough limestone walls that caught the light and reflected it back in glittering fragments. It felt smaller than it was, but the effect was comforting rather than claustrophobic, and even without seeing the altar made of the same rough-hewn limestone as the walls, Zerafine could feel the presence of the god in His sanctuary. It felt like coming home.

Two men and one woman kneeling around the altar looked up as they entered. "My name is Zerafine of Dardagne, and I'm here as special emissary from Atenar to investigate the disturbances in Portena," Zerafine said. It was a formality; they knew who she was. She saluted the woman, who had to be Berenica, *tokthelis* of Atenas and guardian of the Portena shrine. Her white hair was at odds with her faintly lined face, though Zerafine knew her to be over sixty years old. She was short and heavyset and her large hands were steady as they saluted — superior to subordinate, incorrectly, because despite Berenica's higher rank and seniority, Zerafine was currently the *Marathelos* of Atenas's plenipotentiary, invested with full power to act on his behalf. A telling reaction, but not one worth calling her on.

Berenica gave her a long, cold stare. "Be welcome to this sanctuary," she said. Her voice was high, unexpectedly high for such a large woman, Zerafine thought. It was a beautiful voice, and Zerafine could imagine how it might sound performing the chants of High Holy Week. Right now it also sounded unwelcoming, which irritated Zerafine. She had been afraid the proud old woman would not be happy about being outranked, even temporarily, by the *Marathelos*'s representative, especially since Berenica hadn't been the one to ask Atenar for help, and it seemed her fears weren't unfounded. Berenica was more likely to be a stumbling block than an ally.

"We were about to begin the rites of evening, if you'd care to join us," Berenica said, her tone of voice a challenge, her look a chastisement that Zerafine had simply blundered into the sanctuary without giving notice. Zerafine shucked her load and gave it to Gerrard, who ducked back into the antechamber to wait. As Berenica led the chant, Zerafine responded automatically. With her hands tucked into the wide sleeves of her robe and her hood pulled well over her face, she was free to think without giving anything away. The city council had asked Atenar for help; that meant the situation was serious. They had sent for someone with the *Marathelos*'s authority; that suggested the problem was a matter of judgment and political intrigue. Zerafine had never seen this assignment as a reward, but if she didn't know better, she would now have seen it as a punishment.

It did make her wonder, as she knelt at the altar, what the *Marathelos* had been thinking when he gave her the assignment. She was certainly capable of handling rogue ghosts, had made a name for herself doing so, but political machinations were not her forte. And the *Marathelos* had been—could she call it coy?—at any rate, not very forthcoming about the details. *Ghosts*, he had said, then added, *but not like any other*, and described the translucent figures plaguing Portena. That was all. With luck, Berenica's pride wouldn't keep her from being more forthcoming than her spiritual superior.

"May we be the light that guides His spirits home," Berenica concluded, and with final gestures, palm to palm, the service was over. Berenica led the way into the antechamber, Zerafine trailing behind the two men.

"Please join us for an evening meal," Berenica said, pushing her hood back and making a formal salute. "We're all anxious for news from Atenar. Or, if you'd prefer, someone will show you to your quarters and arrange for food to be brought. If you're too tired." Her voice held the tiniest hint of a challenge, as if tiredness after a long journey was a sign of spiritual weakness. Despite her irritation, Zerafine had to admire the woman's nuanced communication, her mastery of that wonderful voice.

"Not at all," she replied. "Gerrard and I would be happy to share your meal." She put just enough emphasis on Gerrard's name to show she'd noticed no one had bothered to ask for it.

Berenica again led the way, out of the shrine and to the house on its left. Full dark had fallen in the time it had taken to complete the evening ritual, and the half-moon cast a pale blue light over the street. More light came from lamps burning behind the household walls farther on, but at this end of the street only two houses were lit, and one of those was behind the gate Berenica now approached. A man dressed in dark shirt and trousers opened the gate before she reached it, and she swept through without a word.

The courtyard was given over to a large and well-kept garden, with many shade trees and benches set artfully beneath them. Zerafine could imagine how comfortable it would be during the heat of the day. The house, by contrast, bore no ornamentation beyond a lintel carved with an abstract design, but the interior blazed with color: jewel-toned hangings from across the sea, chairs comfortably upholstered with brightly-dyed wools, a rug that came from Zerafine's home country of Dardagne, vases etched in intricate patterns that were Portena-made. Beyond the large sitting area stood a low table of some exotic wood, surrounded by cushioned stools, upon which was laid an elegant meal. The man who had opened the gate, who'd come in behind them, removed cutlery and glassware from a curiously carved and painted cabinet and proceeded to rearrange the place settings for five instead of three.

"Is this your home? It's lovely," Zerafine said to Berenica, and felt the woman's tension relax just a little. *She must have expected a*

13

criticism of how luxuriously she lives, she thought, *and if I were as rigid as she appears to be, I would have given it to her.* True, it was a little...ostentatious...but it wasn't Zerafine's job to judge Berenica — or did she think that was part of Zerafine's purpose here? This contradiction in the *tokthelis*, this external austerity wedded to hidden luxury, baffled her, and she wondered again if they would be able to work together, because Zerafine had neither time nor inclination to cosset the woman's injured pride.

Berenica quickly introduced the two *theloi*, Ricenz and Darlen, pretending that she hadn't forgotten to do it earlier just as she'd "forgotten" to ask for Gerrard's name, and they seated themselves around the table. Zerafine guessed Berenica chafed at having to eat with Gerrard; *sentaren* didn't rank any lower than *theloi*, but among the older *theloi* it was tradition to eat separately, and Berenica appeared to be as traditional as they came. Unfortunately for her, she couldn't say anything about it without being rude, since Zerafine outranked her, even if temporarily. It gave Zerafine a wicked little ember of pleasure deep inside; she could show good manners, but she didn't think she liked the old *tokthelis* any more than Berenica liked her.

They ate in silence, as was also tradition among the older *theloi* of Atenas: roast duck, new potatoes, artichokes roasted in olive oil, with a light red wine Zerafine, not normally a wine drinker, enjoyed very much. She was conscious of being covered in road-dust and probably smelling of sweat; they had been offered water to wash their faces and hands and feet, but nothing else. Of course no one would want to wait dinner on their guests' ablutions, but Zerafine felt scruffy surrounded by such opulence. Even the utensils were of fine steel with carved olivewood handles. How on earth could Berenica afford such extravagances? Could Portena really have so many ghosts? She felt certain Berenica was actually snubbing her under the cover of silence, and her irritation flowered into mild dislike.

Dinner was followed by a light sherbet garnished with mint

14

leaves—an ice house was another extravagance, but a welcome one—and chilled water for a palate-cleanser. Berenica rose from the table, a sign to the rest that they should follow, and moved to take a seat on one of the upholstered chairs. Zerafine chose to sit directly opposite her, Gerrard standing at attention behind her. Her chair was just the slightest bit shorter than Berenica's; more accurately, Berenica's seat was just that much taller than all the rest. Zerafine caught Darlen and Ricenz trading a glance of shared amusement as they sat on a nearby couch, and once again had to suppress her irritation. So, they liked seeing the young upstart humbled, did they? She owed Berenica at least the respect due her office, but her subordinates had no such protection.

"We've already seen one of the so-called ghosts as we made our way here," she began, pretending Berenica hadn't just opened her mouth to speak. *It's time you learned I'm not someone you can manipulate to your benefit.* "Perhaps you can explain in more detail what's been happening in Portena. I'm afraid the report we had at Atenar was...rather terse."

"There's little to tell," Berenica said. "People are seeing images that interact with their surroundings, but have no substance. They fade after only a minute or so, often much less. And to the best of our observations, none of them are recently dead. You can imagine the outcry when someone sees his dear old mother, dead five years past, walking toward him on the garden path."

"But they can't possibly be ghosts," Zerafine said.

"Not at all. Real ghosts are only visible because of the *seicorum* they accrete, and they certainly don't take the shape of people. It's not as if the citizens of Portena know nothing about real ghosts. This is a large city; we console some seventy or eighty ghosts every year, most of them by request of the family. But there's no convincing them that these...these *apparitions* cannot possibly be ghosts. Fortunately, we've learned what they actually are."

This was unexpected. Zerafine raised both eyebrows at Berenica to invite her to continue.

15

"They're hallucinations, of course," she said. "Figments of madness. The *theloi* of Sukman have declared their god's involvement, and people are beginning to be convinced of the truth."

"How interesting. If the truth is already known, then why bother to summon an emissary?"

Berenica appeared taken aback by the directness of the question. "I don't know why the Council does anything. They know I am too busy with the duties of the shrine to involve myself in mundane matters."

"You certainly seem well-informed for someone who hasn't taken an active role."

"I've had to make statements about Atenas's non-involvement in the situation, of course. It was my responsibility."

Yes, and thank you so much for muddying the waters with your groundless assertions, Zerafine thought. The apparitions might not be ghosts, but that didn't mean Atenas wasn't involved. But saying so would just make an already tense conversation openly antagonistic, so she merely said, "I'm sure you did your duty," which was satisfyingly patronizing without giving Berenica grounds to openly accuse her of disrespect.

"It's getting late. We shouldn't keep you from your rest," Gerrard said, breaking the silence in which he'd followed their exchange with fascination. Berenica looked at him as if she'd forgotten he existed, then rose from her chair so the rest could follow. Technically, as the *Marathelos*'s vicarious presence in Portena, Zerafine should have been the one to dismiss the gathering, but she was willing to throw the *tokthelis* a bone, at least this time.

"The Council offered to house you, but we thought, as you are a *thelis* of Atenas, to provide you with lodging in one of our properties," Berenica said. She led the way out of the yard and to the house across the street, the other one that had lights burning in the courtyard. "I've arranged for servants to care for your needs, though I'm afraid they may have turned in for the night. I hope you don't mind."

Oh, that was a masterful stroke. Zerafine mentally applauded. Turn the insult of not offering guest quarters in Berenica's own home into a gesture over which she could not take offense; make Zerafine's late-evening appearance justify the failure to give her full hospitality on her arrival. She'd have to take care not to underestimate Berenica again.

"Not at all, you're too kind," was all she said. "Thank you very much. You'll excuse me if I don't join you for morning ritual. I'll be far too busy on the *Marathelos*'s business." With that parting shot, she and Gerrard entered their temporary home.

The servants might have gone to bed, but they had left lights burning in hand-sized lanterns made of wrought iron and translucent white glass. The interior layout was almost identical to Berenica's, minus the colorful décor; it looked as if it were rarely used. On the other hand, it had been well swept and dusted, and the unornamented furniture looked comfortable. Zerafine's explorations led her first to a bedroom and then to a cavernous bathing chamber which appeared to have both hot and cold running water. Ah, civilization.

"I want the room with the chickens," Gerrard said, looking over her shoulder into the bathing room. He had removed his armor and helmet and his blond hair stuck up in tufts here and there. He looked as sweaty as she felt. "Sweet goddess of light, if I weren't so tired I'd fall into that thing this minute."

"And smack your brains out on the empty bottom of the bath."

"And I wouldn't even care."

"Wait—what were you saying about the...chickens?"

Gerrard showed her another door farther along the hallway. The bedrooms had been decorated more lavishly than the sitting room—though that still wasn't saying much—and someone very fond of poultry had had their way with this one. The bedspread covering the narrow bed had been embroidered with rooster heads. A mural of a pastoral scene adorned the wall opposite the bed, with chickens heavily featured therein and a proud rooster stretching out its neck to crow from atop a fence post. The wooden clothes cabinet was carved with a pair of chickens that, when the doors were shut, appeared to kiss. Even the oaken bedposts were tipped with small, perfectly carved chicks.

"You're not serious," Zerafine said. "It's like a farmer's nightmare in here."

"There is the chance that I'll have dreams about ghostly chickens trying to lay eggs in my hair," Gerrard admitted, "but it's got a sort of whimsy to it, don't you think?"

"My room has flowers. Lots of flowers. Berenica is a very nasty person indeed. She practically had to host us, to show the Council that there are still matters in which she has control, but she won't provide more than the bare minimum of hospitality to avoid insult."

"I didn't like that story she told. They aren't ghosts, but we're needed here anyway to tell people they aren't ghosts? Either she's stupid or she thinks we are."

"I'm guessing the latter. She certainly believes she can lead me around by the nose—not to mention believing her efforts toward controlling me would matter. I don't think she understands what I'm doing here. She's so wrapped up in herself that as far as she's concerned, the traditional role of the *theloi* of Atenas as consolers of the dead is all that matters. It infuriates her that she can't just say 'they aren't ghosts' and have the problem just disappear."

Gerrard blew out a hard breath. "Are you sure we can't just poke around a little, give the Council an answer they'll like, and move on? This really isn't what we're trained for."

"I know, but I accepted the *Marathelos*'s commission, and I mean to do him proud. I at least need to speak to the Council. I'm not sure whether they simply want me to find out what's going on, or if they expect me to do something about it. Either way, we'll stay as long as it takes for me to fulfill my word. But more importantly, we've been traveling rough for four months and I think we're due a rest."

"We stopped at Atenar two weeks ago."

"Yes, but we only stayed overnight, and the holy city doesn't have nearly the amenities of Portena."

"The city's going to be hottest during Ailausor," Gerrard said.

"It will still have theater and good restaurants and sport and a lovely bath with a cold water tap."

"I forgot about the bath."

"Well, keep forgetting, because I plan to bathe first tomorrow morning."

Chapter Three

"It'll cost you a thal a day," said Karra. Her lean, brown face showed no fear at dealing with one of Atenas's servants, though admittedly she was dealing with *sentare* and not *thelis*. Zerafine was used to letting Gerrard handle the money aspect of their partnership, though he had a tendency to over-tip; he was in every other way very careful about their expenses.

"A *thal*?" Gerrard exclaimed. "Six parses and not a soldi more. You don't make more than that on the girl's labor in a day." He'd left his armor and helmet behind, since their business here was unlikely to involve consoling ghosts, but his bulk was still intimidating. Or should have been; the sharp-faced woman seemed not to think him a threat.

"I still have to pay for her upkeep," Karra said. "Nine parses, then."

"Seven and a half. We'll pay for her upkeep."

"That hardly covers my costs! She's one of my best runners. You'll pay eight and be grateful for the bargain."

Nacalia watched the byplay with eager curiosity. She was probably nine or ten years old, sharp-faced, with curly black hair and a spattering of what were either freckles or dirt. She'd need a bath and some new clothes if she were going to be a representative of Atenas, even indirectly.

Gerrard appeared to be thinking hard, though Zerafine knew him well enough to tell that he'd already come up with a plan and was about to sell it hard. "You know, the girl won't earn any tips while she's with us," he said. "How about we call it ten parses on the condition you split it equally with her."

Karra's eyes gleamed. "Deal," she said, and stuck out her hand to seal it with a shake. Gerrard gripped her hand briefly, then dipped into his pouch and pulled out six large silver coins. "For the week," he said, "and we'll settle up at the end of our stay for however longer we keep her."

Karra handed half the coins to Nacalia and stowed the rest away somewhere on her person. "Don't think about cheating me," she warned Gerrard.

"I'm sorry, did you just suggest that we might?" Zerafine said mildly.

Karra's face went pale under her tan. "No, *thelis*," she said after a moment's pause to collect herself. "No offense meant."

"None taken, I'm sure. Come along, Nacalia." Zerafine turned on her heel and walked away, leaving her companions to catch up to her.

Nacalia giggled and skipped like the child she was instead of the tiny adult she'd been the night before. "Oh, madama, I never saw Karra looking like that before! One parsis less than she wanted! She's hard mean most times and nobody bests her at nothing, I swear. Thank you for taking me on, madama!"

"You're welcome, Nacalia, and please stop bouncing," Zerafine said. "Thank you. Now, you should call me *thelis* in public, not madama, and you may call me Zerafine in private so long as you don't mix up the two. People will think you're being rude. This is my *sentare*, Gerrard; you call him *sentare* or Gerrard."

"*Sentare*," Nacalia said, pronouncing all three syllables distinctly. "Is that like a bodyguard?"

"Something like," Zerafine said. "Bodyguard and traveling companion and ghost-wrangler. Now, it's the baths and the clothier's for you. You can't work for me and look like a ragamuffin."

"New clothes," said Nacalia, stricken. "Mada—I mean, *thelis*, I can't wear new clothes in my mam's quarters, I'll get stuff thrown at me. I don't favor letting you down right off, but I just can't."

"It will be more convenient if you just stay with me for the duration. If your mother doesn't mind."

Gerrard looked mildly shocked at the idea that they might invite a street urchin to share their quarters, but kept his mouth shut. Nacalia looked surprised, then eager. "Oh yes, *thelis*, mam will be fine pleased to have me out of her hair for a bit. Only —" She cast her eyes down. "I need to take this lot home to her, as she depends on me to help."

"Take us to the Capitol building first," Zerafine said.

Though the main street leading away from the city gate seemed to cut straight to the heart of the city, Nacalia had a fondness for side streets that intersected crazily and dodged through parts of the city ranging from very poor to upscale and wealthy. As they crossed an intersection where shifty-eyed young men loitered in every doorway, Gerrard moved closer to Zerafine, his attention pulled in all directions. "Should I be worried?" Zerafine asked in a low voice. Her eyes lingered on a man in a dirty smock who leered at her, then blinked and let his mouth fall open in a slack-jawed gape.

"I think I need protection more than you," he replied in the same tone. He shifted his grip on his longstaff. "We need to make Nacalia aware that we can't pass unmolested through these neighborhoods. I'm trying to look as inoffensive as possible without looking afraid. You, on the other hand, seem to have them worried."

"Just so they don't get worried enough to strike out at us."

Nacalia darted back. "Hurry up, *thelis*," she said, dancing impatiently. They quickened their step and soon left the young men behind. Minutes later they were in a better part of town and could subside to a slower gait.

"Nacalia," Zerafine said, "why did you choose that route?"

Nacalia looked at her as if she were stupid. "It's the fastest, see?"

"It's more important that we not go places we'll attract attention than that we get to our destination quickly."

Nacalia's face fell. "I didn't think about it. I ha'nt guided people so much as I run errands. I can go anywhere," she said proudly.

"Well, we can't, so can you remember that? We're really very impressed with your ability to find the fastest route," Zerafine said, because Nacalia looked so discouraged. "Obviously when I send you on errands you can take whatever route you like."

"But everyone's scared of you. You ha'nt got to worry about no one hurting you," she said.

"Sometimes it's when people are really scared that they try to hurt others," said Zerafine, her face grim. "People believe a lot of false things about Atenas, like that He kills people, or that His *theloi* are a sign of death."

"He doesn't?"

"No. He welcomes the spirits of those who die and brings them into His courts. But that doesn't stop people from believing otherwise, because death is frightening."

"I a'nt afraid of you," Nacalia reassured her. "I know you won't hurt me."

"Thank you, Nacalia."

"We really should be going," Gerrard reminded them. "And no bad neighborhoods this time. I don't have a red robe to protect me."

"Are you scared?" Nacalia said disdainfully. "'Cause I wouldn't be scared if I had hands like yours. You must be a big sissy." She darted away.

"Sometimes you have really bad ideas," Gerrard said, glaring after the girl.

"Some *sentare* you are, letting a little kid get the better of you. I think she's got you pegged."

"Sissy," he muttered, but followed Nacalia.

Another ten minutes' stroll brought them to the heart of Portena. It had been destroyed by fire during the plague and had been rebuilt less than fifty years ago, and was therefore more orderly than the market district, or even the more residential areas they'd passed on the way. Zerafine had traveled the known world for six years and did not consider herself a provincial, but the straight lines and perfect right angles of the streets that led to the great plaza made her feel a little out of place, a country girl gawking at the city's immensity. Buildings of dark limestone interspersed with others of bold white marble lined both sides of the road, all of them elegant and enormous enough for a god to feel comfortable in. They passed the temple of Arieta, with its ever-burning hearth in a pavilion open on all sides, and a building that was not a temple but had Marenda's symbol carved into its lintel—some sort of theater, possibly. Down one of the cross-streets Zerafine saw what was probably a bank, and in the other direction were some lawyer's stalls; the trappings of civilization, laid out neatly for anyone's use—anyone, that is, who could pay.

The Capitol building was not at the center of the great plaza; that honor was reserved for the temple of Kalindi, chief goddess of the Pantheon, standing on a hill high above the city that was the center of Her worship. The Capitol lay on the extreme northern edge of the plaza, a domed gilt-and-marble edifice with a porch that encircled the building. Zerafine led the way up a short flight of stairs and through the main doors into the cool darkness. She stood just inside the door for a moment, letting her eyes adjust, and Gerrard took a few steps past her and said, "Sweet goddess of light. It's incredible."

Zerafine went to join him, looking upward, and drew in an astonished breath. She had heard that this new Capitol building, built to replace the one destroyed in the fire, was a marvel of modern engineering, but she was not prepared for the sight of the world-famous Rotunda, two hundred feet across and topped by a high dome that seemed to float above the pillars supporting it. A balcony ran the circumference of the room, just below where the dome began, that looked high enough for a person to reach up and touch the murals painted inside the dome. She couldn't help but gaze in awe at those depictions of the twelve days of creation, the whole divided into twelve parts to show the acts of each of the gods of the Pantheon. Atenas, naturally, was absent from the proceedings; the records at Atenas's holy city of Atenar said that He

24

sat apart and watched creation unfold so that Death would have no hold over the new world until its formation was complete. The Unholy Wars had been fought, centuries ago, over whether or not His withdrawal had been a good idea.

Gerrard said, "Look at those panels. That marble is so thin it lets light through." Beside him, Nacalia gawked with her mouth hanging open.

"Kalindi be praised, you're here," said a woman high on the balcony. "Wait, I'll join you." She disappeared from view and soon emerged from one of the smaller doorways spaced evenly around the Rotunda. "I'm Paola, Councilwoman Vessa's assistant. I'm sorry we weren't on hand to greet you, but we had no word of your arrival."

"I'm a few days early," Zerafine said. "I should have sent word, but we arrived late last night and I would like to begin my work as soon as possible. Should I arrange to return when the Council is assembled?"

"No, many of them are here this morning, including our Chief Councilman, Castinidou Rodennos. Please, come with me, they'll be happy to meet you."

"One moment," said Zerafine. She took Nacalia aside. "Go home and take care of any business you have there. Meet us back here in one hour." Nacalia took off, skidding a little on the marble floor.

"She's going to just disappear with our money, you know," Gerrard said.

"Have a little faith," Zerafine told him.

"I'd rather have my six thals back."

"If she weren't reliable, that woman wouldn't keep her on," Zerafine said. "When I told the child she'd need new clothing, she was more worried about how I'd feel than excited at getting new clothes. And, as I believe I've mentioned before, she's not afraid of me. Not only will she come back, Gerrard, she's going to be here *early*."

25

They followed Paola through a door at the back of the Rotunda, which led to a hallway off which other, narrower doors led. Double doors at the end of the hall opened on a low-ceilinged room hung with draperies of blue and gold, furnished as a large sitting room with several long, low couches in matching upholstery. Several people turned at their entrance; all of them looked surprised, then stunned, then either relieved or afraid. Zerafine had learned not to interpret this reaction as guilt; despite what she'd told Nacalia, sensible people feared the *theloi* of Atenas, but not because of their relationship to death. Atenas's *theloi* were sometimes also called on to act as judges — arbiters of justice whose judgments were both fair and incontrovertible. Even the most honest people had things in their past they weren't proud of. And it was both as emissary and as investigator of truth that Zerafine had come to Portena.

"Madama *thelis*, welcome to Portena." A tall, portly man in his fifties stepped out of the crowd and made his salute, equal to equal. "I am Castinidou Rodennos, chief councilman. We are all very grateful to Atenar for sending you." The others saluted in turn.

Zerafine returned his salute exactly. "Zerafine of Dardagne," she said. "My *sentare*, Gerrard of Kionnar."

"I didn't realize Atenar sent its traveling *theloi* as emissaries," said a younger woman. Her long fingers played with a charm on a silver chain around her neck. Her round eyes and plucked eyebrows gave her a permanently surprised expression, but the look she directed at Zerafine was calculating. *So, the Council isn't entirely united in its decision to send for me. Thank you, unknown woman, for showing me the kind of antagonism I should look for. Also, you're a snob.*

"The spiritual component of Portena's problem requires a specialist not only in arbitration, but in consolation," she improvised. It might even be true. It didn't taste like a lie, anyway. "Gerrard and I have had more years in the field than any other currently active pair." Six years, but they didn't need to know that; to the uninformed, it seemed like such a short time, but saying "two hundred and twenty-seven consolations" sounded so much like bragging.

"Then we are doubly grateful," said a middle-aged man, soft around the belly but still very handsome. He exchanged a quick glance with the round-eyed woman. *Something else going on there,* Zerafine thought.

"Let me introduce you to everyone. Vessa, representative of district four." A large, attractive woman who wore a white ankle-length tunic and several pieces of tasteful and expensive jewelry nodded at her. "Alita Talarannos, representative of Talarannos hill. Her husband Gordou Kerynnos, representative of Kerynnos hill." This was the round-eyed woman and the middle-aged man. Married, huh? How had the Council let that happen? Surely it was too much concentration of power in one place. "Vidinou Akennos, representative of Akennos hill." This was a man about Castinidou's age, almost too lean, with the beaky nose of a bird of prey and the soft eyes of a rabbit, and Zerafine was starting to get an idea of just how power in Portena was distributed. Akennos of Akennos hill? Really? "And this is Cerilia, representative of district one." Cerilia had pale, almost Northern skin, an overbite and a nervous expression. She was one of the ones who'd shown fear at Zerafine's entrance.

"Let's sit down," said Castinidou, "and we'll lay out our problem for you." Zerafine took a seat, Gerrard standing behind her with his longstaff in resting position, and amused herself watching how everyone surreptitiously tried to avoid sitting next to her. Everyone, that is, except Vessa, who seated herself beside Zerafine without a trace of fear.

Zerafine took out her letters of introduction and handed them to Castinidou. Castinidou took his time perusing the letters, one from the *Marathelos* and one from *tokthelos* and First Lecturer Arland, the first giving Zerafine plenipotentiary powers on the *Marathelos*'s behalf and the other attesting to her ability to perform those responsibilities. Zerafine wished she'd been able to read (and

META

edit) Arland's letter before he sealed it away; he could be overly enthusiastic about his favorite pupils, and it was not beyond possibility that he'd promised she could lay fifteen ghosts to rest in a single hour.

"The *Marathelos* speaks very highly of you," Castinidou said, tucking the letters inside his linen tunic—very finely made, Zerafine noted. "We're glad he's taking our problem seriously."

"Why don't you tell me what you already know about the situation?" Zerafine requested.

Castinidou leaned forward and rested his elbows on his knees. "Five weeks ago we had the first reports of what we came to refer to as apparitions," he said. "People claimed to see dead relatives or friends, or sometimes just strangers, who appeared and then vanished at random. These apparitions don't try to interact with living people; in fact, they behave as if they are responding to another reality entirely. They move their lips as if they're addressing someone who isn't there—you understand they make no sound. They walk up stairs that don't exist. They walk through walls. Even though they haven't tried to hurt anyone, it's been unsettling.

"Over the last five weeks, the sightings have grown in number. The apparitions—they last longer between appearance and disappearance, and some are even recurring. The citizens are increasingly frightened that they represent some kind of divine chastisement of our city. Some people believe they are ghosts, no matter how often they're reminded of what ghosts really are. Some believe these are the actual spirits of the dead escaped from Atenas's realm who have returned to places they are most familiar with. Others believe, as *tokthelos* Genedirou claims, that they are figments of Sukman's madness made manifest in the world. Since we've seen Genedirou successfully get rid of apparitions, we—" he gestured to the others—"are inclined to believe him."

"Some of us think that the logic of these appearances, their consistency, implies that the third theory cannot be true," said

Vessa, giving Castinidou a sharp look.

"But if Atenas has lost His grip on the spirits in His realm, His *theloi* would know about it," said Gordou.

"Genedirou has also claimed, at times, that the apparitions are a form of communal madness," Vessa said, addressing Zerafine. "He's enjoying his increased importance and will say anything to maintain that power."

"Genedirou gets results," said Gordou, "and whatever his personal motives may be, at least he's able to act, which is more than anyone else in the city has done. Alestiou refuses even to make a statement—"

"*Both* theories have merit, and neither can be definitively proven," Alita said, her voice raised. "Or, I should say, have not yet been definitively proven." She inclined her head in Zerafine's direction. "And just suppose the truth is neither one? You see, *thelis*, how confused our situation is."

"Is there anything else you can tell me?" Zerafine asked. "Even the smallest detail might help guide my investigation."

Gordou said, "We've encouraged people to report sightings and have collected hundreds of them from throughout the city. A cursory analysis seems to show clusters of apparitions in a number of places in the city, mostly in the lower-income neighborhoods. We don't know what it means, but we can save you time running around collecting the information again."

Vessa said, "Paola has that information. I'll have her bring everything to you."

Zerafine nodded. "Not to be too blunt, madamas and sirrahs, but what exactly do you expect from me? I can investigate and with luck find the truth about your problem, but am I to solve it also? By the *Marathelos*'s instructions, my services are at your disposal."

"A spiritual problem will require a spiritual solution," said Castinidou after a pause. "I hope you're not saying you're unwilling to see this through."

"On the contrary. I don't want to overstep my bounds. This is your city, and you are the ones responsible for it. I don't want to usurp your authority."

Castinidou looked relieved. "Of course. Then, yes, we would like you to implement whatever solution you deem necessary—as far as that's possible, of course. And please consider our resources at your disposal."

With that, the meeting appeared to be over. They rose and exchanged salutes again, then Vessa drew Zerafine aside to confer with Paola. Zerafine noticed that aside from Castinidou, none of the others seemed happy to let Vessa have a private conversation with Atenar's emissary. But Vessa only said to Paola, "Please get the emissary all the information we've collected," and then, when she had gone, said, "Don't be swayed by how certain each of us are about our pet theories. I believe the truth will be something different from either one." She went back to join the others, leaving Zerafine confused. Had Vessa just put on a show to get the others to reveal their partisanship?

"We really are pleased to have you in our city," Alita said, coming up with Gordou on her arm. "I hope you'll have time to take in the sights. It would be a shame for you to miss everything just because you're working too hard."

"I'm sure my investigation will take me all over Portena," Zerafine replied.

Alita looked up at Gerrard, who continued to stay close to Zerafine. "I've never met a *sentare* before," she said, almost purring. "You're so quiet."

"I'm not sure what to say in such company," Gerrard said in his deepest, most heavily accented voice, and Zerafine had to stifle a smile. He was playing the dumb Northerner again, something that amused him when he wanted to be underestimated. Good for him. Let this council underestimate them both. Alita wore the superficially pleasant smile of a woman who believed her conversational companion was beneath her, but she had it aimed at both of them. *You're still a snob.*

"So what is it you do, exactly?" Gordou asked him. Zerafine answered for him.

"Oh, this and that. He keeps ghosts away from the public when I'm preparing for a consolation, acts as a bodyguard when someone gets antagonistic, keeps me entertained on the road—" From the way Alita's thin, plucked eyebrows went up, Zerafine guessed she'd said something wrong. Had she just implied that she and Gerrard were lovers, or was Alita just prone to think that way? Oh well. Explaining that she was too busy to think of sex, and certainly wouldn't think about sex with her best friend, would just make it worse.

"You must have an interesting life," Vessa said, inserting herself between Gordou and Alita as if she didn't notice they were there. "I wonder that you were willing to give it up, even temporarily, for our little problem."

"I go where the *Marathelos* tells me," she said cheerily, then found Paola at her elbow with a folder crammed full of papers. "And now I think I should be off to begin my investigation."

Back in the Rotunda, Gerrard said, "I think—"

"Not yet," whispered Zerafine. "I wouldn't put it past them to try to eavesdrop, and I have no idea how far sound carries in this room."

So they went outside, where they found Nacalia loitering at the foot of the stairs. "I ha'nt been here long," she said, "'cause I had to keep moving on account of they don't like my kind hanging around."

"I don't think anyone will bother you now as long as we're here," Zerafine said. "Well, Gerrard? What did you make of that?"

The advantage of Gerrard acting like a big dumb Northerner was that he could watch everyone without attracting attention. "Alita and Gordou would like to seem independent, but it's clear they're lock-stepped. Strange that they both managed to be elected to the Council."

"I thought that myself. Anything else?"

"Castinidou's taking the lead, but I think he's being marginalized. He should have been the one to head off that argument, not Alita. Vessa's playing her own game, but she supports Castinidou. This is just instinct, mind, but I don't think she's got the chief councilhood in her sights, and Alita does."

"Did you notice all the family names? I think Portena's famous democracy is a crock."

"I'd like to know more about the district representatives and how they're chosen. Did you notice they didn't have surnames, unlike the Hill representatives? That one woman didn't even speak. See, I can't even remember her name."

"Cerilia. She was so nondescript I forgot she was there."

"She never even gave any indication that she wanted to chime in. She might be someone else's puppet, but who knows? Also, who's Alestiou?"

"Are you joking? He's the *Marathelos* of Kalindi. Only the most important prelate in the known world!"

"Excuse me for not being on speaking terms with the man to know his first name. So why won't the *Marathelos* of Kalindi make a statement on the matter? I bet two-thirds of the people in Portena owe primary allegiance to the Queen of Heaven. His weighing in could be a huge step toward calming things down."

"That would be another thing to investigate. I wonder what the protocol is for me calling on him? Does the *Marathelos* of Atenas trump the *Marathelos* of Kalindi? Atenas being outside the hierarchy?"

Gerrard shuddered. "Can we please not find out? Besides, we're boring the whelp with all this political talk. Let's get her cleaned up."

Their next stops were, in quick succession, a shop selling reasonably priced but well-made clothing and a public bathhouse. Zerafine supervised both transactions and made sure the girl scrubbed her skin and hair well. Nacalia did have a sprinkling of freckles across her cheeks and the bridge of her nose, and her clean hair hung in loose ringlets past her shoulders. By the time she was washed and groomed and neatly dressed, with the exception of her ratty old leather sandals—Nacalia refused, as she said, to break in a new pair—it was only half past nine.

Zerafine weighed the heavy folder in her hand. "How close are we to Sukman's temple?" she asked Nacalia.

"It's just a few streets over," the girl said.

"Let's see if we can talk to Genedirou as long as we're here. It sounds like he's had more personal interaction with these apparitions than anyone else." Zerafine adjusted her hood. "I have a feeling that this is going to be a long day."

Chapter Four

Sukman's temple was on a corner where two smaller streets off the plaza met. It sat far from the road's edge, as if it had been caught in the act of sidling away from an accident. Its walls were painted a brilliant white, but they were walls of wood instead of stone. Large glass windows pieced together from random colors adorned each side of the building, surmounted by silver spirals that were the god's symbol. It was said that if you looked long enough at Sukman's windows, a pattern would emerge, but it would be a pattern only madmen could see.

Zerafine said, "You two wait here and I'll see if I can talk to the *thelos*. Maybe we can get this whole thing straightened out before lunchtime." She went up the steps into the sanctuary.

The colored windows let in light that cast crazy shadows over the unvarnished wooden floor. Despite this, the room was dim, and Zerafine had to pause to let her eyes adjust. Other than a travertine basin on a wooden pillar carved with indistinct figures, the room was empty. Two doors and a hallway led off the main room. Zerafine crossed to the basin, making the floorboards creak in an unmusical tune, and touched the rim: bone dry. The carved figures turned out to be grotesques of human faces, melting from one expression, one face, to another. Zerafine felt profoundly uncomfortable looking at them. She turned and went into the hallway.

She found a comfortable, if shabby, sitting room furnished with uncushioned chairs of some dark wood, a desk, and a cold fireplace. A man in a frayed shirt and ancient trousers looked up from the desk when she entered. She saw him register the red robe and cowl and swallow whatever he had been about to say. "*Thelis*," he said instead, rising. "You must be the emissary from Atenar. I thought the forbiddance we laid on the building was active. Please, come in."

34

He gestured to one of the seats next to the fireplace and took a seat across from her. "Why would you place a forbiddance on a temple?" she asked. She hadn't even noticed it. That might say something about the power of Sukman in this city.

The man rubbed a hand across his receding hairline. "We've been overrun," he said. "It's the only way to get some peace in the mornings. We take it down around ten o'clock so the people can come for Sukman's protection. It's been madness here for the last three weeks—no irony intended. I'm Rovalt."

"Zerafine of Dardagne," she said. "I would like to talk to your *tokthelos*, if possible."

"Genedirou's up Kerynnos hill banishing another one of these apparitions," said Rovalt. "But he'll no doubt go elsewhere before he returns here for the noonday ceremony. The god only knows where the madness will strike next."

Zerafine leaned forward slightly. "Rovalt, what are these things?"

He shrugged. "They appear with no warning and they seem to interact with things and even places that aren't there. Some of them vanish within moments, but others wander around until Genedirou banishes them. Genedirou says Sukman is punishing the city, but then he would say that—" Rovalt shook his head. "It's a question of whether they're real or simply a mass hallucination. We've used up a bale of *ceratis* trying to learn Sukman's mind on this, but either he's madder than usual or he's just not talking. For all we know, he *is* punishing the city, but for what?" He rubbed his scalp again.

"But Genedirou is able to banish them?"

"He's devised a ceremony in which he propitiates Sukman for his intervention. Or something. Genedirou says it's too complicated for any but the *tokthelos* to understand. He's probably right. It makes no sense to me."

"Do you think he'd be willing to talk to me about it? If it's too sacred—"

"Maybe, but you never know. It's worth your asking, I

35

suppose."

"The Council also told me that the apparitions seem to concentrate in certain spots. I don't suppose you know anything about that?"

Rovalt shrugged. "I know we get a lot of complaints from down by the temple of Hanu and Kanu, near the docks. People there are always sending runners, but...Genedirou doesn't have time to answer every call..." which was code for *Genedirou doesn't want to waste his time on low-class people with no money*. Zerafine wondered if the ritual was really as complicated as Rovalt believed, or if Genedirou was just trying to keep all the power and prestige for himself.

Rovalt stood. "I'm sorry, but I have to prepare for the first ceremony now. If you come back around one o'clock, Genedirou will be able to spare you some time."

"Thank you, Rovalt," Zerafine said, rising and saluting him. "I'll see you again soon."

Rovalt saluted. "I'll make sure Genedirou knows you're coming."

Zerafine returned to the street to find both Gerrard and Nacalia waiting for her. Both had mulish looks on their faces. "What's going on?" she asked.

"*He* wouldn't let me buy a seed cake with my own money," Nacalia said, with a jab of her thumb toward Gerrard.

"I told her not to wander off," Gerrard growled. "She's making it sound like I'm a monster."

"Let's *all* go have a seed cake," said Zerafine, rolling her eyes, "and then we're going to see if we can find a ghost. Not a real ghost. Damn. Now I'm doing it."

"You don't want to go back to the house and go through those notes?"

Zerafine waved the folder in his direction. "Would *you* want to?"

"Good point."

She shepherded her companions to a nearby food stall, where they bought deliciously sticky cakes drenched in scented honey. Then they had to stop at the fountain to wash their hands and faces. The black-veined marble fountain rose ten feet in the air and the spray of water jetting from its top added three feet to its height. Men and women carrying pottery jugs stopped in the act of filling them to stare at the newcomers, though it was not obvious who attracted more attention, Zerafine or Gerrard. The red robe drew nervous glances, but Gerrard, well over six feet tall, broad as an ox and white-blond from the summer sun, got his share of attention as well; in the case of some of the women and a couple of men, it was appreciative attention. Gerrard wiped droplets of water from his beard — another thing that set him off from the mostly clean-shaven and dark-haired Portenan men — and acted as if he didn't notice the stares. Possibly, Zerafine thought, after living ten years in the South, he didn't.

"Where to now?" Gerrard asked.

"We're going to find the temple of Hanu and Kanu," Zerafine replied.

Nacalia sucked in a breath. "That's not the best part of town, *thelis.*"

"We'll have to depend on Gerrard to protect us," Zerafine said. Gerrard snorted in amusement. Nacalia stared up and further up at the *sentare* as if weighing their chances.

"I *guess* he'll do all right," she said. "But I bet you're the more frightening one."

Gerrard winked at her. "You figured it out. I follow her around so she can protect me."

"You're not as dumb as you look," Nacalia retorted, then danced away as Gerrard sputtered in mock rage and amusement.

"You're sure we need the whelp?" Gerrard asked Zerafine, who was trying not to laugh.

"Fairly sure, yes. I think she has a crush on you."

"Me? No, it's you she wants to hero-worship. I'm the

inconvenient lunk hiding behind your robes who trips over his own feet and probably eats too much."

"You may be reading too much into her attitude. Anyway, you do eat a lot."

"I need to regain my strength from tripping over my feet all the time."

Nacalia led them through the vast central plaza and past the temple of Kalindi, queen of the gods, with its bright golden roof and pillars of rose-colored marble. It was the only building in the plaza that hadn't been damaged in the fires. At least one hundred steps led up the side of a manmade hill to the temple portico, but a steady procession of worshippers made the journey nonetheless. Other temples clustered around: the pillared block of Endelion, the ornately carved and painted pavilion of Marenda, Sintha's unadorned but elegant temple, its spire challenging the heavens, surrounded by offertory boxes of coins mixed with luck tokens. Another wide street led south from the plaza, and Nacalia went that way.

They passed the grand amphitheater famed for its races and wrestling matches and soon found themselves in a much less grand part of town. The road continued to be well maintained, but the buildings showed signs of age and wear. Five- and six-story apartment buildings leaned into one another for support, as though their weathered wood and mortared stone weren't enough to hold them up. Women called to each other from open balconies, shaking out laundry or preparing food. Zerafine saw someone dump a chamber pot out of a third-story window. "I thought Portena had indoor plumbing," she said.

"Most places, yes, but they ha'nt got around to everywhere, and it's the poorest places get things last of all," Nacalia said. "We got ours last Sukmor and mam's so grateful she could cry, if she ever done cry over things."

The temple to Hanu and Kanu stood in a cleared-out space within sight of the dock gates. Its stone façade gleamed with newness; Zerafine estimated its age at no more than forty years, more post-plague construction. The relief carving over the doorway picked out in bright colors depicted the twin gods wrestling, neither winning, neither relenting.

"You want to go in?" asked Gerrard.

Zerafine shook her head. "The *thelos* of Sukman said this was one of the loci for so-called ghost appearances. I want to see more of them--with luck, one that lasts for more than a minute."

"We're just going to stand here and stare at people?"

"Do you have a better idea?"

"You there!" a strident voice exclaimed. "You need to move on!" A skinny, gray-haired man dressed in the blue and brown robes of a *thelos* of Hanu, or possibly Kanu, was waving at them from the doorway to the temple. Zerafine asked, "Is something wrong?"

"Is something—Young lady, we can't have *theloi* of the god of Death hovering near the entrance to this temple like...like *gore-crows*, or the like. Take your walking mountain and the imp and be about your business."

Zerafine felt her temper begin to rise and had to sit on it, hard. "Actually, you may be able to help me with my business," she said as politely as her anger would allow. "I'm looking for one of the apparitions that have been plaguing Portena. Do you know where I might find one? Perhaps an area around here where they're common?"

"Young lady, I have no idea what you're talking about. I've never seen one of those delusions and I don't care to. Ask at one of Sukman's houses if you're so interested."

"The *thelos* of Sukman directed me to this district. If you haven't heard anything, could you possibly direct me—"

"Young lady—"

"*Thelos,*" Zerafine said, her voice low and cut with ice, "if you call me that again I swear by my god I will call down a curse upon you the likes of which your gods have never dreamed. I have been polite and respectful to you and I demand the same respect in return. Now, one last time and I'll remove my objectionable presence from your doorstep. I am looking for an apparition. You give a good impression of stupidity, but I doubt even you are so insulated from reality that you don't know what I'm talking about. There is an area here where many of those presences have been seen. Tell me where it is, or who can give me that information, and I'll be on my way."

The *thelos* had turned as gray as his hair. "*Thelis*," he said, "I apologize. I truly don't know where you can find what you seek. But if you ask the dock master, I believe she will be able to help you."

"Thank you. Atenas's blessing be far from you," Zerafine said, giving him the most cursory salute and turning away without waiting for his response. "Dock master?" she said to Nacalia, whose mouth was hanging open and eyes were wide as dinner plates. "Go on, we're running short on time." Nacalia nodded and trotted away, almost too fast for Zerafine and Gerrard to keep up.

"I think you scared the kid," Gerrard said.

"Good. I don't think she takes me seriously. I mean me as a *thelis* of Atenas. She needs to be clear on what it is I do."

"Make threats you can't deliver on? Or does Atenas now curse people for simple rudeness?"

"I know. I shouldn't have lost my temper. Or lied to him about the curse." It had been a small lie, more of a threat than a lie, but it still tasted bitter in her mouth. She adjusted her hood. The *seicorum* lining made the outer wool layer even heavier, and the mid-morning sun promised to burn as hotly as ever. She was already beginning to sweat through her undershift and into her ankle-length sleeveless linen tunic.

The southern gate was wider even than the one they'd entered by the previous night. Its massive, brass-sheathed doors lay flush with the wall and were only closed in time of war; traffic passed through Portena's harbor day and night. Near the gate, it was obvious that this was an area that catered to sailors and travelers. Even at this hour of the day, the taverns were bustling, and scantily clad women leaned out of upper windows, beckoning to all passersby, male and female. Gerrard waved at a busty, horse-faced redhead who whistled at him and then called to someone behind her to "take a look at the big one there." Zerafine nudged him. "Stop encouraging them," she said. The redhead called out something about Gerrard's size that had nothing to do with his visible attributes. Zerafine thought his sunburn deepened for a moment and grinned at him. "Told you," she said.

Outside the gate, warehouses lined the city walls, great flat-roofed buildings with doors broad enough to admit two oxcarts abreast. The dock master's house, its boards painted a weather-beaten blue, lay directly opposite the gate at the edge of the docks. All the traffic that came through Portena's harbor had to pass by it. Zerafine led the way up the steps to the door and knocked. After a moment, a plump woman threw open the door, said "I told you —" and then gasped. She made a quick sign of warding, and Zerafine heard Gerrard make a noise deep in his throat that was just this side of being a growl. Zerafine didn't take offense at people's superstitions, but Gerrard had never gotten used to having warding gestures flicked in their direction.

"Are you the dock master? I was told you might be able to help me," Zerafine said. The woman recovered herself, blushed, and thrust her hands behind her back.

"I thought you were my husband," she said. "Please come in, *thelis*. You must be the emissary. It's good to know someone's taking our problem seriously."

They entered the warm, stuffy dimness of the house, and took seats in the tiny front room. The woman started to sit behind her desk, thought better of it, and came around to lean against it. Nacalia sat on the floor, arms wrapped around her knees, next to Gerrard's feet. She reminded Zerafine of a cat they'd had in the dormitories at Atenar — small, independent, but quick to seek shelter with the biggest person around.

"I'm Solina, madama *thelis*," the woman said. "You're here about Baz?"

"I don't know a Baz," Zerafine replied. "I'm looking for some of these apparitions and I was told I could find one here."

"That's Baz," Solina said. She sounded relieved. "We've seen other apparitions, but he's the only one that's come back again and again. I know what the *theloi* of Sukman say, but it's *not* madness; Baz never hurt anyone, and we all know it's his ghost."

Zerafine bit back a sharp reply. Instead, she said, "Baz was a friend of yours?"

Solina laughed. "Not so much a friend as a lovable pain in my ass. He was a sailor off the *Bouncing Biancha* who spent his pay faster than he could earn it whenever he came into port. Hard worker, when he was sober, and treated the women nice. He fell overboard when the ship was at sea and drowned. We all knew about it, had a little service for him at the temple, and then four weeks ago people started seeing him around the docks. Figured it was just drunken foolery at first, but then *I* saw him on the first of Ailausor, right by warehouse twenty, acting like he was toting a load just like always. And I don't drink, madama." She poked the air in Zerafine's direction for emphasis. "We've asked for *tokthelos* Genedirou to come, but he's too busy to pay any mind to our part of the city. And *tokthelos* or no, madama, I'm not best thrilled at being told I'm suffering from a temporary madness. My wits are as good as the next man's. What else could it be but some new kind of ghost?"

Zerafine was impressed by the woman's emphatic speech even as she totted up the flaws in her argument. Ghosts couldn't travel over water; if Baz had left a ghost, it would have appeared on the ship immediately, not waited until it had returned to port. And the plain fact was that there *were* no other kinds of ghosts. Ghosts were fragments of memory desperate to regain a body, not immaterial illusions of people. Was Genedirou telling people that the "ghosts" were a form of traveling madness?

"I'd like to see Baz, if possible," she said.

Solina nodded. "He's usually at pier 7 around this time of day. We might have to wait a while," she warned.

They walked down the docks to pier 7, which was empty of ship and ghost alike. Zerafine pushed back her hood and let her hair fan across her back. In all directions, sailors scrambled up and down rigging, bare-chested men hauled loads into waiting carts, and drovers guided their wagons through warehouse doors or the gate to the city. The briny odor of seawater mixed with the bite of hot tar and the stink of animal waste. No one seemed to be paying attention to them, or if they were, they were unusually discreet about it. It was nice to feel anonymous for a few minutes.

Zerafine turned her attention out to sea and was startled to find a stranger had joined their party. He was bald, with a tremendous mustache drooping down both sides of his mouth, and wore ragged trousers and a stained linen shirt. He seemed not to notice them, but sat down on the edge of the pier and kicked his bare heels above the water.

Solina clutched Zerafine's arm. Her earlier fear of the *thelis* had vanished. "That's Baz," she whispered. She sounded excited and terrified at the same time.

Zerafine exchanged glances with Gerrard, who gave a typical shrug. "He wasn't there one second and he was the next," he said in a low voice. "No fading in, no noise or flashing lights or...I don't know what else you might expect. Just standing there." Nacalia peered out from behind Gerrard, her eyes wide.

Zerafine knelt down beside the apparition. He seemed more solid than the woman they'd seen in the market, but there was still a translucency to him that made it clear he wasn't human. She waved her hand in front of his face and got no reaction. She sat down beside him and said, "Hello, Baz." The man ignored her. He pursed his lips and began to whistle soundlessly, his feet waving, his hands propped behind his back. Zerafine thought for a moment, then, before she could talk herself out of it, swung herself to sit on Baz's lap.

She looked down and saw her own body overlaid with Baz's suddenly more transparent one. Other than that, she felt nothing. Baz seemed nothing more than an image, but she couldn't help feeling that if she could just—

--and Baz disappeared, and Zerafine inhabited her body alone. She felt no different, felt no lingering effects from Baz's presence. She scrambled up to face Gerrard, his face crimson, who shouted, "What in Atenas's name were you thinking? That thing could have killed you, or scrambled your brains, or worse!"

"I didn't think of that," she admitted. "It just occurred to me that if it were a ghost, I should be able to communicate with it. It's not a ghost," she added.

Solina's face fell. "So what is it?"

"I don't know. Not a ghost. Not some kind of madness. An illusion, maybe. And you're not going crazy, Solina. Baz hasn't hurt anyone, has he?" Solina shook her head. "Then I think you should just try to ignore him—yes, I know it's going to be hard, but I don't know what else to tell you. I can promise you, though, that I will figure it out."

Chapter Five

"That's a risky promise," Gerrard said as they walked back toward the central plaza. "Last I heard, you have no power over figments."

"It's not a mere figment, Gerrard," Zerafine said. "But I didn't have time to fully open myself to perceive it. I felt as though, if I could just get the right angle on it, I would understand what it was. We really need to talk to Genedirou. If he's capable of banishing these things, that might give us something to go on."

"I suppose it will really annoy Berenica if we don't finish quickly and move on."

"Who's Berenica?" Nacalia asked. Relieved temporarily of guide duties, she was amusing herself by dancing ahead of them and swinging back around in large swooping circles.

"That's madama *tokthelis* to you, whelp," Gerrard said. "Anyway, who says Genedirou is interested in help from a *thelis* not even of his faith?"

"Mam says the *tokthelos* of Sukman is crazy," Nacalia chirped. "He's as loony as a bag full of cats. He's got a head full of butterflies drunk on rum. He—"

"The *theloi* of Sukman are not crazy, Nacalia," Zerafine chided her. "You'd better not talk like that when we get to the sanctuary."

"Better not to talk at all, disrespectful whelp that you are," Gerrard said with a grin, tousling her wild black locks.

"No, sirrah," she said, and then added, in a tiny voice, "They won't make me crazy, will they?"

"You don't have anything to fear from them, little one." Zerafine shaded her eyes. "What on earth is that?"

They were at that moment passing the temple of Kalindi. Not so far ahead, a roiling mass of people thronged the plaza, their movement centered on one point. Gerrard nudged Zerafine, and the three climbed the temple steps to the first landing to get a better look. The central point turned out to be the temple of Sukman. From their vantage point, they could see a small figure emerge from the sanctuary and raise its arms as if in benediction upon the crowd.

"Should we join them? I'd like to hear what he has to say," said Zerafine.

"I'd feel happier if we weren't part of that crowd. I don't like how they're crushed together," Gerrard replied. "Besides, you can guess what he's saying. 'Behold, the displeasure of Sukman is upon you, be humble and donate more, yea verily.'"

"Don't blaspheme," Zerafine chided him, but with a smile. "Though I admit the *thelos* Rovalt implied something like that. Or, at any rate, that Genedirou would like for this to be Sukman's responsibility. But I think we should give him the benefit of the doubt. It's not easy to serve Sukman at any time, much less under these circumstances."

They watched as the small figure led the crowd in some sort of complicated ritual dance, the sound of chanting carried to their ears by the light wind. At their distance they couldn't make out the words, though since this was a ritual of Sukman, the words might not make any sense. When the crowd began to disperse, Gerrard led them down the stairs and across the plaza to the temple. The worshippers they passed seemed exhausted and not a little downcast. Unusual, Zerafine reflected, given that temple ceremonies were supposed to make one feel better, not worse.

A steady stream of worshippers continued to file up the steps and into the sanctuary. Zerafine shamelessly used the power of the red robe to push her way past the line of people, Gerrard and Nacalia trailing in her wake. At the basin, Rovalt was anointing each worshipper with water and a murmured blessing. His ceremonial robe of silk and velvet patchwork was far nicer than the clothes she'd seen him in that morning. He caught her eye and nodded toward the office they'd met in earlier that day. Zerafine cast her eye on Nacalia, who appeared suitably subdued, then led their little group down the hallway.

Genedirou was a tall, middle-aged man whose lean physique was interrupted by a small potbelly that threatened to grow larger. His crazily embroidered robe hung open over a loose shirt and long trousers, and his feet were bare. He stood next to the empty fireplace as if in contemplation, ignoring their entrance, then looked up a moment later as if he'd only just heard them come in. Zerafine was fairly certain he was simply being dramatic. "Welcome, *thelis*, Rovalt told me you were coming," he said, his voice gravelly in a pleasant way. "I am *tokthelos* Genedirou."

"Zerafine of Dardagne," she replied, saluting him as an equal. "My *sentare*, Gerrard of Kionnar." She didn't bother introducing Nacalia; he wouldn't expect her to. "Thank you for taking time to meet with us."

"Anything for the *theloi* of Atenas," he said, indicating that she should sit; Gerrard, naturally, continued to stand at attention, and Nacalia hid behind him. Genedirou took the seat opposite her. "Though I have to tell you, meaning no offense, that I'm surprised you've bothered to remain, seeing as how this is clearly the responsibility of Sukman."

"No offense taken," Zerafine said, excusing herself a little white lie. "But it was the Council who requested an emissary from Atenar, not the temple acting on its own initiative, so I'm obligated to conduct an impartial investigation." She resisted the urge to put emphasis on the word "investigation." "But I'd like to know what you think."

"An investigation?" Genedirou sounded surprised, which was natural, but also a trifle angry, which was not. "What do you mean, investigation?"

Zerafine cocked an eyebrow. She decided to pretend disingenuousness. "Investigation is part of my responsibility, you know. I interacted with one of the apparitions just half an hour ago. I was surprised to find it had no substance—"

"No substance apparent to mortal eye, yes," Genedirou said. He clasped his hands together in his lap. "You were very fortunate

47

in your encounter. These figments of Sukman's madness have been known to drive people mad themselves. I'll have to ask you not to interfere with them again. For your safety."

Patronizing and *pulling rank, eh? We'll see how far that will take you.* Zerafine smiled. "What do you mean, 'figments of Sukman's madness'?" she asked, making no promises.

Genedirou sat back in his chair. "Our Lord is, of course, profoundly mad," he said. He sounded more like a bored schoolmaster than a *thelos*. "We care for those He touches, though we cannot cure them, and we attempt to reach Him in His madness by embracing madness ourselves, though temporarily. Now, however, Sukman's anger at this city's pride and selfishness has manifested itself in these illusions, visible to some as a warning to all. I have been able to banish many of these illusions, though at great cost to myself, and my *theloi* labor daily to guide the people in worship that Our Lord might turn His wrath away."

"Have you any idea what Sukman might want? What could possibly turn His wrath away?"

Genedirou gave Zerafine a narrow-eyed look, but she returned it with one of innocent concern. "More humility in their treatment of others," he said. "More generosity in dealing with their fellow men and women. Sukman's mind is hard to read at the best of times, but in this time of greater madness, it's almost impossible to know the truth. The outpouring of support for our temple is certainly a heartening sign."

"I saw the noonday ritual," Zerafine said, "though I regret I was too far away to observe closely. I imagine worshippers have also been very generous to the temple."

Genedirou nodded sharply. "Money is of little consequence to us; you've seen how we live. But Sukman's work is always aided by...financial support." He clasped his hands so tightly that his knuckles showed white against his olive skin.

"I understand," she said with sweet, false sincerity. "Sirrah, I thank you for your time. You've certainly cleared up a lot of my questions."

Genedirou rose when she did, and saluted her perfunctorily. "I hope your visit here won't be entirely wasted on our problems," he said. "And that your...investigation...will be swiftly concluded."

"Oh, we've decided to stay here for a few weeks anyway," Zerafine said cheerily, and was rewarded with Genedirou's tightening all his facial muscles at once. "We've been traveling for so many months, I think we've earned some rest, even if it *is* during the height of the summer heat. I find Ailausor to be so *draining*, don't you?"

They exchanged a few more inconsequentialities, then Zerafine took her leave. The three were silent as they crossed the sanctuary, still full of people, but Zerafine took a moment to salute Rovalt, who nodded in return. Back on the street, they walked for a while in silence, Nacalia running ahead, until Zerafine said, "Well?"

"He's milking this thing for all he can get out of it," Gerrard said. "He was *definitely* not happy that you were meddling in what he thinks of as his affairs."

"Agreed. I would bet he has no idea what these apparitions really are."

"And yet he has some way of making them disappear and stay disappeared."

"So it might still have something to do with Sukman."

Gerrard scratched his beard. "Possibly. My impression is that Genedirou really believes Sukman is behind it all, but he's sort of flailing around and has happened upon something that works."

Zerafine sighed. "If it's true that Sukman is responsible, then that makes it none of our business, except that the *Marathelos* gave me the responsibility, which makes it my business again. And the Council wants me to be part of the solution, whatever Genedirou says. So it's my business twice over."

"I'll be happy when this is all over. Almost nobody involved really wants us here. Even the Council wishes we weren't necessary." Gerrard stopped. "Where are we?"

"I don't know. Where is *Nacalia*?"

They had been following her without thinking, and now found themselves in a warren of tiny streets and tall apartment houses of lath and stone. Nacalia had vanished. Gerrard cursed. "I knew I should have been paying closer attention to her."

"She wouldn't have run off and left us."

"No, but she might have gotten too far ahead. She's sort of flighty sometimes."

They moved to the side of the road and watched the traffic for sign of their little guide. After about five minutes, Nacalia ran up to them from a completely unexpected direction. She was wide-eyed and harried.

"Where did you run off to?" Gerrard thundered.

"Don't growl," Zerafine said. She crouched down to Nacalia's eye level. "The girl is terrified."

"Can't imagine *her* being afraid of anything on these streets," Gerrard muttered.

"Madama *thelis, sentare,* I...I got lost!" Nacalia exclaimed, and burst into tears.

"Oh, little one, that's not so bad—"

"It *is, thelis,* it *is!*" Nacalia was beside herself. "I ha'nt never been lost on these streets, not once my whole life long, and I turned a corner along the way to your place and I swear it wa'nt there, and when I turn around the road I come down was the wrong road. Took me an age and some to find my way back to you." She wiped her eyes and her nose. "I swear it, *thelis.* Don't send me back!"

"I believe you," said Zerafine, glancing at Gerrard, who merely shrugged, "and I'm not going to send you back. Let's stick closer together this time, and if anything happens, at least we'll all be together. But I'm sure you won't get lost again."

Chapter Six

They didn't get lost. In just a few minutes' time they were back at the Atenas compound, as Zerafine had begun to think of it, with no trouble. A traveling coach of great size and gaudiness stood outside their door, its perfectly matched bearers lounging around the gate. Gerrard tensed and looked ready for action, but the men only straightened to attention as the little party approached, with one man stepping out of the way as Gerrard reached for the gate.

As they approached the house, they could hear the murmur of voices within. Zerafine motioned for Gerrard and Nacalia to remain silent, and she went quietly forward until she could make out words.

"—old sour-patch like Berenica, so just sweet-talk her and keep her out of the way." That was a woman, young but not too young, with a sharp edge to her voice.

"Kalindi save me from old sour-patches I have to flirt with," said a second person, male, of indeterminate age. "She'll probably keep herself out of the way, eager for her comforts and not interested in our problems, emissary or not."

Zerafine raised her eyebrows. She threw the door open and swept in, Gerrard a step behind. "This old sour-patch is most definitely interested in your problems," she announced. "But I'll be happy to stay out of your way if that's what the situation calls for. I am nothing if not at your disposal."

She'd caught both her visitors by surprise, their mouths agape and their faces flushed. Both were dressed in semi-formal tunics and knee-trousers. The young woman wore her dark hair cut short and her face carefully made up despite the heat. The man, possibly in his early thirties, was taller than his companion by a few inches and was remarkably good-looking, with high cheekbones, a well-chiseled nose, and startling blue eyes in a darkly tanned face. He ran one hand through his curly black hair and said, "Madama *thelis*,

51

I beg your pardon. This is very embarrassing—"

"Not for me," Zerafine said cheerfully.

"—really just unforgivable, please accept our apologies," he continued. "I'm afraid we were expecting someone much older, given your responsibilities, and we—"

"We're used to dealing with Berenica," the woman said, as if that explained everything.

"I hope you're more respectful of her to her face," Zerafine said, frowning. This was fun.

"We are, *thelis*, we really are," the woman said. "But even you must admit—"

"Nothing," said the man. "Berenica is a fine woman and it was inexcusable of us to make such comments in your house."

"But not elsewhere," Zerafine needled him. He ran his hand through his hair again and smiled. "You're having us on," he said.

"Just a little," she admitted. "I am Zerafine of Dardagne and this is my *sentare*, Gerrard of Kionnar."

The man gave her a nod, acknowledging that she'd won again—he should have introduced himself first. "My name is Dakariou. I'm the council liaison assigned to work with you. This is my assistant, Giara."

"Welcome to Portena," Giara said, still flushed with embarrassment.

"Welcome to my home, however temporary it is," Zerafine said. She gestured toward the sitting room. "Please be seated."

A man wearing a long ribbed tunic in black and red came out of the kitchen bearing a tray of tall blue glasses. Zerafine and Gerrard had left early that morning, apparently too early for the servants to be awake, and this one seemed to be trying to make up for his failure to rise on time. At least his manner was perfectly correct; he offered the tray to each of them in turn, properly starting with their guests. The glasses were filled with cool tea, with chunks of ice floating in each. Tiny rounds of sliced bread smeared with a dark substance sat on a plate in the middle of the tray. Dakariou and Giara each took one, Zerafine thought out of politeness rather than hunger. Zerafine took one as well and nodded to the man. "That will be all," she said, exactly as if she'd told him to bring refreshments. Gerrard took a position by the wall and did his best to pretend to be furniture. Nacalia was nowhere in sight. Zerafine hoped she'd have the sense to stay still. The man bowed and withdrew.

"Council liaison," Zerafine said. "I met with some of the Council members this morning. What does your role entail?"

"You've seen them?" Dakariou shook his head. "I truly am behind in my business, then. My only excuse is that you came upon us so suddenly. I throw myself upon your mercy." His expression was so self-deprecatingly comical that Zerafine smiled.

"I'm only interested in finding the truth as quickly as possible," she said. "Your help will be invaluable."

"I hope so. The Council has instructed me to work with you, to report to them on your findings and provide any assistance they can offer. The idea is to streamline the process so you can spend your time on your investigations, not on endless meetings."

"Councilor Castinidou told me the two theories were that the apparitions are spirits escaped from Atenas's courts, or figments of Sukman's madness made manifest. We've also heard it said that these are a new kind of ghost, which I can assure you is not true."

"*Tokthelis* Berenica said the same," Dakariou said.

"And you didn't believe her."

Dakariou flushed, but smiled at her. "I don't wish to speak ill of such a respected member of our community," he began, "so please forgive me for my bluntness. The *tokthelis*'s honesty — in fact that of all of the *theloi* of Atenas — is well known, but her response to this crisis has been to sit back and watch events unfold. You must know that's why you were brought here to investigate; Berenica should be our investigator, but she will not, or cannot, look into the problem herself."

"And you believed her assertions were based on...what?

Wishful thinking?"

"Rather, assumptions based on hearsay and secondhand reports." Dakariou took a sip from his glass. "As I said, I would rather not call her character into question."

And yet that's precisely what you've done, Zerafine thought. But his assessment of Berenica's character matched her own. She was beginning to like this man.

"What do you make of *tokthelos* Genedirou?" she asked.

"Again, I'd prefer not to speak ill—"

"Dakariou, please don't stand on ceremony with me," she asked. "Let me make this easier for you. Whether or not Sukman is involved, Genedirou intends to turn the situation to his advantage. He's been encouraging people to believe that worshipping Sukman—better yet, donating to His temple—will keep the apparitions away. He has some method of banishing them that he uses to bolster his position and improve Sukman's standing within the Pantheon, at least here in Portena. He probably doesn't wish anyone harm, but he certainly has no stake in ending this, as you called it, rash of appearances."

Dakariou leaned back and gave her a smile, a real one, not the flirtatious half-glances he'd been using on her since she came in. "You've spoken to him," he said.

"I have. I'm guessing you haven't had much cooperation from him."

"Not in the least. His interest is in using me as a way to get at the Council, to improve his secular as well as ecclesiastical standing."

"To his credit, I think he's doing this as much for the sake of his god as for his own status. He doesn't seem to have diverted any of the funds toward making his life more comfortable."

"I don't like him much, but I agree with you there. Even so, it doesn't begin to solve our problem."

Zerafine noted that "our." "So, in your opinion, what needs to be done?"

Dakariou smiled again. "I think your role as, as you put it, impartial third party will go a long way toward easing pressure on the Council. Until now, people have been leaning on them to validate one theory or the other; with you around, the people will be less inclined to throw the blame at the government."

"That's certainly how my presence benefits the Council. Shouldn't we be more concerned about how it benefits the people?"

Dakariou gave her another genuine smile. "I'm talking like a politician again, aren't I? The truth is, at this point most people don't know whom to listen to. Genedirou is charismatic, but with the apparitions being mostly passive, it's hard to believe they're a form of madness. People want some kind of official declaration, and they want it from someone who doesn't have an axe to grind. Genedirou will make a stink about you poking your nose into his affairs, but even he can't challenge your right to investigate. And, to be honest, you're far more attractive than either Genedirou or Berenica, and people will respond to that." He wasn't smiling now, but there was an intensity in his eyes that made Zerafine blush. She considered telling him what she'd learned about the non-physical nature of the apparitions, but decided against it. It would be better, she thought, to learn more about them before sharing information that made no sense.

Instead, she said, "I think I will have to find an excuse to be at one of these banishments of his. Does he ever give advance notice? I'd think he would want an audience."

"A performance is exactly what it is," said Dakariou sourly. "He makes sure the Council knows about his banishments so they can witness them. All in the name of open honesty, but he really wants to be seen as someone with power."

"I'd take it as a kindness if you'd send me word," Zerafine said. "I may not always be here, but I'll find a way to check in occasionally."

"Certainly, if you'll do me a favor in return. Will you keep me apprised of your progress? I'd like to be able to give *something* to the

Council."

"Agreed," Zerafine said, and reached out to seal the bargain, clasping Dakariou's hand. It was warm and smooth and sent an unexpected tingle down her spine. Dakariou had a firm grip that lingered, perhaps, a little longer than necessary. It seemed the council liaison still felt the need to flirt with her. She found she didn't mind all that much. It had been a long time since anyone had looked at her that way.

The three rose and exchanged pleasantries for about a minute, and then Dakariou and Giara excused themselves. Zerafine showed them to the door, which she closed behind them, and then leaned against it, her forehead pressed against the black wood. "Can we be done talking to people for the day?" she asked, hearing a plaintive note in her voice that surprised her.

"I don't trust him," Gerrard said. Zerafine turned to look at him. He sounded almost angry.

"I trust him as far as our interests coincide," she said. "He seemed very forthcoming about his role in all of this."

"He's trying to get on your good side by flirting with you."

"So? He's handsome and I don't mind being flirted with, given that I know what he's up to. Besides, with a face like that, I think he does it by reflex."

"I liked him," Nacalia said. She'd found a seat in the corner and had silently been observing the proceedings. "He's handsome and she was pretty. I liked how she did her face."

"Let's find you a place to sleep, whelp." Gerrard scooped the girl up and carried her, squealing in mock fear, down the hallway opposite the bathing chamber. Zerafine sat in her abandoned chair, dropped the folder of reports on the floor, and put her face in her hands. Berenica, Genedirou, Dakariou. Spirits with no tangible form; apparitions of dead people — damn, she hadn't thought to ask if any of them had become actual ghosts when they died. That would have been a pertinent question. Well, it could wait until tomorrow. She was sweaty and needed another bath.

The servant reappeared from what she imagined must be the kitchen and bowed, very low. "Madama *thelis*, I must apologize for my inexcusably lax behavior —"

"Please don't," she said, and then, hearing how abrupt she sounded, added, "People have been apologizing to me all day. Can we just skip to the part where you've apologized and I've excused you and told you to be more alert in the future? My name is Zerafine. What's yours?"

"Aesoron, madama *thelis*," he said, again bowing low. "The *tokthelis* has assigned me to your household." A small, thin woman appeared in the kitchen doorway. "This is Fidonia, your cook. We are ready for your instructions...perhaps you would like to order dinner?"

"What time is it? It can't be much past two. Shall we say — Gerrard, when do you want to eat?"

"Now," he replied from far down the hall.

"Ignore him, he's always hungry. Can you give him something now, and have the evening meal ready at seven?"

"Whatever madama *thelis* wishes," Aesoron said, bowing yet again.

"Thank you. What madama *thelis* wishes is that you call her simply *thelis*, and please stop bowing. I think we shall get along just fine, don't you?"

Aesoron began to bow, caught himself, and nodded instead. Zerafine shucked her robe and peeled off her slightly sweaty hood and cowl. "Hang these somewhere until I find a place that can clean them properly, would you?"

Aesoron took them without flinching. "I can take care of that, *thelis*."

"Can you? Excellent. I'll need them again in the morning. Now I'm going to bathe and probably take a nap. If I'm not up by six, please wake me then." In Atenas's name, having servants again was lovely. Zerafine went down the hall to find Gerrard, who was watching Nacalia bounce on a large bed covered with a blanket done in an eye-watering pink and turquoise pattern.

"Nacalia, don't bother the servants," he said, and took Zerafine's arm to lead her back down the hall out of earshot. "I'm starting to worry that we've done the wrong thing by her," he said in a low voice, scratching his beard. "The first thing she told me, when I showed her that room, was that her whole family lived in a space only twice that size. She's never had a bed she didn't have to share. What's going to happen to her when we leave?"

"It never occurred to me that we weren't doing her any favors," Zerafine admitted. "But what are we supposed to do? We've already contracted for her time, and it would break her heart if we sent her away early—and not, I think, because she'd miss the luxury. I'm getting fond of her myself."

"Do *not* suggest that we adopt her."

"Not on your life! But we need to consider making other arrangements. We put her in this position; we're responsible for her now." Zerafine scrubbed at the hair at the base of her neck, which felt stiff with sweat. "Maybe I should cut my hair short like Giara's."

Gerrard eyed her skeptically. "You'd regret it come the winter," he said. "Besides, you have nice hair."

"Thank you. I'm going to wash it now and then take a very lazy, very long nap. Then I'm going to go over these notes. Pity me."

"So I can consider myself off duty for the afternoon?"

"What, I'm a duty now? Thanks so much."

"You have no idea how much work it is keeping you out of trouble." Gerrard ran his fingers through his hair, which made it stand up in wiry tufts, unlike Dakariou's smooth curls. "I may go get a haircut or something.

"Take Nacalia with you, then."

"Do I have to?" Gerrard asked plaintively.

"You do if you ever want to find your way back here again."

"There is that," Gerrard said. "Did someone say something

about food?"

Chapter Seven

They spent the entire next day following up on the material in Vessa's notes. She had been thorough, if not systematic; it took Zerafine an hour to organize and collate everything. As promised, the notes included a map that plotted out most of the complaints the Council had received, and they did indeed cluster around four spots in the city. Since those spots were also mostly equidistant from each other, Zerafine agreed that it couldn't be coincidence. They visited each of these loci of activity: one was sited in the center of a shopping district, one in a middle-class neighborhood, a third just off the plaza, and the last lay in a part of town where the houses were so overbuilt that only a thread of daylight filtered between the buildings to reach the street. Zerafine couldn't see anything they had in common.

Of even more help were the detailed reports some enterprising assistant, probably Paola, had compiled, noting time, place, duration, and type of fourteen of the more than one hundred reported apparitions. They were helpful because, in contrast to the mapped clusters, they showed absolutely no commonalities beyond being apparitions of people who had died in the last five years. They ranged in age from an eighty-year-old grandfather to— disturbingly—an infant who lay in the street and soundlessly squalled for ten minutes before vanishing and reappearing exactly twenty hours later. This last bit of information they discovered from going to the neighborhood themselves. Zerafine had had the idea of finding out whether the apparitions, or rather the people they represented, had created ghosts when they died. Five hours of trekking across the city, a journey dramatically reduced by Nacalia's ability to find the shortest route to anywhere, turned up the useless fact that only two of the fourteen had become ghosts. Zerafine wasn't sure what it would have told them if all had been ghosts, or none, but either way it came to nothing. Either way, the day was a complete waste.

They returned home to find two invitations. The first was from Dakariou, telling them that Genedirou would be performing a banishment in Naklos the next morning at ten. Nacalia said it was a neighborhood on Talarannos hill and would be easy to find. The second was from Berenica, inviting Zerafine to dinner. Zerafine groaned inwardly, but penned a response and sent Nacalia scurrying to deliver it. She went to change into more formal, less sweat-stained clothing. Unfortunately, her options were limited; they took very little with them on their journeys, and she was forced to make do with the selection of clothes left behind by other visitors.

"That is an ugly dress," Gerrard said, truthfully if not tactfully. The gown was an unflattering green with a slightly lumpy weave.

"I swear, first thing in the morning, we're going to trade in some of that *seicorum* you're hauling around and buy some decent clothes. I don't even care if we leave them behind when we go. In fact, we'll be doing future residents a favor." She coiled her hair high on her head and pinned it with a beaten brass comb that was unexpectedly beautiful. Possibly Berenica had overlooked it in her quest to remove all things attractive and tasteful from the house.

"First thing tomorrow afternoon. Tomorrow morning we get to watch Genedirou put on a show."

"Agreed." She traded grimaces with her *sentare*, then crossed the street to Berenica's home, where she was welcomed by the same dark-clad man as before. Inside, Berenica greeted her. She was alone; apparently this was to be a more private meal. Berenica waited for Zerafine to take her seat, then sat opposite her. The servitor brought them tossed greens with a light oil and vinegar dressing, then withdrew.

"I understand you've been working hard," Berenica said.

Zerafine wondered where she got her information. "Doing my job," she said brightly.

"Indeed."

They ate in silence for a while, Zerafine unable to think of a conversational gambit, Berenica closed-off and silent with her own thoughts. "I met the council liaison yesterday," Zerafine finally said.

Berenica's frown deepened. "An impertinent young man."

"I found him engaging. He certainly had a lot to say about our situation."

"Don't be too quick to take his word. His appointment was political. I wouldn't be surprised to learn that he's using you to his advantage."

Zerafine wiped her lips on her napkin. "That's all very well, since I intend to use him too," she said. It wasn't entirely true, but she felt a little rattled at Berenica's direct approach. She had assumed the old lady would be more subtle.

"And what have you discovered?" Berenica said.

"That if Sukman is involved, it's not in the way Genedirou believes," she said. She could be direct, too. She added, "You must have realized that Genedirou has much to gain from this as well."

Berenica's eyes narrowed. "I told you that I haven't seen fit to poke my nose into this business beyond what our Lord demands."

The servitor returned to clear their places and bring out some lightly poached sea bass in some kind of creamy sauce. His timely appearance saved Zerafine from saying something a lot more pointed in return. "*Our Lord* requires us to be arbiters of justice as well as consolers of the dead," she said. "My role in this goes beyond simply making pronouncements about His part in all of this."

"Are you accusing me of negligence?"

"I'm not accusing you of anything. You don't appear to have done much to be accused of." *Oops.*

Berenica sucked in a deep breath. "Do not you *dare* to pass judgment on me, *thelis*," she said. "My conscience is clear. I've declared that Atenas has nothing to do with it and I resent your implication that my part has been inadequate."

"*Tokthelis*, I have no intention of calling your work into question." Zerafine swallowed a handful of nasty words and said,

"I apologize for implying otherwise. I think you may misunderstand why I was sent here. This is not about Atenas's role in the problem. The *Marathelos* is concerned about the entire situation, this...rash of appearances." Her mouth quirked up, remembering Dakariou. "The Council requested an emissary; he believes I will be an effective neutral party—"

"Which is to say that I am not!"

"Which is to say that he respects the work you do here and does not think it wise to pull you away from your regular duties. After all, you can't go hunting all over town *and* perform consolations *and* fulfill the daily ritual duties." *You arrogant cow, you have no idea how much I want to throw your words back into your smug face.*

Berenica subsided only a tiny bit. "You've certainly seen fit to throw your weight around, given that you're only a young *thelis* and unranked."

"I bear the rank of the *Marathelos*. Would you care to take it up with him?" Zerafine drew a deep, calming breath. "Remember that when I leave here, you will still be *tokthelis*, and I will once again be a lowly *thelis*." That might have been too obvious, but she was tired of fencing with the old woman when she wasn't allowed to use the point of her blade.

Berenica held her gaze for a long, long moment, then sat back in her chair. "True," she said. "We do all have our parts to play. Please, eat." The sudden change in conversation made Zerafine's head whirl, the more so because Berenica's conversation from that point was full of pleasant trivialities, as though they hadn't been at each other's throats moments before.

Dessert was another light sherbet and then Berenica offered an after-dinner coffee, which Zerafine declined, pleading tiredness and an early morning. They parted on superficially civil terms, but Zerafine was seething underneath. The feeling grew as she crossed the street, until when she reached her front door her jaw was clenched and her head ached.

In the seconds it took to swing the heavy black door open, she regained enough control that, instead of raging when she stepped inside, she merely said, "Gerrard. Let's walk."

Gerrard was in the middle of playing some ratty old board game with Nacalia. He looked surprised, but stood up and joined her anyway. Nacalia leaped up to follow, but Gerrard, accurately gauging Zerafine's mood, said, "No, we won't go far. You get ready for bed."

Outside again, Zerafine stormed off down the street, Gerrard lengthening his stride to keep up. "I take it you and Berenica aren't best friends now," he said.

Zerafine rounded on him, causing him to pull up short or run over her. "She *should* have been an *ally*," she raged. "There is no reason, none at all, why she shouldn't want to help me, but instead? She's a bitter old hag who can't stand that someone younger and smarter and prettier than her gets all this power and makes her look bad, at least as far as she believes—"

Gerrard put his finger to her lips. "Try not to scare the neighbors," he said. She slapped his hand away.

"I came out here because for all I know those servants of ours are spies for her. You see what she's got me doing? I'm suspicious of two people who are probably perfectly nice and honorable. That's what she's done to me."

"She's certainly made you bitchy enough," Gerrard snapped. "No need to hit me."

"Oh, like you even feel it, you big—" Zerafine stopped. "Oh, Gerrard. I'm so sorry. You're right, I'm being bitchy. I'm just so *angry* at her, and I'm angry at myself. We spent all day learning absolutely nothing, and I really don't know what I'm doing. Maybe we *should* give it up."

Gerrard put his hand on her shoulder, then withdrew it quickly. "Sorry. I was afraid you might hit me again."

"Oh, shut up."

He grinned, then gripped both her shoulders. "I was thinking, right around the tenth or eleventh apparition today, that it was all a waste of time because we kept coming up with nothing. But what we've really done is narrow down the possibilities. That means we're actually making progress. And given the number of possibilities we've had to eliminate, it's pretty obvious the Council hasn't given much attention to this. I'm really starting to feel like we're the only ones who want to know what's going on."

"Us and Dakariou," Zerafine said.

He grimaced and released her. "Him too," he said. "But even he has an agenda. I don't like that you're so high up on it."

"I'm not worried about him," she said. "I'm worried about what's going to happen when we inevitably confront Genedirou about *his* agenda. Dakariou did have a point about not upsetting the balance in the city."

"Maybe confronting him won't be necessary."

"Maybe." They turned and walked back to the house. "But I wouldn't count on it."

Chapter Eight

The banishment took place on an estate halfway up Talarannos hill. Zerafine rode there in an enclosed sedan chair. She and Gerrard had argued about this, since Zerafine hated to travel anywhere except under her own power, but Gerrard had won by pointing out that she didn't want to arrive sweat-sodden and exhausted. She had to concede his logic.

Now she watched the city pass by through the gauzy curtains of the conveyance Nacalia had hired. It smelled strongly of roses; no doubt she'd be perfumed when they reached their destination. Gerrard paced beside her, easily keeping up with the bearers. They'd looked so relieved when they learned he wouldn't be riding with her.

"This neighborhood is beyond wealthy," Gerrard said in a low voice as they began their ascent. "I mean, Berenica's compound is certainly upscale, but I'm afraid I'm going to start gawking like the uncouth Northerner I am. That last place had fire-breathing stone gargoyles on the gate posts!"

"Conspicuous consumption," Zerafine agreed. "I can't imagine how the owners of this place we're going to must feel about having an apparition in their backyard. So pedestrian of us to trample over their property."

But when they arrived at the estate and were ushered in, a plump woman dressed in an intricately woven blue and purple gown hurried to greet them and identified herself as the lady of the house, Serrana. "Thank you so much for attending," she said, giving them a weak but genuine smile. "I really don't know what we'd do without dear Genedirou, but it's so comforting to have a *thelis* of Atenas present. Somehow it makes everything more real."

She led them through the house while, behind her back, Zerafine and Gerrard exchanged equally surprised glances. Fear of them was common, respect understandable, but pleasure was rare.

66

The garden was cool even in the mid-morning sun. Shade trees provided cover from the heat, and lemon and orange trees added their tangy scent to the air. Late summer flowers bloomed everywhere, and cobblestone paths wound through neatly trimmed grass past the occasional bench. It was a tidy little gardener's paradise.

Genedirou hadn't arrived yet. He'd probably want to make a grand entrance. Dakariou was there, though, talking to Councilwoman Vessa, Alita Talarannos, and a man Zerafine didn't know. Dakariou greeted her with what she thought was genuine pleasure. Possibly she'd underestimated him.

"Madama *thelis*, you've met Councilwomen Vessa and Alita, so let me introduce you to *Marathelos* Alestiou, *thelos* of Kalindi and Council representative from the temples. *Marathelos*, Zerafine of Dardagne." Salutes were exchanged all around. Vessa gave her a pleasant smile, Alita an arch one.

Marathelos Alestiou was a skeleton of a man, tall and dark, with long white hair worn gathered at the nape of his neck, held in place with a band bearing the circle of Kalindi. Zerafine bowed low before him; he was the highest ranking *thelos* of the chief goddess of the Pantheon, first among equals—as if anyone believed that. One glance was enough to tell Zerafine that this was not a well man; his hands trembled as he saluted her, the skin paper-thin, and his face had lines of pain at the corners of his mouth and eyes. If a man of his rank, and that ill, were here to witness the banishment, the Council must think the situation very dire.

"It's good to meet you, emissary," he said. His voice was as frail as his appearance. "And this must be your *sentare*."

Gerrard's mouth quirked. Dakariou turned quickly and said, "Of course, I'm so sorry, I should have introduced madama *thelis's* companion, Gerrard of..."

"Kionnar," Gerrard rumbled. Zerafine had to stifle a grin. Her *sentare* was back to playing the dumb ox. Had Dakariou genuinely forgotten to introduce him, or was he playing a deeper game? Either way, Zerafine provisionally rated him down again.

Serrana personally brought drinks to her guests. Not wedded to tradition, or just nouveau riche? In any case, she was a sweet and likeable person, and for her sake Zerafine hoped Genedirou wasn't faking his ability to banish an apparition.

Just as she thought this, she noticed what seemed to be a thickening of the air, something like heat waves, but with more substance. The next moment, a child stood there, tossing a fist-sized ball up and catching it, toss and catch, over and over. Zerafine plucked the sleeve of the person nearest her, who turned out to be Vessa. "Look there," she said.

Vessa looked, and started. "It's here," she announced. Aside from her initial startled reaction, she didn't seem either surprised or afraid. Zerafine remembered that the councilmen and women had witnessed more than a few of these banishments. Serrana squeaked and stepped behind a tree.

"Where is Genedirou?" Alestiou said.

"I am here," Genedirou said grandly, stepping past them all and approaching the child. He made a show of examining it from all directions, tapping his chin and saying "Hmm" on occasion. Finally he straightened up and said, "I believe I can banish it. If you would all step back — I'm afraid the space here is so constrained, I will have to make some adjustments to the ritual." They all obediently took a few steps back.

Rovalt came past them, holding a stemmed silver cup inscribed with spirals. He and Genedirou both wore their ritual robes, crazy patchworks of different fabrics and different shapes, but nevertheless invested with a mad dignity. Genedirou took the cup and held it while Rovalt searched in his robes, finally coming up with a pair of copper tubes stopped with wax. Rovalt peeled the wax away with his fingernails and poured first one, then the other into the cup. Genedirou held it to his nose and inhaled deeply, then drank the mixture down and flung the cup aside.

They all waited. Nothing happened. Genedirou's eyes were

closed and his breathing heavy. They waited a few minutes more. Zerafine found herself holding her breath. The perfumed air was heavy with a new, unidentifiable scent. Then Genedirou opened his eyes. His pupils were pinpoints, almost invisible in the dark brown of his eyes. He began to stretch, arms over head, one leg lifted until his foot reached his chest. His body seemed to move independently of his mind's control. His fingers fumbled with the catches on his robe, undoing them at random, and then he threw his robe to the ground.

He was completely naked underneath.

Zerafine wanted to laugh, but something about his movements made him seem dignified, even though the outline of his ribs was clearly visible in his concave chest and his potbelly hung over his manhood like a ripe melon. At that moment, Zerafine actually respected Genedirou; any man who could so thoroughly expose himself (in every sense) could not be acting entirely out of self-interest.

Genedirou began to wander through the garden, oblivious to his audience, who were sometimes forced to step out of his way. He stood on his head. He took positions out of classical and modern dance. He made obscene gestures that Zerafine simply could not look away from, however unsettling they were. He looked ridiculous and he looked like a man touching the face of the Divine. Zerafine was so caught up in his movements that it wasn't until he had nearly reached the illusory child that she realized his random movements were actually tracing out a sigil: the spiral of Sukman. Genedirou was invoking the presence of his god. She felt an unusual pressure behind her eyes, began to taste colors, hear impossible sounds. Sukman was there. She felt sure that if she could see Him, she would go mad. She wondered what the others sensed.

She closed her eyes and drew three cleansing breaths, opening her heart's eye. What she was trying might be dangerous, but she wanted to see what Genedirou's banishment actually did. From this perspective, the child tossing the ball vanished. In its place was a tangle of hair-thin threads, a knot about the size of a walnut that glowed with the same light a spirit did. She couldn't see where the threads began; they faded into invisibility only a few inches from the tangle. But she was certain they were attached to *something*.

Genedirou was entreating Sukman for a boon. She could sense his mind, chaotic and unformed, merging with the god's, for the moment completely insane. He wanted Sukman to touch the world, just *here*, just *now*, fill this one spot with his madness. And Sukman agreed.

She felt Sukman's attention turn to the little knot. It broke apart under His touch, the threads unwinding in a chaotic dance that ended with their ends waving free like the fronds of an undersea plant. Sukman's presence withdrew and the pressure behind her eyes dropped to nothing. Free from the restraint of His presence, she looked more closely. The fine threads were nearly invisible, but as she watched, she saw two of them entwine again, and the glow grew infinitesimally stronger.

Gerrard said, "What's wrong?" She looked up at him, further up than normal, and realized she had sat down on one of the benches. She felt dizzy. So that was what it was like to be in the presence of a god. "Did you feel any of that?" she asked him.

"I felt as though my ears needed to pop."

"I want to talk to Genedirou."

"Genedirou? He's not going to be in a position to talk to anyone for a while. Still lightheaded from those drugs, I'd guess."

"Sukman was there, part of Him anyway. It was... indescribable." She shook her head. "I think the apparitions are spirits, or partly spirit, but I've never seen anything like it before. The important thing is that Genedirou's not doing what he thinks he's doing. I don't think his banishments are a permanent cure."

"Does he not know, or not care?"

"I'd...rather give him the benefit of the doubt. Either way, he's got to be stopped. Refine his ritual, whatever. Who knows what could happen if an apparition he supposedly banished returned?"

"Panic, if that mob outside the temple is any indication."

"I'm afraid you're right."

With Gerrard's help, Zerafine stood and approached Genedirou. Someone had brought him his robe and he leaned heavily on Rovalt's arm. He looked as if he'd wrestled ten men the size of Gerrard. "Genedirou," she said, and when she had his attention, she saluted him. "That was impressive. It was certainly not what I expected."

"I live to serve our city," he replied. "I hope you understand that." There seemed to be a double meaning to his words that Zerafine couldn't understand. Did he know she'd been watching?

"I understand many things now," she said. "We will speak more later. You clearly need time to recover."

She turned away before he could respond. It was possible he didn't know what he was doing, but by the look in his eye, he knew more about the apparitions than he was willing to admit.

Chapter Nine

But Genedirou wasn't available later that day; he was out performing another banishment. He was also gone the next morning. When they returned in the afternoon, Rovalt told them Genedirou wasn't in the temple. He was lying.

"I don't know why, but he's avoiding me," Zerafine said. They stood in the shade of a booth across from the temple, enjoying a cool drink. "I assume that means he knows his banishments are temporary and is afraid I'll intervene."

"Maybe he just doesn't want to discuss his sacred ritual with you. It *did* summon a god, after all."

"He knows he's doing something wrong, and I intend to find out what."

"You'll worry away at him like a terrier is what you'll do. Though I don't like the man, so I don't know why you shouldn't."

"I have to catch him first." Zerafine finished her drink and handed the cup back to the stall keeper, who took it warily, but at least didn't throw it away to prevent her contaminating his next customer. "I'm tired of trying to wait him out. There's another approach I want to try."

"What's that?"

"Baz. I want to see if I can learn anything more from him — it — now that I've seen what to look for. And if Baz doesn't show up, we can talk to Solina again and see if he's appearing on a schedule."

"You're not going to recreate that ritual, are you?" Gerrard looked horrified.

"I'm not quite brave enough to dance naked in front of a hundred sailors, so no," she said. "Besides, it would be blasphemous to try to reach the apparition with some other god's ritual. No, I'm going to try approaching it like a consolation. The symbolic part, anyway."

"And *that's* not blasphemous?"

72

"I'm not going to invoke the god, I'm just going to see if it responds to symbols that aren't invested with a god's presence. You suggested that Genedirou might have just stumbled on something that works. I'm wondering if what he stumbled on was the secret of getting an apparition's attention, the symbolic part, and Sukman's involvement was something he came up with later."

"That doesn't explain how Sukman, through Genedirou, was able to affect the apparition."

"One mystery at a time. If I can learn something through Baz, that's one more piece of information I can use on Genedirou."

"Or against him."

Zerafine remembered the exhausted, half-naked *thelos* in the garden. "I'd like to avoid being his antagonist. If we're going to fight, let it be his fault. I almost feel sorry for him."

It was a good day for a long walk. The sky was partly overcast, dimming the sun's rays, and a cool breeze found its way between buildings now and again. Their route took them through a residential neighborhood raucous with children's shouts and the sound of men and women calling out greetings to one another from their doorsteps. The noise was enough that the sounds of real, terrified shouting didn't register with Zerafine until a woman's scream shattered the air.

They ran toward the sound of the screaming, pushing through increasing numbers of people, until they burst into a part of the street that was completely clear. Clear, except for a woman screaming and wringing her hands, and a man curled on the street, pelted repeatedly by *seicorum* the size of a man's doubled fist flung about by a ghost. An enormous, enraged ghost. *Right, my actual job,* Zerafine thought, disoriented.

Gerrard cursed and pounded toward the ghost, sliding across the cobbles for the last few feet and using his weight and momentum to push the man out of the thing's range. Zerafine ran after him, pulling her hood over her head and saying a few curses herself; he was completely unarmored, hadn't so much as worn his *seicorum* helmet since they'd arrived in Portena. Gerrard had landed on his knees and had his arms over his head, but held his ground. As long as the ghost had a target, it wouldn't try to attack anyone else. She leaped over him and reached out to embrace the ghost with her arms.

It was furious. She'd never seen such anger, such passion, from a ghost before. It fought her, its body of gigantic *seicorum* stones flying past with such force she had a moment's fear, against all reason, that her cloak would not be enough to protect her. That momentary lapse sent it flailing wildly in all directions, and she had to breathe deeply, once, twice, a third time, to regain her control.

Its memories were so fragmented that at first they made no sense: flashes of color and sound only, nothing coherent. It was like trying to reassemble one of Sukman's windows, all irregular pieces, none of them seeming to match. Sukman. Intuitively, but counter to logic, she drew the silver spiral in her mind and turned it gold. She would never, never have used this symbol, which should have driven a ghost mad, or madder. Yet in her mind she held it out, willing the ghost to see it as an acknowledgement of its pain and fury. The storm abated just enough for her heart's eye to catch hold of a memory more solid than the others, a memory of satin sheets — but nothing more. Carefully, she used the spiral to seek out memories that connected to the first: guilt, fear, anger, pain. The woman had died in agony, some illness her people couldn't afford to ease, or an illness with no possible relief. She had been mistress to many different men over the years, a woman kept in luxury, discarded when sickness began to show itself on her body. Her name was Zenia.

Zerafine could not bind all Zenia's shattered pieces together, but what she could do was enough. She gave her Kalindi's peace, Kandra's blessing, and the triple arch that would take her to Atenas's court. She imagined the woman's relief; the consolation had been as much a promise of merciful judgment as the offer of a path home, and it was Zenia's irrational fear of what awaited her at

Atenas's hands as much as the pain of her death that had created a ghost.

Chunks of *seicorum* struck the cobblestones in a sharp, rattling rain. She let out a sigh and calmed herself, wiped her eyes; her hands were trembling. Then she pushed back her hood, wondering why Gerrard didn't move, and found him lying at her feet, blood running down the side of his face, unconscious. Nacalia darted in and wrapped herself around his waist, sobbing.

"Somebody find me a healer!" Zerafine shouted, dropping to her knees and checking his pulse, her own pulse hammering in her ears. Yes, unconscious but alive, thank Atenas. The stone had caught him just behind the ear. She saw that the ghost's victim was in even worse shape; the screaming woman had flung herself over him and was keening a different note now. Zerafine left Gerrard and pushed the woman aside, checking the man's head and body, feeling his wrist. Alive — injured, a few bones probably broken, but alive. No new ghosts would be created this day — at least, not if the healer came quickly.

"Quickly!" she shouted at Nacalia, because it looked as though every onlooker in that crowd had been turned to stone. Nacalia started, then leaped to her feet and ran off. Zerafine cradled Gerrard's head in her lap and willed him to wake up. He looked white under the sunburn and she could barely see his chest rise and fall with his breathing. *He'll be fine*, she told herself, *this is nothing*, but her hand ached and when she looked at it, she realized she was gripping the front of his tunic so tightly the blood had stopped flowing to her fingers.

It felt like forever before Nacalia pushed her way back through the crowd, leading a man and a woman in green and blue tunics. Two healers. What a stroke of luck. They conferred quickly, and then the man, who bore Kalindi's sun on the back and front of his tunic, laid his hands on the ghost's victim's head and threw his head back in prayer. Zerafine had never wished so hard for the sun to come out just then, blessing his work, but he seemed capable of managing on his own.

The woman, whose robe was unmarked, felt Gerrard's pulse, turned his head to see where the *seicorum* stone had struck him, lifted his eyelids to look at his pupils. Just then he groaned and twitched away from her hand. Zerafine felt an enormous weight lift from her chest. "Did you get it?" he asked hoarsely.

"I did, no thanks—no thanks to your big dumb ox body getting in my way," she said, feeling a tear slide down her cheek, quickly wiping it away before it could fall on his face.

His eyelids fluttered. "You're sort of blurry," he said.

"That's because you've had your brains rattled a bit," said the healer. "Do you feel dizzy? Nauseated? Have a headache?"

"Of course I have a headache, I got hit in the head by a lump of *seicorum* the size of my fist. Have you seen the size of my fist?"

Zerafine laughed. It was only a little wobbly.

"If he can make jokes, he's probably going to be fine," the healer said. "But stay there for a minute, sirrah. I want to see how bad that cut is."

Gerrard lay there long enough that Zerafine's legs started to go numb. The cut turned out to be small but bloody, easy enough for the healer to deal with. Finally she allowed him to stand. It took both of them to get Gerrard to his feet, and he wavered a little bit, enough that Zerafine inserted herself under his arm to give him support. Not that her short frame would make much difference if he decided to go down again. But he seemed stable enough.

"Keep him awake," the healer told Zerafine, "and if he starts feeling sick or dizzy, or has trouble keeping his balance, get him to one of Kalindi's *theloi*. I'd say let Jerontius take care of it now, but I'm afraid my colleague is exhausted." They all looked at the little man with the suns on his tunic, who sat on the curb looking more ill than his patient, who was lying on the ground talking emphatically with some of the members of the crowd. He stopped talking long enough to look at Gerrard, then struggled to his feet. The healer tried to make him sit, but the man persisted.

"You saved my life. I can't begin to repay that debt. Thank you, thank you," he said, clasping Gerrard about the shoulders. The woman—his companion, possibly his wife, held out a heavy sack. "They all helped gather it up for you. You're all right, yes? I can't believe you were willing to pull me out of there, and at such a cost to you! You're not badly injured, I hope?"

"I'm fine," Gerrard said. By the still-ashy cast to his skin, he was lying. He took the bag filled with *seicorum* and said, "Half of this is yours, by right."

The man flushed and stepped back. "I couldn't possibly take it. I can't allow myself to benefit from simply being in the wrong place when it showed up. Perhaps the healers...?"

"Good idea," Gerrard said. He dug through the pouch until he found something he liked. "Look," he grunted, and showed the stone to Zerafine. One corner of the irregular chunk was stained dark with blood. "I'm keeping this one." Zerafine grimaced.

Gerrard then approached the healers and gave them each a large handful of *seicorum*, which turned out to be a double handful for them. He tucked the bag with its remaining contents into his belt. "Excuse us," he rumbled, and led Zerafine through the crowd. Nacalia followed close behind, her hand gripping the hem of Gerrard's tunic.

"Sorry," he said when they'd left everything behind. "I'm just feeling a little—dizzy." He tottered over to sit on the rim of a convenient fountain. He used some of the water to splash his head. Pale red trails of water ran down his scalp and into the neck of his tunic.

"We need to get you to a divine healer," Zerafine said, but he shook his head, and winced.

"No, I was only dizzy because there were so many people there," he replied. "I'm going to be fine. The nice healer said so."

"We should go back home and do this another day."

"And give me time to think of reasons why we shouldn't? You really want that?"

"What I *want* is a *sentare* who isn't going to pass out on the docks."

"At least you'd have a crane handy to get me up again."

"Could you take this seriously, please?"

"Zerafine, I *am* taking this seriously. I'm not stupid and I'm not foolhardy. If I thought I was in the least bit incapacitated, I would be the first to go to a *thelos* for healing. Could you stop behaving like a mother hen?"

Zerafine, stung, retorted, "You didn't have to see yourself lying there with blood all over your head and a face like death! You scared the life out of me! I thought—" She stopped, feeling the tears well up again.

Gerrard looked at her, then reached out to hold her close. "I'm an idiot," he murmured into her hair. "I'm a big dumb ox. Forgive me."

Zerafine nodded into his chest. He was large and warm and solid and she felt at peace for the first time in—how long had it even taken? An hour? Five minutes? She wrapped her arms around his waist and hugged him.

"I'll stop mothering you," she said, wiping her eyes, "if you swear you won't push yourself and you'll tell me if you start feeling strange."

He held her tighter. "Promise."

Something about the way he said it made her feel awkward, and she stepped away. "I do feel hungry," he added. "But that's not strange, for me."

She laughed a little too loudly, trying to cover up her discomfort. "Nacalia, find us something to eat," she said. But as they walked along, eating roast lamb off wooden skewers, she had a hard time not keeping an eye on her *sentare*.

Chapter Ten

Baz wasn't on the pier and Solina wasn't in the dock master's house. A little asking around turned up a sailor who said that she'd gone into town on an errand and should return shortly. They decided to do some shopping in one of the nearby markets, its booths crammed with goods from all corners of the known world. Gerrard found a new belt to replace the one he'd been wearing for two years. Zerafine wavered between an ivory hair clasp and a pair of delicate earrings of interlocking golden rings. In the end, she bought both, even though Gerrard had to change some of their *seicorum* for money to pay for them. She put the earrings on immediately, enjoying the way they tinkled when she turned her head. She considered buying Nacalia a present, seeing how avidly the girl eyed a stall selling necklaces of beaten bronze, but remembered her conversation with Gerrard about Nacalia's prospects when they left, and decided against it. Instead, she bought her an overpriced cone of toasted pine nuts.

"It's strange," Gerrard said as they left the market. He weighed his coin pouch before tucking it securely away. "I got a surprisingly good exchange rate for the *seicorum*. The moneychanger seemed eager to have it. Maybe Berenica and her *theloi* are squirreling it away for the winter."

"You've seen how Berenica lives. I can't imagine frugality is in her vocabulary."

"Well, the ghost rate can't have gone down here, or we'd have heard about it."

"And ghost hunters are even bigger spenders than Berenica. You're right, that's strange."

"It's not like I'm complaining. I always forget how expensive it is to live in a big city. I'd hate to think how much it would cost if we had to rent an apartment, or a house."

"Especially since the Council isn't paying us for this job—did

79

you realize that?" Zerafine sighed. "Let's see if Solina is back."

She wasn't. They ambled back down to pier 7, still empty of ghosts, ships, sailors, or cargo. Probably everyone knew about Baz. Zerafine took her hood and cowl off and sat on the pier, dangling her feet over the edge. The tide was high enough that the waves flowed over her feet and dampened the hem of her long tunic. With the overcast, the sun was just warm enough to be pleasant rather than broiling. The salt breeze coming off the ocean mingled its briny scent with the hot tang of tar and the stink of ox dung, and Zerafine tipped her head back and closed her eyes. For ten soldi she'd take off her robe and sandals and go wading through the surf.

"Zerafine," Gerrard said, his voice guarded. She opened her eyes to find Baz sitting next to her. Gerrard stood about a foot away, Nacalia peering out from behind him. "What's your plan?"

"Let me think." She rolled up her sleeve and reached out, slowly, inching her outstretched fingers closer until they brushed the edge of the apparition. As before, Baz showed no sign that he — it — was aware of her. She reached further and sank her hand to the first knuckle into the image. Still nothing. She felt nothing, either — it might have been a little warmer than its surroundings, but that could have been her imagination. She closed her eyes, drew a cleansing breath, and attempted to reach the same state she'd been in when she'd witnessed Sukman's appearance at the banishment. There, again, was the knot of threads she'd seen before.

"I'm going to touch it," she said, not sure if she were speaking on the spiritual plane or in her own voice, then brushed her fingers over the surface of the knot and felt a thrill go up her arm. It felt alive in the sense one might say the night was alive with movement; it hummed with energy. It showed no reaction to her touch. She traced the threads lightly with her fingertips, feeling her way along where they emerged from the knot. She could still feel them under her fingers for a short distance after they became invisible. It was like stroking a horse's mane, although it was the finest, silkiest mane imaginable. But eventually they faded into nothing. She still had no idea what the knot attached to.

Now, what symbol would reach it? Nothing of the gods, certainly; if that wasn't blasphemous, it was certainly dangerous, if only because too powerful a symbol might cause it to react violently, or destroy it. Or her. She thought for a moment, then settled on the circled cross, a circle divided into four parts, unity from many. Among other things, it meant finding common ground. She drew the symbol in golden fire on her wrist, pushed her first two fingers into the knot, and let the symbol roll down her hand into the creature.

She screamed. It was as if her entire hand had caught fire. The last thing she saw before dropping out of her meditative state was the knot coming apart explosively, loose threads flying in every direction. She snatched her hand close to her chest, drawing in great sobbing breaths. Through dry, burning eyes, she saw the apparition of Baz shred into a million pieces that vanished with the wind.

"What happened?" Gerrard demanded. "Let me see." He crouched beside her and peeled her arm away from her chest.

"It feels burned," she said through gritted teeth.

"It looks fine," Gerrard said. He forced her fingers open and hissed. Burned like a brand into her palm was the circled cross.

"I guess I got its attention," Zerafine said weakly. The pain in her arm had already subsided, and despite the raw lines of the burn, her hand felt fine. "It didn't like the symbol."

"Didn't like that symbol, or didn't like any symbol?"

"I don't know, and I have no inclination to find out. That *hurt*." Zerafine stretched and rotated her arm at the elbow. "I think I just performed my very first banishment. Wait a minute." She breathed deeply and once again opened her heart's eye. Unlike Genedirou's banishment, no trace of the knot remained, no loose waving threads, not even barely visible ones. It seemed to have completely vanished.

"It's gone," she said. She stood up and dusted off the seat of her robe. "No residual spirit."

"I can see why Genedirou wouldn't have gone that route. Painful, huh?"

"Yes. I wouldn't want to go through that again, even as transitory as the pain is." She massaged her arm, then let it fall to her side. "I think—" she began, then stopped.

"You think what?"

She pursed her lips. "Everything that lives has a spirit," she said. "People, trees, animals, everything."

"Yes, Zerafine, I took the same classes you did back in Atenar."

"Shut up and listen. I'm trying to work out how these apparitions could exist in the first place." She rubbed her chin meditatively. "The knot of threads at the heart of each apparition is attached to something. It's not an independent spirit the way you and I are. It's part of something bigger. But if this apparition and the one Genedirou banished come from the same source, that's pretty damn big."

Gerrard shook his head. "And it would have to be invisible, too."

"Maybe not. You know how people talk about Portena like it's a living thing? Maybe it is. Maybe all these people living here for all these centuries have given it a life of its own. Not a life exactly, but an independent spirit."

"Is that even possible?" Gerrard scratched his beard. "It's kind of a stretch."

"Well, I'm not attached to the idea. It's just a theory. But it makes more sense than that there's a two-mile-long invisible creature sitting on top of the city."

"Or under it."

"They have sewers. It would have to be pretty far down."

Gerrard stretched. "Shall we try to tackle Genedirou with our new information? Assuming he's willing to speak to us?"

"Oh, I thought of a plan for that." Zerafine grinned.

"This is either a very clever plan or a very stupid one," Gerrard said.

"It all depends on whether Genedirou is actually in there." Zerafine adjusted her hood. They were concealed along one side of the temple, out of sight of the door. Just a few more seconds....

Nacalia skipped down the temple stairs. As instructed, she ignored them and ran to the fountain to get a drink. About a minute later, Genedirou left the temple and descended the stairs. When he'd gotten a few feet from the temple, Zerafine and Gerrard emerged and flanked him on both sides.

"*Tokthelos* Genedirou. You're a hard man to reach," Zerafine said.

He gave her a sour, disdainful look. "So, you'll 'be at the temple in five minutes,' will you? I should have guessed you would stoop to trickery."

"You've engaged in a little deception yourself, though, haven't you?" Zerafine said. He continued to glare. "Genedirou, we can have this conversation on the street or we can have it in your office. I'll let you choose." After another glare that, had it been steel, would have killed her, Genedirou turned and led the way back into the temple.

Once in his office, Genedirou sat behind his desk and moved some papers around in what seemed to Zerafine a completely unnecessary maneuver. He looked tired, as if he hadn't slept well. "Well, *thelis*?" he said, not meeting her eye. "My time is short. Say your piece and move on."

"I'd like you to explain to me what happens during a banishment," Zerafine said.

He smiled a smug smile that made Zerafine's temper rise. "I'm afraid I can't discuss such sacred matters with someone not of my faith," he said.

"Then tell me what happens to the apparitions when they're banished. Surely that can't be considered a sacred matter?"

Genedirou considered that. "Not at all. Sukman releases them from their hold on our sane reality, and gathers them into His bosom." He gave her a pious look that she was positive was faked.

Zerafine sighed. "Genedirou, if you were just going to feed me a line, why have you been avoiding me? You've wasted both our time."

Genedirou stood, his face flushed. "Are you accusing me of lying?"

"Not yet. You might just be obtuse."

"How *dare* you come into my temple, into my sanctuary, and make such accusations! Get out at once!" He threw up his arm and pointed dramatically at the door, his pointing finger missing Zerafine's forehead by a hair's breadth.

Zerafine didn't flinch. "I saw what happened, Genedirou—really saw it. I know Sukman didn't take that apparition away. I know the elements of it are still there and that they've already started reassembling. Don't you realize your so-called banishments are only temporary? What's going to happen if one of them comes back?"

"You understand *nothing*," Genedirou seethed.

"Is that because you refuse to tell me anything?"

"My banishments are a *gift*. What no one realizes is that madness always lurks just beneath the surface. If people understood that, they would not be able to live with that truth. Those things, those apparitions, they exist to allow Sukman to show His power and His mercy to this city. Sukman will not allow His gift to be undone."

"Are you certain of that? Sukman *is* mad, after all. What if He changes His mind?"

"Blasphemer!" Genedirou was nearly purple now. "I do Sukman's will for the sake of the city!"

"And it's just a happy coincidence that Sukman's will also enriches your coffers? I don't think you're as impartial as you want me to believe."

"Believe what you will. I am still the only one doing anything about this blight on the city. And I refuse to stop serving this people just because some upstart unranked *thelis* who — "

"*Shut up,*" Zerafine said, slamming her palms down on Genedirou's desk. "I don't care about how you're building your prestige and I don't care that you're lining your temple coffers. What I do care about is that *you are in my way.* It's my job to figure out what these apparitions are and put a stop to them, not put on some exotic show to impress the masses. I'll give you credit for taking action, but your solution is temporary and I think you know that. Go on performing your banishments, but I'm going to find a permanent solution, and when I do, I will shut you down. So enjoy your fame while you can." She turned on her heel and stormed out of the room, out of the temple, and out of the plaza.

"Slow down, holy avenger," Gerrard said. "I thought he was going to pop a vein."

"Slow *down,*" Nacalia said, running beside her. "I can't keep up and you're going to get lost."

"I'm too angry to slow down," Zerafine said, but cut her pace to a slow lope instead of a brisk trot.

"I hope you're not going to treat everyone you encounter that way," Gerrard said. "I think you may be drunk on power."

"Are you being serious, or joking around?" Zerafine asked.

"A little of both. You were pretty hard on Genedirou."

"I know." Zerafine sighed. "I lost my temper. It won't happen again."

"It will probably happen again."

"I know. But I'll do my best to keep it from being so...violent. Did I just make a huge mistake?"

Gerrard took her arm, forcing her to stop. "You may have made a personal enemy, but you weren't wrong in what you said. Genedirou's so happy with his newfound importance that he doesn't really care about the truth. It wouldn't matter so much except that he's positioned himself as the authority on apparitions. If you learn something that contradicts him, getting people to believe you will be that much harder. So you're right, he's in your way, and he has to understand you aren't afraid to step over him. Or push him aside."

"Even so, he just seems so fragile, once you get past the bluster."

"Let it go. It's done, and you can't take it back. So either forget about it or learn from it."

"That's very wise." She stopped. "I forgot where we were going."

"Home," Gerrard said. "No, wait." He took Zerafine's right hand and looked at the palm. "We should get that removed. It's unsettling. To the temple of Kalindi, which thanks to you means backtracking a mile."

Zerafine made a face at him. "I admit I'll feel happier when it's gone," she said.

It took fifteen minutes to return to Kalindi's temple and five minutes for a divine healer to remove the brand. She looked uninterested in how a *thelis* of Atenas had come by such a thing. Zerafine stood outside the temple when it was over, gazing out over the city. The sun had burned away the overcast and the hills cast their long shadows over the streets and houses, gray streaks over white walls and red and black roofs. The temple dome behind her gleamed golden in the afternoon light. Zerafine breathed in the clear air and felt the day's trials fall away from her shoulders.

"I had someone check out my head, so we can leave whenever you're ready," Gerrard said, coming up behind her.

"That was smart." She adjusted her cowl, but chose to leave her hood down. "This place really is beautiful," she said.

"It's the oldest city in the known world," Gerrard said. "It's seen over nine hundred years of war, plague, expansion, life and death. And it's still here."

"Part of me thinks it would be nice to settle here. You know, if Berenica weren't *tokthelis*. But I'd hate to give up traveling."

Gerrard shrugged. "Everyone has to settle down sometime, and this would be as good a place as any. Better, probably. We could buy adjoining houses and send our children to the same schools."

Zerafine shivered. The idea of settling down, of children, gave her a strange discomfort that she found she didn't want to share with Gerrard. Instead she said, "Let's go home."

Nacalia was uncharacteristically silent on the walk home. When they were finally indoors, Gerrard said, "Nacalia, is something bothering you?"

Nacalia looked at the floor. "Somebody tried to make me tell them what you were doing."

"When was this?" asked Zerafine, startled.

"When you were in the temple and I was at the fountain. He came up to me—"

"Who did?"

"Some man." Nacalia shrugged. "He said, did I want to earn some money, and I said I was already hired, and he said, extra money, so I said what for." Nacalia gave them a defiant glare. "I wa'nt going to take it, I just wanted to know should I run away from him. Some men, they want more off runners than just running."

"I understand," Zerafine said. The idea made her sick to her stomach.

"He said all I had to do was write out where you go and who you talk to and leave it in a place he'd show me. I said I couldn't do that, and he must've figured I couldn't write, which I *can*, so he said he would meet me every day and I could tell him and he'd give me a parsis every time."

"What happened when you told him no?" Gerrard asked, and Nacalia grinned. She seemed relieved that they hadn't even considered she might say yes.

"He offered me more money. He was stupid. Should've known that would ring all kinds of bells with a runner. Nobody pays more than they have to." Nacalia shook her head. "Then he told me if I di'nt, he'd find me and beat me up, but I just laughed at him and said he ha'nt got nobody could get at me with you around." She included them both in her brilliant smile. "Then I kicked him and ran away, but he was gone next I checked the fountain. So I waited, but then *thelis* was so angry when you came out, I forgot until now."

Zerafine and Gerrard exchanged looks. "So who do you think would be interested in our movements?" Zerafine said.

"Well, it definitely wasn't Genedirou," said Gerrard. "He's not that subtle. And if he were going to hire a man to beat someone up, that someone would be you." He sat down on one of the couches and began pulling off his boots.

"Dakariou? He's subtle enough, but I keep in contact with him. He'd have to be truly paranoid to want us followed, too."

"I don't know. He's a political. That might be reason enough." He nudged Nacalia, who was sitting on the floor following their conversation with interest, with his bare toe, and said, "You need to take yourself off to bed, whelp."

"But I'm *interested*," she complained.

"When we figure it all out, we'll tell you the whole story," he said. "Scoot." Nacalia made a face at him, then slouched off toward her room.

"Speaking of politicals," Zerafine continued, "could it be someone on the Council? We already know Alita doesn't want us here. But the same thing applies—we're already telling them what we find out." She sat across from Gerrard and put her chin in her hands. "So either somebody is incredibly paranoid, or somebody is afraid we might turn up a secret, and since the only thing I've done since I got here is investigate the apparitions, it's probably a secret related to them."

Someone knocked on the door. Aesoron sailed past and opened it before either of them could even stand. He spoke briefly to the visitor, then closed the door and returned to them, bearing a folded sheet of paper. "For you, *thelis*."

The paper was heavy cream-colored rag paper sealed with

black wax. Zerafine broke the seal and opened it. "A party? *Tonight?*"

"You're kidding." Gerrard took the invitation out of her hands. "Trust Dakariou to give short notice."

"Council members, ecclesiastical leaders, wealthy members of the community.... We can't not go. If one of those people is behind Nacalia's mystery man...."

"I'll send Nacalia for a sedan chair." From the hallway, Nacalia hooted with delight. Gerrard glared in her direction. "I'm positive the hallway is not your bedroom, whelp."

Nacalia peeked around the corner. "I never learn things if I do what I'm told." She bounced over and accepted a handful of coin, then ran out the door. "Be *careful,*" Zerafine called after her. She hadn't forgotten the stranger's threat. "I don't recall agreeing to the sedan chair," she said to Gerrard.

"Let's skip to the part where I remind you that this is a fancy party and none of the women will be arriving on foot."

"I hate it when you're right."

"Unfortunately, it's not our biggest problem. The only thing you have to wear is that green thing, and the only thing *I* have to wear is that orange tunic that makes me look like a pumpkin."

"Ah, but what we *do* have," Zerafine said, pointing at Gerrard's belt pouch, "is an *awful* lot of money."

Chapter Eleven

"An awful lot of money" turned out to be just enough to convince a clothier's to reopen just after closing and to pay for two sets of expensive dress clothing. They'd have to exchange more *seicorum* soon. Zerafine leaned toward a tunic and trousers ensemble in red, but at the last minute decided to forgo her usual color and chose a gown of silver gauze over a long violet tunic. Finding clothes to fit Gerrard was much more difficult, but in the end the proprietor unearthed a bespoke, unclaimed pair of black trousers and a thigh-length tunic in midnight blue that was only a little tight across the shoulders. Suitably costumed, they set out for the Capitol.

The Capitol was a handsome building by day, but at night, transformed by the light of five hundred lamps, it glowed. Zerafine, always confident when in her robes of office, now felt intimidated and small beneath the expanse of the dome. A quartet of musicians on the balcony played something modern, barely audible over the conversations below. A cluster of bulbs shining with Kandra's light hovered near the top of the dome, illuminating the murals more clearly than they had been in the natural light of day. The gods looked over the gathering below; whether they were pleased or not was impossible to tell.

Zerafine soon realized that without her robes, she was not only intimidated but insignificant. No one recognized her, not even with Gerrard by her side; it seemed people rarely looked beyond the robe to the woman wearing it. She had never been this invisible. Gerrard squeezed her hand and was off. They'd agreed to work the room separately, thinking that people might be more forthcoming if neither of them had their formidable companion. Now she wished he'd stayed by her side.

"Madama *thelis*." Dakariou greeted her with a pleased and admiring smile. "I would almost not have recognized you, without your robes, had it not been for your exquisite beauty," he said, offering her a glass of wine. She smiled, acknowledging the flattery. Her heart lifted. Something about his smile made her feel warm inside. "I'm glad you were able to come on such short notice, but then it was short notice for everyone. There was another banishment this morning. It didn't go well."

Zerafine remembered Genedirou's haggard appearance and felt guilty. "How so?"

"The apparition didn't go quietly. It took Genedirou some effort to make the ritual come off. A lot of people were frightened. This impromptu gathering is to reassure the people who matter that the problem is in hand." Dakariou frowned. "Frankly, I'm not sure it won't do the opposite. There's a sense that the Council isn't in control, and that's bad."

"Bad for the Council, certainly."

"Bad for everyone. If the people lose faith in the Council, well, who can they get to replace them? I don't want to sound elitist, but there aren't many who are prepared to do that job."

"You being one of the few?"

Dakariou's eyes widened, then he laughed. "I continue to underestimate you," he said, "and I won't insult you by suggesting you're too beautiful to be clever. Though, in truth, I don't think you realize how lovely you are."

Zerafine felt herself blush. The way he looked at her now had nothing of flirtation in it. "I meant no insult," she said.

"Oh, it's no secret I have political ambitions," he said, "but I'm intelligent enough to know I'm not ready for that kind of power. Later, when we've solved this problem, perhaps. Though if we don't solve it soon, my aspirations are meaningless. I don't suppose you've learned anything that might help?"

She thought again of Genedirou, and of Nacalia's mystery man. "Nothing I'm prepared to share at the moment," she said. "I've learned very little that makes sense, and I hesitate to draw conclusions from such scant evidence."

"I understand," he said, surprising her. She'd expected him to press harder. "And this is hardly the venue for serious discussion. Shall we meet tomorrow afternoon? Say, two o'clock? I've received more reports from around the city, and perhaps we can see if your new information makes mine more comprehensible."

"Agreed. At my home, then?" She took his hand and once again felt that disquieting thrill. His eyes lingered on her face, and she realized that, flirtation or no, he genuinely thought her beautiful. Had it been so long since she'd thought of herself as a woman, and not just *thelis*?

"May I escort you? There are people I'd like to introduce you to, and frankly—" his voice dropped—"I look forward to giving your name and title and watching their eyes pop out of their skulls. Without the robe, you look...extraordinary...but they will all know that putting off the robe does not mean putting off your mantle of office." He offered Zerafine his arm, and without hesitation she laid her hand on it.

Dakariou was an ideal escort for this kind of gathering. He knew the name of everyone in the room, their families, their positions, their interests, and he conversed on all of these with such subtlety that everyone he met walked away feeling appreciated. Zerafine knew his charm was all about politics, but she was coming to appreciate that for Dakariou, politics came as naturally and unselfconsciously as breathing. Was he using her? Probably, on some level. But she was increasingly certain that on all the other levels Dakariou reacted to her as a person, a woman he was interested in, and she liked it.

Dakariou introduced her to the councilors who hadn't been present at that first meeting. Sure enough, every councilor from the hills shared a surname with the place they represented. But the district councilors, despite their plebeian origins, seemed forceful enough to hold their own against the wealth and family power of those from the hills. Even the mousy, bland Cerilia appeared lively. Vessa, in particular, met her counterparts' gazes with a directness

Zerafine was beginning to like. The outspoken district 4 representative dressed in what Zerafine was coming to think of as her trademark white gown, this one of silk embroidered with pearls. She extended her hand in greeting to Zerafine, then drew her aside from the other councilors.

"You look so different without the robe," Vessa murmured. "Are you enjoying being the woman of mystery?"

"I surely can't look *that* different," Zerafine laughed.

Vessa shook her head. "You can't imagine how many people have asked me if I know who you are. Everyone here grew up together and any new face is cause for comment, but it simply doesn't occur to them that a *thelis* of Atenas could be so young and pretty. Not that Berenica is unattractive, but I think you know what I mean."

"I do. Most people expect the *theloi* of Atenas to have some outward difference to indicate the god we serve. They must be disappointed that we aren't all hideous and, well, ten feet tall."

"Not so much disappointed as startled. I think—but you would know better than I if this is true—that people, being determined to fear something, would like to have a reason to justify their prejudice." She sipped her drink. "Are you finding the south much different from Dardagne?"

"I've lived in the south since I was twelve, so it's hard for me to remember. Dardagne's not a large country, probably not much bigger than three city-states combined, and the Autarch was always a distant presence. And it's not that far north, so the climate is mostly the same, maybe a little rainier during the winter season."

"I imagine your companion—your *sentare*, correct?—had more of an adjustment to make. What is a Northerner doing this far south? I believe he's only the second one I've ever seen in my life."

Zerafine smiled. "Gerrard's never said and I've never asked. I get the impression, from how he doesn't say things, that his religious beliefs made him something of an outcast among his people. Northerners, aside from being insular and reluctant to travel far from home, don't care for the worship of Atenas. Our *theloi* are only tolerated because Northerners have as much need for ghosts to be consoled as anyone else, but Atenas forbid someone might choose to worship Him if they didn't have to."

"How odd. And how...provincial, I think I'd call it." Vessa sipped her wine again. "May I ask you a personal question?"

"Certainly, but I may not be able to answer."

Vessa looked across the room. "What is your relationship with your *sentare*?"

Zerafine followed her gaze and saw Gerrard. He was in conversation with three beautiful girls, laughing at something one of them said, and they laughed in turn. He towered over the crowd, and in his dark blue tunic, with his blond beard and hair neatly trimmed, he looked like a warrior out of some Northern saga. Something about the scene made her chest ache, and when she spoke, her voice sounded strange to her ears. "He's my closest friend," she said. "We've been together for six years now, tracking ghosts, and there's no one I'd rather have guarding my back."

"I see," said Vessa. Zerafine looked at her, struck by something odd in her voice, but Vessa merely looked curious. "I don't know if I could keep my relationship with any man merely professional, being that close for so long."

"I suppose it's never occurred to either of us to see the other in that light," Zerafine replied, still feeling that ache in her chest. It had been just the two of them for so long. It occurred to her, watching her *sentare* flirt, that he wasn't going to want to trail along after her forever. What would happen if—when—Gerrard became romantically involved with someone? What would that woman think of his being so close to another woman, however platonic the relationship? And yet—he'd talked about settling down someday, building lives side by side. It was obviously something he'd thought about already. Zerafine was unsettled to find herself annoyed at that imaginary woman's intrusion into their life.

"Do *theloi* and their *sentaren* ever become romantically

attached?" Vessa asked. Zerafine nodded.

"It's not common, but it's not all that rare," she said. "One of my friends, Vivienne, even fell in love with her *thelis* when they were both still novices. They asked to be assigned together. The other couples I've known, they fell in love after being partnered. It's funny how few of them ever split up. You would think that being in one another's constant company would put too much of a strain on a relationship, but it almost never happens that way."

"One rarely thinks of romance and the *theloi* of Atenas in the same sentence," Vessa said with a smile. "It seems even I have my prejudices."

"Say, rather, that you still have things you can learn," said Zerafine, and they both laughed.

"May anyone join this conversation? You seem to be having such fun," said Castinidou Rodennos. He was resplendent in a short robe embroidered with gold thread, lying open over a white tunic and matching trousers.

"Not at all," said Vessa. "In fact, I'm afraid I must leave you to Castinidou's care, *thelis*, as I see one of my associates is trying to attract my attention." She floated away, and Zerafine and Castinidou faced one another. At a loss for words, Zerafine took a long drink of her wine. She would have to be careful how much she drank tonight; she had a terrible head for alcohol.

"You seem to be enjoying yourself," Castinidou said. "I felt obligated to make sure you weren't lost in the crowd, but Dakariou has taken care of that."

"Yes, he's been very good to me," Zerafine replied. "If you watch, you'll see that he's never very far away, just in case I run out of people to talk to."

Castinidou laughed. "I believe you've made an impression on him. He suddenly became very interested in the investigation when you arrived."

Zerafine blushed, but a more suspicious part of her brain filed that away under "curious." He might be behind Nacalia's mystery man after all. "That's very flattering," she said.

"I just hope he's been useful to you," he said. "I don't suppose you have any news for us?"

"Not yet. I'm sorry."

Castinidou frowned. "I don't mean to be critical, but you've been here, what, five days already? I was hoping you'd have made some progress by now."

"I have made progress," Zerafine said, trying to sound even-tempered, but feeling both resentful and guilty, not a good combination. "I'm just not sure what it means yet."

"I had hoped you and Genedirou might be able to work together, but it seems he's got his hands full with all these banishments."

Zerafine blushed again, wondering what Genedirou had told the councilor. Was that meant as a criticism? "I'm afraid that's true," she said. "I understand he had a very difficult banishment this morning."

"On my property, yes. The thing fought Sukman's will for several minutes."

"Have you been present for many banishments, then?"

"Too many to count. My estate seems to be overrun with the things. I've been grateful to Genedirou for his willingness to keep returning. I almost feel guilty, bringing him back so often."

A warning bell went off in Zerafine's head. "I don't suppose someone *has* kept count of the actual number?"

"Oh, I was exaggerating. There have been forty-three apparitions—no, forty-four as of this morning, mostly one-time appearances. Genedirou has banished six of them."

"That's...quite a lot." It was a lot. It was more than double the number reported for the Rodennos estate in Vessa's notes. "I wasn't aware your situation was so serious."

"It's not nearly as many as have been reported in the lower city, so I feel grateful for Sintha's blessing on us. We've always been a lucky family."

"How so?"

"Oh, our financial ventures are usually sound, that sort of thing. And we live high enough above the city that we seem to suffer less from the occasional outbreaks of illness that pass through. My parents, for example, were wise enough to shut our estate off from the world during the plague. Very few of us got it. Unfortunately, I was one of those, but I was, again, fortunate enough to survive." A shadow passed across his face and was gone. "Sintha seems to smile on us, and we show our gratitude in every way possible."

"Did you help fund the construction of the new temple? Or is that too impertinent a question?"

Castinidou laughed. "It would be a slight to the goddess to be ashamed of the blessings she's brought us. Yes, we funded the new temple, and my nephew Akelliou designed the building itself."

"I don't believe I've met him."

"He's around someplace, probably flirting with one of our neighbors' wealthy daughters." He smiled, but Zerafine thought she saw strain in it. Perhaps their family relationships weren't as blessed by Sintha as everything else. "Have Dakariou introduce you, but be careful — Akelliou will try to charm you away from him." He winked and turned to go, but bumped into someone tall and lean. "Oh, I beg your pardon, *Marathelos*."

"Not at all," Alestiou said. "I was so intent on speaking to this young woman that I hardly noticed you." Had Castinidou not already been leaving, it would have been a firm dismissal. Zerafine noted that the area immediately around Alestiou remained empty, as if he carried with him a protective barrier that kept others at a distance. She knew exactly how it felt; her robe granted her the same protection. She wondered if the *Marathelos* felt lonely; she at least had Gerrard.

"Sirrah *Marathelos*, greetings," she said, bowing low. The prelate returned her salute and drew her aside, into an alcove near the back door.

"How is your work progressing, daughter?" he asked.

Zerafine looked up at him, weighing the odds that he might be involved in some conspiracy. He looked even more tired than he had at the banishment. She noticed again that his hands trembled. "Not well," she told him. "I think I've stumbled on something bigger than just the apparitions, but I have no idea what. And it seems that someone believes I know more than I do."

Alestiou nodded. "In an ideal world, we would all be working together to save our city," he said. "You look surprised. Do you not realize that Portena is in danger? I know very little, but I do know that there is worse to come. Kalindi, praise Her, speaks in riddles these days, and I wish I could give you some key to unlocking your mystery, but I cannot. I am very much afraid that your answers will only come after some new disaster has befallen us."

Zerafine swallowed. Her mouth was suddenly dry. "You speak in riddles yourself, sirrah," she said.

Alestiou smiled, weary but compassionate. "I have very little time left," he said. "I think you know this. I've given you what I can. I ask you now to return the favor."

Her lips parted. "I—"

"Do not say no, daughter. This is between me and your god. You are merely His vessel."

She took his trembling, parchment-skinned hands in hers. "May Atenas's blessing be upon you," she whispered, bowing her head. She felt the illusory folds of her hood fall heavy around her.

"Thank you," he said, his voice barely more than a whisper itself. She felt tears come to her eyes.

"And thank you for your warning," she replied. "I think you have told me more than you know."

Alestiou pressed the tips of his left middle and index fingers against her forehead. "Kalindi's blessing, for what good it may do you," he said. "Clarity and vision in the dark days ahead." He was gone before she could move again. She stood facing the wall, willing her eyes to dry before anyone could see.

"Are you all right?" Gerrard said from behind her. She smiled. Trust the *sentare* to know when she was in distress.

"No," she said. He put his hand on her shoulder, and she reached up to cover it with hers. "I—we can't talk about it here. Later."

"Do we need to leave?"

"I'm not done here. I've found a thread and I'm going to pull it. How are you doing?"

"Finding that there's a certain kind of young woman who appreciates a tall, muscular, thick-headed Northerner who speaks with a strong accent. It remains to be seen whether their conversation means anything."

She felt the ache in her chest again. "Keep talking, then," she said with an effort. Her eyes were dry, her voice steady.

"Mind if I steal her away, *sentare*?" Dakariou asked. Zerafine turned, but Gerrard merely nodded and walked away. She felt deflated, though she couldn't have said what she'd expected. Dakariou offered his arm and a dazzling smile, and Zerafine linked her arm with his. If her heart was heavy, she could at least pretend to enjoy herself.

Chapter Twelve

Mingling with the crowd proved to be the right medicine. She had another glass of wine and felt her sorrow for Alestiou, and the ache in her heart over Gerrard, subside enough that she could laugh and converse and even flirt a little, mostly with Dakariou. He was easily the most handsome man she'd ever met, his close-cropped black curls framing that wonderful face, his eyes even bluer by lamplight than by day. And he kept smiling at *her*. Part of her mind worried that she was falling under his spell, but the part of her ruled by wine and excitement wanted to believe otherwise. Conspirator or not, this evening she was going to accept him at face value.

Even so, she wasn't so dazzled as to forget her true purpose. Gently steering Dakariou herself, she spoke first to Vidinou Akennos, then to councilor Vidannos—she couldn't remember his first name, but it was the surnames, and the estates they represented, that mattered. It was a wild guess, but it paid off: both men told her that they'd called on Genedirou often, and both gave her counts of apparitions that were far higher than those reported to the Council. Their numbers, and Castinidou's, were also far higher than any other single location she'd investigated. *Three out of the five--let's just call them "ruling houses" and forget about the democracy pretense--underreported? Something's not right here.*

She needed to talk to Alita or Gordou, preferably not together. It took some doing to locate Alita on her own, but there she was, chatting with four other women. Gordou was nowhere in sight. Zerafine would have preferred to tackle him, since he seemed to be the weaker personality, but Alita it would have to be. Making her excuses to Dakariou, she maneuvered through the crowd until she was behind Alita. Then she backed into the woman with a solid bump.

"Oh, excuse me—why, councilor Talarannos, I do beg your

pardon!" Zerafine felt the wine bubble up inside her. She'd have to keep it from running this interrogation. "How lovely to see you again. Ladies, I'm Zerafine of Dardagne, it's so good to meet you all."

The women exchanged glances, then politely made up reasons to be elsewhere. They definitely recognized her name. Zerafine kept her lazy, hopefully drunken smile on her face. "I was so pleased to be invited to this party," she said. "I've been so busy with my investigations that I haven't had time to simply relax, you know?"

"It's barely a party," Alita drawled. "At best, a gathering with drinks. But I'm sure it must seem fabulous to you, what with traveling the dusty roads and all." Her smirk showed clearly what she thought of people who didn't have the decency to stay put in a gracious home the way the gods intended. *Good*, Zerafine thought. *The more you look down on me, the less likely you'll be to see through my ploy.*

"Oh, most definitely," she said. "But small or not, it's surely a relief to simply mingle and chat and not have to think about all the apparitions running all over the place. Madama, I've heard how beautiful your home is. I simply can't bear thinking of Genedirou doing his little ritual all over your garden." A calculated guess; Alita had to live in the nicest estate in the city.

"Genedirou is an upstart," Alita sneered. "He's only been to my estate three times, but every time he comes, I die a little inside. Still, one can't have these things on one's property. The man is a necessary evil."

"I *completely* agree," Zerafine said, finding, to her surprise, that she didn't agree at all. "How many apparitions have been? Forty? Fifty?"

"Only about fifteen. We've been lucky, I suppose."

"Sintha does seem to watch over some families more than others." Only fifteen? That was exactly the number in her notes. What was Alita up to? "Was that what brought you and Gordou together? Luck? Your families must have been so happy to approve the match."

"Gordou and I have known each other since childhood. Falling in love was simply the next step. I don't believe men and women can ever really be friends without physical attraction stepping in." She flicked her eyes in Gerrard's direction. And *that* was a deliberate insult. Zerafine decided she'd had enough of the woman.

"I have to say that hasn't been my experience, but I am so happy for both of you. Daring to fall in love like that, I mean, without considering how powerful your two families would become. It's nice to meet someone for whom political considerations come second." Zerafine fixed Alita with her eye and watched the woman's face blanch. She'd meant only to needle her, but it seemed she'd struck a nerve. Too bad she didn't know which one.

Alita took a deep breath as if to speak, then turned and walked away without another word. Snobbish *and* rude. So, her number matched the one in the reports, did it? Something was wrong there, and Zerafine's instincts told her that Alita, not the other three Councilors, was lying. But she had no way to prove it.

Zerafine finished her glass of wine and realized she couldn't remember how many she'd had. At least three. That was more than her limit. She looked around for Dakariou, intending to make her goodbyes, and instead found Genedirou holding court just inside the front door, wearing his ceremonial robe and a typically smug expression. She was going to have to walk past him to get out, and Atenas knew how he'd react to her presence.

But—maybe she didn't want to walk out unnoticed. If she dared risk making him angrier with her, he might have an answer for her. Alita claimed only three banishments; Genedirou knew whether or not that were true. The question was, would he even talk to her? Maybe he would, if she could arrange the right conditions. She could only hope that Gerrard was paying attention, because she would have to leave immediately, whether or not it worked.

She moved through the crowd at an angle, judging that

Genedirou's audience was thinnest on the side near the front door. Perfect. She slid forward until she stood at the front of his ring of listeners, and waited for him to notice her. It didn't take long. Genedirou had no trouble recognizing her without her robe. She held her breath, hoping she'd judged him properly and that he wouldn't risk his dignity by starting a fight in public, and that his pride wouldn't allow him to ignore her. She wasn't disappointed.

"Madama *thelis*," he said, coldly, grandly.

"Sirrah *tokthelos*," she replied.

"Still conducting your investigation? Why don't you lay down your robes and rest? Oh, I see that you already have." The audience tittered, but only here and there. They sensed that he'd tried to insult her, but couldn't quite work out how. It was clear that most of them didn't realize who she was.

"No, I came to congratulate you, sirrah," she said, a look of perfect sincerity on her face. She saw his certainty waver. He was probably wondering where the attack would come from.

"I had no idea what a busy man you are, until tonight," she continued. "Councilor Castinidou told me how often you've been at his estate, banishing apparitions."

"Very busy," he replied, looking confused. "I have to force myself to enjoy gatherings such as this one, so I will not exhaust myself."

Zerafine wanted to roll her eyes, but she continued to smile as though she meant it. "Six banishments at the Rodennos estate, seven at Vidannos, what a *busy* man you are," she cooed, trying to make the inoffensive numbers sound as insulting as possible. Genedirou bristled, but still couldn't figure out where she was going with this.

"And only three at the Talarannos estate — are they lucky, or are you slipping?" she said, and was rewarded by a slow, dismissive smile.

"How uninformed you are. There have been no banishments at the Talarannos estate," he said. "Perhaps you should spend less time at parties and more in your...*investigations*."

Zerafine stared at him in genuine astonishment. All around her, Genedirou's listeners laughed, but she pushed through them and left the Rotunda. Letting Genedirou embarrass her in public might be a long-term blunder, but he'd given her what might be the key to the problem. She touched the spot where Alestiou had pressed his fingers against her forehead. Kalindi's blessing? Or simply her expert manipulation of Genedirou's pride? No banishments at Talarannos. Alita had lied, but not the way Zerafine had expected. The apparitions were linked to four of the five most powerful families in Portena. Zerafine just had to figure out how.

"Please, *please* let me hit him," Gerrard said. He took her arm and steered her toward the chair. "Why did you let him laugh at you? He's going to make you a figure of ridicule all over the city. No one's going to respect you after this."

"It will pass," she said. "Let's get home and I'll tell you what I've learned."

It was almost impossible for her to keep her mouth shut on the journey home. Probably they could trust the bearers, hired from an independent transportation company, but the fewer ears heard this, the better.

Rodennos, Akellos, Vidannos—all underreported. Talarannos—not only over reported, but completely without banishments. Would Gordou's estate be over or under? She'd bet the former. But why? What possible benefit was there in misrepresenting the numbers?

She dragged Gerrard into the house almost before he'd finished tipping the bearers. He said, "You'd better have learned something impressive, because you're going to look like a fool once it gets around that Genedirou showed you for the arrogant upstart you are."

"I—that's not what happened!" She dropped onto one of the couches and began to massage her feet. Walking all day was one thing; standing for hours was another.

"That's what's going to be said. These stories grow in the

telling. And I know Genedirou can't make you look foolish, so you have to have done it to yourself."

"I had to get him to talk to me. After this afternoon there's no chance we'll get anything more out of him. Besides, half those people didn't know who I am."

"What was so important that you had to ruin your reputation to get it?"

"Don't exaggerate. I have confidence in Dakariou's ability to spin any story coming out of that party to our advantage. Just listen. Genedirou said there haven't been any banishments at the Talarannos estate."

Gerrard sat across from her. "So?"

"So Alita told me there had been three. That's the number that was in the report. All five of the, so to speak, ruling houses had totals between two and five in the report and no more than twenty-five apparitions. But Castinidou and the heads of Vidannos and Akennos told me they'd each had something closer to forty-five or fifty apparitions and six or eight banishments."

Gerrard scratched his beard. "So three of them are underreporting and one is boosting her numbers. Why?"

"I don't know. I don't even know if they're doing it or if some clerk employed by the Council is trying to make the numbers match. But it's suspicious, don't you think? You want to bet if we asked Gordou, we'd find the same pattern?"

"Given how lock-stepped he and his wife are, I don't see how it could be otherwise."

"Alita reacted oddly when I suggested her marriage might have been politically motivated. I thought it was strange, given that it's no secret she and Gordou support one another's political careers."

"I think there's something odd about their relationship, period. Speaking of Gordou, I had an interesting conversation with him. Which is to say that it was a boring conversation that had interesting implications. He kept asking questions about the investigation, how it was going, that sort of thing. And he had all this "information" for me, most of it outdated, some of it improbable. I think he was trying to send us off on the wrong trail. I just played stupid and nodded and thanked him."

"I wonder if he could be behind Nacalia's mystery man."

"It certainly suggests that he's playing a deeper game."

Zerafine hesitated. "He might not be the only one. Castinidou told me that Dakariou became much more interested in the investigation after we arrived. And he's been our link to the council. I think...maybe we should be careful what we tell him."

"That's what I've said all along. The man is a weasel."

"He is not! But he might have a private agenda."

"I said that too."

"Fine, you're so smart, thank you. We're meeting with him tomorrow afternoon to pool information. I hope it's not a mistake."

"If he's our conspirator, it should be easy to tell. Give him what we know and then talk to Castinidou and see what got back to him." Gerrard rolled onto his back and stretched out on the couch. "I think he's a good man. Castinidou, I mean. How he came to have such a rotten nephew is beyond me."

"Akelliou? I meant to talk to him, but Dakariou forgot to introduce me."

"Oh, he didn't forget. Dakariou's a weasel, but he's smart enough not to let you anywhere near that toad. I had a conversation with him I'd rather forget."

"You know I won't let you get away with not telling me."

Gerrard sighed. "Akelliou has a reputation with the ladies that isn't savory. Because I was pretending to be a dumb ox, I had to act like I didn't understand his insinuations about every woman he cast his eyes on. Including you. Aside from that, he's rude and arrogant and makes no secret that he has no respect for his uncle, whom he actually calls a castrate in public. Not to Castinidou's face; he's not stupid, and he's his uncle's heir. But he's a foul excuse for a human being."

"Why would he say that about Castinidou?"

"I gather it's not a secret that Castinidou is sterile. He had the plague when he was five and it left him infertile. 'Castrate' is just Akelliou's natural charm at work."

Zerafine grimaced. "It must be killing Castinidou to have an heir like him. Even if he doesn't talk like that to his uncle's face, Castinidou has to be aware of it." She took off her other sandal. "I'm so tired I can't think straight," she said. "Did we come up with a plan?"

"The clerk's office," Gerrard said. "Dakariou. The five families. Get an invitation to Alita Talarannos's estate."

"Why the last?"

"What place in all of Portena has been totally free of apparitions? There's even been one in Berenica's back garden. Darlen told me."

"I see. Yes, Alita's estate." She yawned.

Gerrard knelt in front of her. "Are you ready," he said gently, "to talk about what happened with Alestiou?"

Zerafine thought of how frail his hands had felt. "Yes," she said, and told Gerrard everything about her encounter with the *Marathelos*. By the end, she was sobbing. "I don't know why," she said through her tears, "it matters so much. He is in so much pain. But that such a life is coming to an end..."

Gerrard wrapped her in an enormous hug. "I understand," he said.

She clung to him, comforted. *When he falls in love, I'm going to lose this,* she thought, and cursed herself for a fool. What were the odds Gerrard was going to find someone he could settle down with, given the life they led? Besides, maybe it would be she who found someone else to share her life with. Better not to worry about it, she told herself, but Dakariou's handsome face filled her memory, and she wasn't sure that worry was the right word for how she felt.

Chapter Thirteen

The news that Alestiou, *Marathelos* of Kalindi, had died in his sleep came early the next morning via a messenger from Dakariou. Zerafine took the news dry-eyed; she'd finished her crying for Alestiou and now felt a familiar sorrow mixed with joy at the thought of his passing into a realm where there was no more pain. Nacalia cried a little, but without much personal feeling; she'd lived her whole life with Alestiou a powerful presence far in the background, whose actions had no effect on her personally. Gerrard said nothing, but watched Zerafine closely until, irritated, she told him to stop hovering. Instead of taking her bad mood personally, he seemed pleased that she'd recovered her spirits enough to snap at him.

At nine o'clock, they set out on their investigations. Nacalia led the way toward the Capitol, but after a few minutes, she stopped in the middle of an intersection and turned in a full circle. She headed off in a different direction, her back hunched, her attention firmly on the ground. At the next turn, she stopped again.

"What is *wrong*, Nacalia?" Zerafine asked, more sharply than she'd intended. Perhaps her bad mood hadn't worn off as much as she'd thought.

"Can't find the road," Nacalia said, every bit as irritable as Zerafine.

"The road's right there," Gerrard pointed out.

"It a'nt the *right* road," Nacalia said. "This is the road goes off to market way. See here? The stones? The way they poke up like eggs in a basket? Road to the Capitol is all smooth pavers."

"How did we get on the wrong road?" Zerafine asked.

"I don't know!" Nacalia shouted. "We was on the right road to the Capitol and then it wa'nt the same road!" She sat down in the middle of the street, oblivious to the traffic passing around her, without care for the dirt.

"These people don't seem to have any trouble," Gerrard began, but Nacalia cut him off.

"These are who lives here. They a'nt going farther than home or market. Bet they don't even notice. Or they figure they just took a wrong turn."

Zerafine and Gerrard looked at each other over the girl's head. "Could the roads really change, or..." Zerafine pointed down at Nacalia. She was only nine. Even she could make mistakes.

"I a'nt crazy, so stop pointing at me," Nacalia said, not looking up.

"Portena's legendary for its maze of streets," Gerrard said. "Maybe this is why."

"But—streets changing? Stepping into one street and out on another? That doesn't seem possible."

"If you a'nt going to believe me, why did you hire me?" Nacalia shouted.

Zerafine looked down at her small, angry head. "You're right," she said. "I'm sorry, Nacalia. Let me see if I understand. We were on the road to the Capitol, and then we were on the road to the market, yes?"

"I just *said*," Nacalia muttered.

"I mean, you don't see any changes? There's no, I don't know, ripple or fading or anything?"

The small head went back and forth in a 'no'.

Zerafine looked at Gerrard. "Let's see if I can do better. Guide me?"

He took hold of the back of her robe. "Let's move on, whelp."

Zerafine centered herself and opened her heart's eye. She was aware of buildings as immaterial shapes, but people shimmered with a pale glow, spirits safely encased in bodies. Far to the left, mostly concealed by the press, she thought she saw the brighter knot of energy marking an apparition. She was barely conscious of the road as more than a pressure on the soles of her feet, and Gerrard's hand at her back kept her from stumbling. "Tell us when the road changes again," she said.

In just a few minutes, Nacalia turned a corner and said, "Right there," but Zerafine knew before she spoke. The world pulsed, like a heartbeat, and the buildings and the stones of the street glowed briefly red. She opened her physical eyes. "Where are we now?" she asked.

"Three streets south of where we was before," Nacalia said.

"It was like a pulse, or like a muscle flexing," Zerafine told Gerrard. She turned to look back at the street they'd come from; it didn't look any different. "And now, according to Nacalia, that street connects to one it didn't before. What I don't understand is how nobody else notices. I mean, suppose you were shopping at a stall and suddenly you're five blocks away?"

"Only ever happens when we turn a corner," Nacalia chimed in.

"That just means we haven't seen it happen any other way yet."

Gerrard shrugged. "Can you still get us to the Capitol?" he asked, scratching his beard.

Nacalia matched his shrug. "Streets keep changing."

"But you know every street in this city," Zerafine pointed out. "You must know every possible route to the Capitol, no matter what street you're on. Could you assume you're going to have to keep changing your route?"

Nacalia looked up. "I suppose," she said, but she looked more hopeful. "Takes longer."

"We're not in a hurry."

Nacalia led the way with more confidence. This time, Zerafine watched, not the buildings, but their fellow travelers. Most of them kept their heads down or conversed loudly with their companions. A pair of ghost hunters with a shiny new trap crossed the street to avoid her, unable to meet her eyes. A few people, however, would come around a corner toward them and look around in confusion, turning one way and another as if lost. Some even turned around and went back the way they'd come, muttering curses. So some people did notice. Why hadn't anyone reported *this* weird occurrence?

They passed through a nearly empty market, stalls that should have been full of food empty and untended. One of the lone vendors, a woman selling turnips off a cart, gave them a look as empty as her neighbors' booths. Zerafine took a look around at the quiet neighborhood. Unemployed men on the street corner gazed at her narrow-eyed as she passed. She could feel their eyes on her long after they'd fallen behind. It was a relief to reach the Capitol and duck into the coolness of the Rotunda.

Having reached their goal, however, Zerafine realized she didn't know what to do next. After some discussion, she and Gerrard decided to try their luck with the hall that led to the Council chamber. Nacalia, already looking bored, followed in their wake; Zerafine still hadn't forgotten the mystery man's threat. After peeking into three or four rooms, badly startling their occupants, she found an office that contained Paola, a broad desk, and many piles of paper.

"Madama *thelis*," Paola said, surprised. "Were you expected?"

"I'm here to look at the records on the apparitions," Zerafine said. "I assume you've collected more since my first visit?"

"Certainly. Were they helpful?" Paola began to rummage through a stack of papers at least four inches tall.

"Very much so." Zerafine put out a hand to stop the papers from sliding away. Paola murmured her thanks.

"Here they are," she said, handing Zerafine a few sheets of paper. She scanned the top page, noting how the reports had been organized by district or hill, then by neighborhood, in an orderly fashion.

"What I'm actually interested in," she said, "are the reports themselves. They can't arrive at your office this neatly organized."

"Well, no," Paola said, "but we don't keep those. There are so many. We collect them and then list them on this document. And not everything gets reported. The lists from our, um, more notable citizens are complete, but we're certain that in some neighborhoods, people just can't be bothered to tell us about the problem."

"I'm not sure how you can tell that certain, um, notable citizens are making complete reports?" Zerafine said, and instantly felt sorry for mocking the young woman's attempt not to say "the rich people who matter." But Paola seemed not to notice. She was becoming enthusiastic about the topic. She was apparently one of those people who thrived on bureaucracy.

"We do keep track of multiple reports of the same sighting," she said. "We've found that the more affluent the neighborhood, the more likely we are to hear about a sighting. But that makes sense, because—" She cut herself off, mid-sentence.

"Because?" Zerafine prompted her.

Paola looked around as if she expected some invisible person to take note of her words for her future punishment. "Because *tokthelos* Genedirou is more willing to come out for important people," she said in a hushed voice. "So it's to their advantage to report every apparition they see, because then the *tokthelos* will know to take care of it."

"Thank you for your honesty," Zerafine said. "Walk me through the process by which the reports arrive."

Paola looked as though her desire to know why the emissary wanted such information was at war with her keen sense of self-preservation. Self-preservation won. "Someone sends a runner to bring the message," she said. "The runner brings the message to the receiving office—you understand we get messages, requests for the Council and so forth, all day. A clerk puts the message about the apparition into the proper bin. And at the end of the day another clerk sorts through the messages and produces a list like the one you have there."

"I'd like to talk to these clerks," Zerafine said.

Paola opened her mouth to object, closed it, then said, "I think your presence might be a little...disturbing to their work."

"They'll have to deal with it. I promise I won't take much of

112

their time."

Paola led them back down the hall and to a stairway leading down. Gerrard said, in a low voice, "You're wondering about the chance one of them could be bribed."

Zerafine nodded. "This setup sounds like a perfect way to obscure what's really going on up on the hills." She raised her hood. It was a calculated risk; either she'd need the intimidation factor of the red robes, or she'd make a handful of innocent clerks wet themselves in terror.

The low-ceilinged room they entered looked far less orderly even than Paola's office. A handful of men and women were occupied with sorting paper of all sizes, from mere scraps to immense folio sheets. A middle-aged woman wearing spectacles and a frown came to meet them. Her collar bore the circle pin of one of Kalindi's worshippers.

"Emissary," she said coldly. Not madama or *thelis*. Interesting. "What can I do for you?"

"I'd like to see today's apparition reports," Zerafine said politely. The woman raised her eyebrows, but indicated a box on the deep shelf that circled the room. The other clerks had stopped their work and were eyeing her nervously.

Zerafine reached into the box and pulled out a scant handful of messages. Well, it was still early, despite their many detours in reaching the Capitol. She glanced through them quickly. Only one was signed, and she recognized the name of one of the people she'd been introduced to at the Council's party. Another way to make sure the report got noticed, perhaps?

"Which of you received these messages?" she asked.

"Please direct your questions to me, emissary," the woman said. It was Zerafine's turn to raise her eyebrows in surprise.

"Who are you?" she asked.

"Cimelia Argest," she replied as if daring Zerafine to doubt her.

"Are you the one who received the messages?"

"No, emissary." She sounded as if Zerafine should know how

beneath her the task was.

"Then I fail to see how you can answer my question. Again, which of you received these messages?" She could practically feel Gerrard struggling not to laugh.

"Madama *thelis*? We all take in messages. There's no one person handles specific ones," said a timid woman near the back of the room.

"Please stop wasting my people's time, emissary," Cimelia said. Paola made a sound like a gasp being suppressed. Zerafine was surprised to feel the god's curse begin to roil inside her chest. The belligerent woman, she realized, wasn't so much belligerent as genuinely angry at her. *What in the known world does she think I did to her? And why does the god think she's a threat?*

"I'll be the judge of what's a waste of time," she said, politely, swallowing the curse and ignoring the insult. If Cimelia's anger was personal, Zerafine had no time available to figure out why. "Thank you for your help, madama," she said to the timid woman in the back, and turned on her heel to leave, Gerrard and Nacalia close behind. Paola, her mouth agape, scrambled to catch up.

"I am *so* sorry, madama *thelis*. I apologize for Cimelia's rudeness. I've never been so embarrassed," she said when they were back in her office.

"You weren't the rude one, and I took no offense," Zerafine said. It was only a little bit of a lie. "Thank you for your time. You've been so helpful."

"It's my pleasure, madama," Paola said. "Please, if you have any more questions, come by any time." They exchanged salutes, and Zerafine led her little group through the Rotunda, sparing a glance for the gods on the dome high above. It was a pity they couldn't tell her what they saw.

Chapter Fourteen

Out on the street, Zerafine said, "I wanted to punch that woman straight in the mouth."

"Paola?"

"Very funny. I got the strangest feeling that that Cimelia person was angry at me personally and not at my intrusion into her fiefdom. And believe it or not, the god agreed with me."

"I wouldn't know. I was watching the clerks. You realize this was all inconclusive, right?"

Zerafine sighed. "Yes. Any one of them could be throwing away the reports he or she receives. That would account for the discrepancies in three of the estates, and we'd never be able to prove which one of the clerks it was."

"Well, for what it's worth, none of them showed the kind of fear I'd associate with guilt. Just the usual existential dread of the red robe."

"What's existential?" said Nacalia. She was practicing standing on one foot, the other folded across her chest.

"A really big word," said Gerrard. "Much as it kills me to admit it, I don't think Dakariou is involved with falsifying the reports. He'd either have to spend all his time running between the estates or he'd have to find a way to intercept those messages before they get to the Capitol. My instincts tell me the source is somewhere inside the five families. *Someone* has to generate those reports."

"It would have to be someone operating behind the family heads' backs," Zerafine said.

"Well, someone like Castinidou Rodennos is too busy to deal with little details like that. He'd obviously delegate."

"I'm really not looking forward to tackling Alita."

"You think Gordou is a better target?"

"He'd be easier to get around, but he's also our only unknown. At least with Alita we have some idea of what to look for."

"So what's your plan?"

Zerafine stretched. "I'll have to put her in a position where she can't refuse me an invitation to her home. I may have to leave you behind," she warned, and Gerrard frowned.

Nacalia grabbed her sleeve. "*Thelis*, somebody just made this—" she mimed a warding gesture—"at you."

"It's okay, Nacalia, I'm used to it."

Nacalia shook her head. "He looked angry, like he wanted to hit you. There are a lot of people giving you mean looks."

Zerafine looked around. Most people, as usual, were avoiding eye contact with her. But Nacalia was right; there was a sizable percentage of passersby who were looking at her with angry glares. It was unnerving. "I think we should go home," she said, "and look over this new information before we have to meet with Dakariou later."

On the way home, Nacalia again taking any number of detours, it became obvious that nearly half the people they passed glared at Zerafine. One or two even jostled her in the street, which surprised rather than hurt her. Gerrard began making the noises, deep in his chest, that meant he was gearing up to fight someone, anyone, given half an opportunity. He switched his longstaff from his left hand to his right.

They came into a neighborhood market that Zerafine, after a moment, recognized as the half-empty market they'd passed through just hours earlier. What a difference those hours made. The place was alive with activity, and every stall was filled with produce or housewares. The only thing that remained the same was the small group of toughs on the corner, still giving her that narrow-eyed stare.

Zerafine stopped and bought some oranges for them at one stall. "I can't believe how different this place looks. There was almost no one here when we passed through earlier," she told the vendor.

The man was relaxed, inclined to chat, and thankfully didn't seem to hate her. "What a day *I've* had," he said, offering her a small knife to pare her orange with. "I've been coming to this market every day, barring the Last of the Old Year, for maybe fourteen years now. You can imagine how well I know my route, yes? And today I got lost. Found myself wheeling down a road I'd never seen before. I tell you, it was like being lost in my own house, that's how unsettling it was."

Zerafine glanced at Nacalia, who was up to her eyebrows in orange juice. "*Told* you," she said in a muffled voice.

"It wasn't just you, though, was it?" Gerrard asked.

"Goddess, aren't you a big fellow. No, most all of us had the same problem. Strange thing was, didn't see any of these others on the road with me. But all us got lost the same way. Piedrou!" he shouted to a man selling almonds across the way. "You want to tell the *thelis* what happened to you?"

"Ended up in a dead-end street near where I lived as a boy!" Piedrou, an elderly man with white hair and beard, shouted back. "Halfway across Portena! Took me most of an hour to get back here."

"That *is* strange," Zerafine said. "I'm glad you made it here safely."

"Don't know as it was dangerous, just strange," he replied.

They went on, having found a fountain at which to wash Nacalia's face. A few steps later, Gerrard took Zerafine's arm. "We're being followed," he said in a low voice. "Those young men on the corner. Four or five of them."

"Should I be worried?"

"It might come to blows. I don't suppose Atenas is interested in delivering justice?"

She felt no gathering pressure in her chest or throat, no sense of the curse filling her. "No. What is *wrong* with everyone today? I can't remember the last time someone tried to attack us."

"Fifth of last Ormuor."

"I'm disturbed that you remember that so precisely."

"I so rarely get to flex my muscles in your defense."

"Bloodthirsty savage. Have you found a place to make a stand?"

"Alcove on the right, about twenty feet ahead."

Something solid struck Zerafine in the center of her back. Not a rock, something softer...*please, please let it be mud.* The stink reached her nose. *Not mud. Damn.*

They weren't quite to the alcove. Zerafine took a few more steps before turning. *Sweet goddess of light, did that idiot actually pick up a turd with his bare hands?* The five men—three of them were barely more than boys, really—stood several paces away, grinning the foolish grins of men who had started a fight they wouldn't be able to finish.

"Do you have a problem?" Zerafine said coldly. There was always a chance they could walk away from this. No. There really wasn't. Beside her, Gerrard was loosening up for battle. She didn't need to look at him to know that he was grinning too, except his grin was that of a wolf who'd just seen the shepherd walk away from the flock.

"Don't think you ought to be walking around in public like that," said the shortest gang member. His hair was slicked down close to his head, parted in the middle and brilliant with oil. "Don't think you ought to be so bold."

Zerafine took a few steps backward, trying to look casual. "Walk away from this," she commanded. She nearly tripped over Nacalia, who was clinging to her robe with both hands. Only a few more steps and she'd have the alcove at her back. Gerrard moved to put himself between her and the gang.

"Last chance," she warned. One of the men pulled out a length of chain and snapped it between his hands, still grinning. Zerafine shrugged. "Just remember, this was all your idea," she said, and scooped up Nacalia and got them both into the shelter of the alcove as the five men ran at them.

The one in the lead met Gerrard's left fist coming the other way and dropped like a sack of grain. The other four had too much momentum to be able to react to this, and by the time they'd realized they'd lost a man, Gerrard's staff had caught a second thug between his legs and assisted him down a nearby stairwell. The remaining three retreated a few steps, watching Gerrard warily. He stood, balanced neatly on the balls of his feet, twirling his longstaff in both hands, and said, "Come on, boys, who's next?"

What no one ever expected, looking at Gerrard, was that he was so damned *fast* for a man of his size. He did something Zerafine couldn't see, but which enraged the man with the chain wrapped around his fist, because the man snarled and ran at Gerrard, readying a punch. Gerrard twisted under the awkward punch, booted the man in the seat of his trousers, and used his momentum to run him headfirst into the wall. Zerafine shrieked; he'd come within inches of hitting her. "Sorry," Gerrard said, and that moment of inattention was enough to allow the short fellow, the gang's leader, to land a blow in the area of Gerrard's kidneys. He made a pained sound and turned on the man. "That hurt," he said, and smashed the man in the face with the staff, then scythed his feet from beneath him.

The man in the stairwell clawed his way upright, saw the carnage, and dropped back into hiding. The remaining assailant looked terrified, but kept his fists up, hopping from side to side as if hoping to avoid Gerrard's staff by never staying in the same place for more than a second. Gerrard watched him do this for a while, then lowered his staff. "This is just embarrassing," he rumbled.

"You afraid to fight me?" jeered the thug.

"Sorry, was I talking to you? Seriously, what am I supposed to do here? It's like fighting a little yappy dog."

"I a'nt a dog!"

"Fine. Come at me and prove it." Gerrard raised his longstaff again. The man, still dancing, seemed to consider the size difference between his own fists and Gerrard's, then abandoned his friends and took off running.

"You can beat me all you want, can't change what she is," coughed the gang leader, who'd sat up and was vainly trying to stanch the blood coming from his nose, which appeared to be broken.

Gerrard lifted him by his shirt collar with one hand and held him at eye level, letting the man's feet dangle ten inches in the air. "And what is she?"

The man glared at Zerafine with such hatred in his eyes that she took a step backward, feeling the alcove press against her shoulders. "*Murderer*," he said, vicious and low.

"What?" Zerafine exclaimed.

"You killed Alestiou!" the man shouted. "We all know it. Kalindi's people will be avenged on you, gore-crow! Struck him down in full view of everyone, but the truth can't be silenced!"

Zerafine covered her mouth. She felt as though she might throw up. Surely Atenas would not stand for this, but no, His curse still didn't rise to her lips. Angry, bitter, vengeful the man might be, but somehow he was also innocent of evil. Nacalia screamed, "She didn't murder no one, you...you *bastard*! You take it back!"

"Can't silence me," he muttered, then shouted, "The Goddess will strike you down!"

"Put him down," Zerafine said. Gerrard dropped the man, who collapsed on the stones of the road. "I didn't kill Alestiou," she told him. "When you wake up from this dream of vengeance, you're going to remember that the *theloi* of Atenas do not lie. Alestiou was old and sick and in more pain than you can imagine, and the god gave him rest. Tell your friends. Tell the world. And be sure to remind them that Atenas is merciful as well as just, because you attacked a *thelis* of the god of Death and came out alive." She removed her robe and shook the clot of feces off, flicking it at him, then wrapped the robe around herself again. "I'm going home," she announced to the air, and let Nacalia take her hand.

They were all silent for the rest of the journey home, and Zerafine's first act upon arriving was to shuck her noisome robe and hand it off to Aesoron. "I'm really sorry about this," she said. "It's a disgusting thing to present you with."

"I've cleaned worse," he said, smiling his faint smile.

"Well, thank you anyway," she said, and went to her bedroom. Once there, she couldn't think of anything to do, so she sat down on her bed and stared at her sandals.

"Don't start," said Gerrard from the doorway.

"I don't remember giving you permission to come in here."

"I'm not in there. I'm in the doorway. And I'm telling you, don't start."

"That woman Cimelia at the Capitol. She was a Kalindi worshipper. Two-thirds of the people in this city worship Kalindi. And they all hate me now because somebody started a rumor that I killed their *Marathelos*. Gerrard, what am I supposed to do with that?"

"Wait for it to blow over. As you told my favorite thug, they're going to wake to reason at some point and remember what Atenas's blessing is for."

"You can't fight two-thirds of the city."

"I bet I could fight one-third of the city. You'd have to handle the rest. Sorry. You're not ready for jokes yet."

"I'm—Gerrard, I've gotten used to the way people treat the red robe. I forget that there's a reason they're all so afraid of it."

"People are always going to be afraid of death. It's unknown. The best we can do is try to show them why there's nothing to fear." Gerrard sat down next to her, making the bed creak. "But that's not what's bothering you."

She shook her head. "Alestiou had such faith...I felt the god's presence, Gerrard. For them to take something that sacred and twist it into something vile and ugly...I can't tell you how it makes me feel."

"I can imagine. I'm sorry, Zerafine."

She leaned her head on his broad shoulder. "Do you suppose Genedirou started the rumor?"

"He could have, but it doesn't feel like his work. He's a vindictive little wart, but he's respectful of the gods. All the gods."

She sighed. "I hope this blows over quickly."

Gerrard craned his neck to look down at her. "Maybe your beloved Dakariou can spin this too."

"He's not my beloved." *At least, I don't think he is.*

Chapter Fifteen

Dakariou appeared precisely at two. "Did you have any trouble getting here?" Zerafine asked.

"No, why do you ask?"

"Just curious. Let's use the dining table, shall we?" So, the streets didn't move around all the time. Maybe just when it would be most inconvenient. *Now I'm ascribing motive. This city is making me paranoid.*

"You must have heard the latest rumors about you," Dakariou said as he held her chair for her. His hand brushed hers, and from the glance he gave her, it had been on purpose. It seemed Dakariou was interested in making their relationship a little more serious. The idea intrigued her. "And to think," he continued, "that when I woke up this morning I thought my biggest problem would be cleaning up after your spat with Genedirou."

"I must be such a trial to you," Zerafine said.

"No trial at all," Dakariou said with a wink. "Seriously, though, I'm sorry for what's being said about you and Alestiou. As far as I've learned, even before the *Marathelos* passed away there were rumors that you were here to kill him. There's a faction of Kalindi's worshippers—*not*, I should point out, among Her *theloi*—who have turned Alestiou into...I don't know, something of a cult figure, venerated for himself rather than in his relationship to the Goddess. They aren't always rational where he's concerned; I think they believed he would live forever. They were fine with Atenas as represented by Berenica and the *theloi* because they mostly stayed in their compound, but then you showed up, walking all over town, and strange things followed you, and...the stories just went from there. I promise, the *theloi* are doing their best to set people straight, but it might take a while. You should be careful."

"I have plenty of protection," Zerafine said, smiling fondly at Gerrard. He smiled back, but maintained his position of stolid readiness, staff at a diagonal across his chest.

"Even so, don't go anywhere alone. For my sake, if not for yours." Dakariou smiled. "I can't imagine what the Council might do to me if you were hurt."

"I'm grateful for your concern," she said. "I take it the thing with Genedirou is now a non-issue?"

"Might just as well never have happened," he said. "But Genedirou thinks he's scored one off you, so he's satisfied, even though no one else remembers that you even spoke. And a satisfied Genedirou is a Genedirou who's not making trouble for me. On that subject, would you care to explain why you felt you had to get up his nose so very publicly?"

"That's part of what we're here to discuss." Zerafine glanced at Gerrard, who shrugged just the tiniest bit. "This is my analysis of the reports the Council has received about the apparitions around the city." She pushed a well-marked map across the table to him. "You'll notice that, according to the Council's records, there are concentrations of activity in these four places. Everywhere else, they're distributed more evenly. However—" She pulled out a new map. "Last night I discovered that in these four estates, the numbers are either much higher or much lower than has been reported to the Council. This means that here, here, and here—" she pointed at the Rodennos, Vidannos, and Akennos estates—"suddenly have as many appearances as the places of highest concentration down in the city, while the Talarannos estate has had zero. That last piece of information is what I had to get out of Genedirou, because Alita Talarannos lied to my face when I asked her about it."

Dakariou's face had gone very still. "Four of the five most powerful families in Portena," he said.

"You don't seem surprised."

"Oh, I am." But he maintained that blank façade until Zerafine, impatient, said, "Now would be a good time for you to share what you've learned. Unless you're ready to admit that you're in on it."

He startled, then laughed. "Me? No. It's just—you've stumbled onto a connection I didn't realize existed. I'm just working out how much to tell you."

"It had better be everything, unless you want us to tell Castinidou you're a spy," Gerrard rumbled.

Dakariou seemed surprised to hear Gerrard speak. "Castinidou already knows I'm a spy," he said. "I'm *his* spy."

"You've been spying on me?" Zerafine exclaimed. "All this time?"

"No, I really have been your liaison with the Council," Dakariou said. "It's the rest of the Council I've been spying on. Alita Talarannos and Gordou Kerynnos, mostly. And if Castinidou learns I've told you this much, he's going to hang me upside down and beat me until all my secrets come out. But I think—" He paused, covered his mouth, then added, "I think your investigation and mine have just come together."

Zerafine leaned back and made a "go on" gesture with her right hand. Dakariou took a deep breath and let it out, slowly.

"You've probably noticed that Castinidou, while head of the Council in name, doesn't get much respect from some of the younger councilors. A while back—say about two years, right after Alita and Gordou were 'elected' to the Council—"

"Yes, and how exactly did that happen?"

"I'll get to that. Castinidou noticed that they, Alita and Gordou, had started building support among some of the other councilors in a way that indicated that one of them, almost certainly Alita, was angling for his position. Castinidou has been in politics his whole life, so he was able to head them off, but he worried that they might take action in ways he couldn't see. He asked me to keep an eye on them, learn what connections they were making, that sort of thing. I've been following them around ever since."

He leaned in closer to Zerafine. "The first thing I found out was—no, let me back up. The official story is that Alita and Gordou got to know each other better after joining the Council, hearts skipped a beat, and next thing you know they're happily married.

Romantic, no? But I learned later that their attachment was of much longer standing. As in, ten years or more."

"They concealed it until after both were safely elected."

"Exactly. If they'd been married before the election, only one of them would have been eligible to run for office. Instead, not only are they both on the Council, but the circumstances are such that no one wants to be heartless enough to protest in the face of True Love. And it was a plan they were working on for more than ten years, which speaks to a cold-blooded political machination that I'd admire if I were sufficiently cynical."

Gerrard muttered something under his breath. Dakariou flashed him a brilliant smile. "I really had no idea you were anything more than a bodyguard," he said. "It's astonishing, really."

"Back to the point," said Zerafine. "Where do we come in?"

"Five weeks ago," said Dakariou, "the Talarannos and Kerynnos estates started closing themselves off from the outside world. People still come and go, but the doors don't stand open anymore. Alita used to host these amazing parties, and now—nothing. Gordou's all but locked the doors at Kerynnos...he lives with Alita now anyway, but he still oversaw his own estate, and now he's hardly ever there, and the place seems deserted. The official story is that, in this crisis, they don't want to waste time and money on frivolities until the problem is solved. But, coincidentally, five weeks ago is when the first apparitions showed up, and it took nearly a week for anyone to realize it was a serious problem. Something happened five weeks ago that made Alita and Gordou circle the wagons, so to speak, *before* the crisis came."

"Something that might be caused by the apparitions instead of being a result of their appearing."

"I think the reason for the artificially lowered numbers at these three estates is to conceal whatever's going on at Talarannos," Dakariou said. "And before you ask, I don't know what the situation is at Gordou's estate. I didn't bother to watch Genedirou;

he's harmless, if a bit nutty. I have no idea how often, or not, he may have gone there."

"But who would be in a position to change the reports?"

"Anyone." Dakariou ran a hand through his curls. "But assuming that Alita is the mastermind, she's got friends in all five families. Morica Akennos, for one, though she's kind of a strange girl. The Vidannos twins are the same age she is, they might be close. I'm not sure about Rodennos...unless, ew, Akelliou is involved. What a waste of air. I'm told he and Gordou used to be great friends when they were young, but as Gordou got more heavily into politics, he let that relationship drop. Unless that's a ploy, too. I wish I didn't see conspiracies everywhere."

"I wish there weren't so many to see," said Zerafine.

"*I* wish I could get someone inside one of those estates, but the servants are all fiercely loyal to their masters, and the families are all, well, clannish," Dakariou said. He leaned back in his chair and ruffled his fingers through his hair again.

"How interesting. Because I want you to get me an invitation to Alita Talarannos's house," said Zerafine.

"That's impossible," he said. "She doesn't invite anyone in anymore. Not possible."

"Not 'anyone.' The official emissary from Atenar. The person who, if she's told 'no,' is going to put her entire official weight behind finding out why she's just been told 'no.' And, coincidentally, make life a misery for the nay-sayer. I just want you to put all that in diplomatic terms so Alita can pretend it's her idea. I'm certain that if any man can do it, you can."

Dakariou regarded her silently. "I'll do it, on one condition."

"You think you can make conditions?"

"Have dinner with me. My home. Tomorrow night. Just the two of us." He turned that brilliant smile on her. "No politics, no conspiracies, no agenda. Just a pleasant dinner with good conversation."

The idea made her heart beat a little faster. "I wonder if you ever *don't* have an agenda," she said.

The smile went even brighter, but his eyes were totally serious. "Come tomorrow, and find out," he said.

Zerafine considered it for a long moment. She was aware of Gerrard, bristling with disapproval, behind her, but Dakariou was clever and handsome and, amazingly, attracted to her. "I'll come," she said. "But I expect truly excellent conversation."

"You'll have it, madama," he said. He rose from the table and saluted her. "Expect to hear from Alita by tomorrow morning at the latest. I think I can put this in terms that will light a fire under her. And — don't go walking alone."

Zerafine saw him to the door. She expected Gerrard to explode once Dakariou was safely out of the house, and he didn't disappoint her. "*Dinner? Alone? Are you out of your mind?*"

"I thought it was a very rational choice."

"Zerafine, we hardly know the man. He's an admitted spy. You don't know if he's telling you the whole truth. And he wants you on your own. I think that's suspicious."

"Why is that suspicious? What kind of ulterior motives do you think he has?"

"I think he wants more from you than information."

Zerafine snapped. "And what's so wrong with that?" she shouted. "Is it so awful that a handsome, clever man thinks I'm beautiful and wants to spend time with me? Well, Gerrard, it happens that I like him. I like talking to him. I want to have dinner with him and talk about things that aren't apparitions and conspiracies and Genedirou and...and I don't know what else. *Yes*, I think he's got an agenda, but right now I really don't care!"

Gerrard stared at her, his jaw set. "Fine," he said. "Fine. You want to put yourself in the hands of someone you've known less than a week, that's your business. I can't stop you." He stomped off to his room and slammed the door.

Zerafine clenched her fists and screamed, a short burst of sound that sent Nacalia cowering. She was immediately sorry. "Come back, Nacalia," she said. "I shouldn't have done that." But Nacalia had already run off to her room. Frustrated, Zerafine went to her room and did a little door-slamming of her own. Then she flung herself face down on her bed and screamed and beat her fists into the mattress for a full minute. Then she rolled onto her back and stared at the ceiling.

It was just dinner. Gerrard was being totally unreasonable. Yes, Dakariou was a spy. Yes, his motives only coincided with theirs—hers—for the moment, but she was certain he meant her no harm. Quite the opposite, in fact. But a niggling worm of doubt crept into her reflections. She'd only just the other day felt fear, and misery, at the idea that Gerrard might leave her. And here she was, developing a relationship with someone that Gerrard considered a threat. Zerafine tried to justify it to herself—they would leave when this was all over, she'd leave Dakariou behind and think of him only as a pleasant interlude. No reason for Gerrard to worry. *How did you feel when you imagined him in your position?* Zerafine put the pillow over her face. He wasn't the only one being unreasonable.

Zerafine tossed the pillow aside and went to the door. She could admit she'd been wrong—but would she agree to cancel dinner with Dakariou for the sake of peace? She hesitated, her hand on the doorknob, then smiled when she heard Gerrard's door open. He was coming to her.

But his footsteps went on down the hall, and shortly she heard the front door open and close. Zerafine felt her anger rise again. So, he was so angry with her he couldn't even stay in the same house? Her face heated as she realized she had been about to give in when she was certain she was right. *Fine,* she thought, unconsciously echoing Gerrard's words. *Fine. Let him be angry. I'm not letting that influence my actions.*

By dinnertime, Gerrard still hadn't returned, but a letter arrived with the Talarannos mark on the seal. Dakariou had been quicker even than she'd hoped. Alita Talarannos sent her regards and asked Zerafine of Dardagne to join her for a midmorning meal at her estate. Zerafine crushed the fine paper in her hand, feeling excitement despite her heavy heart. This could be the key to the mystery. What did one wear to a midmorning meal at one of the most wealthy estates in Portena? The red robe that went everywhere, naturally.

She and Nacalia were in the middle of dinner when Gerrard returned. They sized each other up, warily. "Would you like something to eat?" Zerafine asked, breaking the silence.

"I ate at a street vendor's half an hour ago," he replied. Zerafine felt her face heat again. He couldn't even bring himself to share a simple meal with her.

"Where did you go?" she asked, more to have something to say than out of any real interest.

"Just around. The gymnasium. Got lost a couple of times."

"You could have taken Nacalia."

"I wanted to be alone."

Silence fell again. Nacalia looked from one of them to the other. "Why are you fighting?" she asked.

Gerrard's mouth set in a grim line. Zerafine said, "We're having a disagreement." Gerrard snorted. Zerafine turned on him. "Well, what would you call it?" she asked, feeling dangerously close to losing her temper again.

"An argument," he said, "in which you won't admit I'm right."

Fighting words. "That's because you aren't. You're being unreasonable."

"I'm supposed to keep you safe. You're making that impossible."

"You want to keep me safe by never letting me go anywhere alone?"

"You think you'd have been safe alone today when those men wanted to beat you senseless?"

"I'm not talking about wandering the streets of Portena. I'm talking about dinner with someone who, you have to admit, has never tried to hurt me."

"Hasn't tried to hurt you *yet*."

"Will you stop being so suspicious?"

"Will you stop being so pigheaded?"

Nacalia climbed down from her chair, crying, and ran to her room.

"Wonderful, Gerrard. You've made a small child cry. I'm so impressed."

Gerrard's eyes blazed. "I'm not the one who started yelling first," he snarled. "You think you're entitled to lose your temper because no one's willing to stand up to a *thelis* of Atenas. It's past time you learned you can't bully people and get away with it."

"And who's going to teach me that lesson? You?"

Gerrard's jaw was once again set like granite. "No," he said. "I think you're too proud to learn that from anyone. I'm going to bed."

Zerafine stared after him, shocked, as he turned his back on her. She was so angry, and so hurt, that she wanted to cry, but she wouldn't give him the satisfaction. She went to her own room, and shut the door, deliberately not slamming it, then disrobed and crawled into bed. She wasn't sleepy, but she didn't think she could face any more of this awful day. She realized she was crying after all.

Chapter Sixteen

The ubiquitous sedan chair arrived at ten the next morning. They'd eaten their breakfast in silence, the three of them, Gerrard and Zerafine unable to meet one another's eyes. Zerafine had spent a restless night replaying every word, every gesture of their arguments, and concluded that they had both been idiots. Unreasonable or not, Gerrard was simply trying to do his job. But she couldn't figure out a way to tell him that, because every time she came close, she remembered the last things he'd flung at her. Bully. Proud. It made her furious and embarrassed and hurt all at once, and she wanted to hit back at him with words she hadn't thought of at the time. A tiny part of her, the rational, unwounded part, pointed out that it was just as well, that there were some words that couldn't be taken back.

The doors set into the high walls of the Talarannos estate loomed high over the heads of her bearers, at least four feet taller even than Gerrard. "Do you know what to expect?" he murmured to her through the gauzy curtains, and she shivered at the neutral sound of his voice.

"Watch the servants," she told him. "They may have secrets to guard, but they probably won't be as good at it as Alita."

"Understood. Try not to eat any poisoned food." Zerafine smiled at that, then remembered she was still angry at him. If he was trying to make things normal between them, she wasn't ready for that.

The bearers set her chair down in the center of a small courtyard. It was paved with enormous granite stones polished smooth from years of use, and surrounded on three sides by smooth-sided stone buildings with tall, blank faces in which only slits of windows could be seen. It was an ancient style of building, and Zerafine wondered how old the estate was.

Alita emerged from the center building, her hands out in

greeting. "Emissary," she said with a smile. "Thank you for coming. I'm honored that you thought my home worthy of a visit." Her smile didn't reach her eyes. Zerafine took her greeting at face value. They'd both be taking the other's measure; just as well to pretend this was an actual social call.

Alita led the way around through a small gate near the left-hand building. Zerafine could see a much larger, much more well-trodden way along the right. The path they took was nearly overgrown with untrimmed trees and grasping shrubs. *So, there's something you don't want me to see there.* She wished she could find an excuse for Gerrard to wander around. But no, he trailed her closely, his hair getting caught in the branches even when he ducked.

Untraveled or not, the path led to a tiny, beautifully groomed garden in which it seemed everything had been designed at two-thirds scale. Trees in pots were sculpted into exquisite shapes; tiny flowers blossomed on all sides, their sweet scent delicately perfuming the air. The table and chairs were the only full-sized objects present.

Alita indicated they should sit. "I'm afraid I didn't provide for your servant," she said. Zerafine guessed that Alita really did believe Gerrard was a servant, which showed that she hadn't done much research on her guest, which further implied that Alita still didn't take her seriously. Very well. She could use that.

"Don't worry about him, I often expect him to stand around waiting for me. I'm sure his life is quite boring," she said, and instantly cursed herself. Would Gerrard have heard that as a subtle dig at him, another volley in their ongoing war? "Thank you for inviting me," she added. She didn't have time to worry about Gerrard now.

"Not at all," said Alita. "I so enjoy showing my home to others. I'm quite proud of the work I've done on it. Antiques are all very well, but I prefer modern comforts, don't you?"

"I know I'm grateful for indoor plumbing," Zerafine said, and they both laughed, probably the only genuine sound either of them would produce during this visit.

A man emerged from the rear of the house, carrying a folding table which he set up beside them. A small woman brought a tray, which she placed on the table, and from which she poured cups of coffee tiny enough to seem made to suit the theme of the garden. "You've had coffee before?" Alita asked. "A delicacy from the south. It hasn't been widely adopted yet in Portena, but I like it." Her tone of voice indicated that she did not expect her uncouth guest to be familiar with upper-class delicacies.

"Oh, yes, and I like it very much," Zerafine said, tuning her voice to match Alita's. "I became accustomed to it while traveling through the southern city-states. It's quite popular in Kavarro and Cazorno." She enjoyed seeing the twitch of Alita's lips as she registered that her patrician drink wasn't so exclusive after all.

The woman servant laid plates in front of them. A basket of various breads and a plate of cheeses appeared next, and then the woman brought out a basket of fruit, melons and grapes and a sweet berry Zerafine wasn't familiar with. The next few minutes were occupied with the ladies helping themselves to the choicest morsels. "I hope you don't mind the informality, but I didn't think it was necessary to stand on ceremony with you," Alita said, but her hesitation in picking up fruit told Zerafine that this was a woman accustomed to having her food put on her plate for her. Perhaps she needed assistance chewing as well.

Zerafine spread soft cheese on a slice of nutty bread and took a bite. "I must admit that my visit is not entirely a personal one," she said when she'd finished chewing. She'd briefly considered talking with her mouth full, just to cement Alita's belief that the emissary was completely without class, but decided that would have been too much. "I've been curious about your estate ever since I spoke with Genedirou. He told me he's never performed a banishment here. I find that astonishing, don't you? You must feel so fortunate." She hoped Alita would believe she'd been drunk enough at the party to forget that Alita had told her specifically how much she hated having Genedirou on her estate when he came to do banishments.

"I do," said Alita. "I don't know how to explain it, except that Sintha, praise Her, must once again be watching over our family." Good, she was willing to pretend that conversation had never happened. Or she really had forgotten it.

"I don't suppose you have any ideas as to what makes your estate special?"

Alita shrugged. "Who can tell the ways of the gods?" she said. "I don't want to sound immodest, but we are a very devout family."

"It's especially interesting," said Zerafine, "when you consider just how many your fellow councilors have had. Castinidou tells me he's had forty-four apparitions on his estate alone. And yet he seems so devout. I understand he paid for the new temple to Sintha. It's quite lovely."

Alita's smile was strained. "You're right, it would be improper to accuse others of inattention to their worship. But then, I suppose I ought to be asking you. Aren't you the one who's been tasked with learning the reason behind these apparitions? Perhaps if you could tell us what they are, we'd know the reason and logic behind their appearances."

Touché. Zerafine drained her cup to give herself time to come up with a response. "I'm coming closer to understanding every day. In fact, the other reason for my interest in coming here is to look over your estate to see if it has any unusual features that might account for its freedom from apparitions." She might as well come right out with it.

"I'd be happy to show you around," Alita said. "Now, if you're finished."

They rose from the table, and Alita gestured toward a gate obscured by vines and bushes. "Let me show you the grounds first," she said.

Beyond the gate lay the bulk of the estate, the modern parts, as Alita had said. Buildings lay scattered along deep terraces cut into the side of the hill, some of them almost overhanging the cliff side of Talarannos hill. The view from the top was magnificent; the city lay spread beneath them like a crazy quilt of silk and wool. From here, Zerafine could see the gilded dome of Kalindi's temple, the marble and tile of the vast library, the bowl of the amphitheater. "Amazing," she breathed, sincere for the second time since she'd arrived.

"We like it, anyway," said Alita, a smug pleasure in her voice. "I'd rather not disturb the family in their homes, but we can walk through the garden."

The houses seemed locked and still—at ten-thirty in the morning? Zerafine noted their locations and wondered where everyone was. Alita came to a stop in front of one of the buildings near the cliff edge. "This one's empty, if you'd like to see an example of the construction," she said. "I'm really quite proud of the workmanship, so I enjoy showing it off."

First they couldn't enter any of the houses, and now here was one conveniently empty? Zerafine stepped into a broad sitting room, the couches scattered throughout instead of grouped. At the far end of the room was a wall of very expensive glass panes, through which the same view of the city could be seen. Zerafine obediently oohed and aahed over the bedrooms, the kitchen, the ultra-modern commode and bathing room, the private garden. With any luck Gerrard was making more of this than she was.

Alita led them all over the estate, but Zerafine could tell she was avoiding certain places: the path on the right side of the main house, for example. They finished in a salon just off the tiny garden, which was comfortably furnished with a number of thick rugs and some tall, cushioned chairs.

"I hope—" began Alita, but she was interrupted by a door opening behind her—a door, moreover, that led to a room Zerafine had not been allowed to see.

"Alita, I need you to look at this," a woman said, then realized Alita was not alone. "Sorry," she said. She was a tall, bony woman with surprising dark blonde hair caught up messily in the back. She wore a stained apron and her hands were dusty with a white powder.

"Emissary, my good friend Morica Akennos," said Alita. Her body was tense. "Morica, this is *thelis* Zerafine of Dardagne, the emissary from Atenar." Was Zerafine mistaken, or did she hear Alita place just the slightest emphasis on the last three words? "Morica has been staying with me for a few days."

"My home is boring," Morica said. "So much more to do here." She had trouble meeting Zerafine's eyes, but not, Zerafine judged, out of guilt. When Morica added, "I learned something new today," Zerafine was convinced that Morica was one of those people for whom a passion became an obsession so strong that normal social conventions were beyond them.

"I'd love to see it later," Alita said. "The emissary will be leaving shortly, and I'll join you then." Her intent was so strong that even Morica realized she was being dismissed. The woman went back the way she'd come.

"My apologies. Morica is a...baker and becomes rather...involved in her work. No doubt I'll have to try one of her new concoctions," Alita said with a smile, managing to convey embarrassment and resignation in a shrug. Gerrard could learn a thing or two from her, Zerafine thought fondly, and then became angry all over again at herself.

"Is she a good cook?" she asked.

"Oh, very. She's just an experimenter, and not all of her experiments go well. May I see you out?"

It was a clear dismissal. Zerafine didn't fight her. She'd learned...well, she wasn't sure what she'd learned yet. But she'd pushed her luck as far as it would go.

The journey home proceeded in silence. Zerafine was dying to talk to Gerrard about what he'd seen. Before, she'd have kept quiet for reasons of secrecy. Now, she just didn't know what to say to him. They didn't have to talk about what had come between them.

She could be professional. So could he.

But the minute they stepped inside their house, Gerrard said, "I need pen and paper." No awkwardness. No standing around waiting for the other to speak first. She got him writing supplies and watched him spread them out on the table. Quickly, and to her eye accurately, he sketched out the Talarannos estate. "Does this look right to you?" he asked, and she nodded. He then began cross-hatching the map, covering huge sections with black lines, until he seemed satisfied. "The blacked-out sections are the places Alita wouldn't let us go," he said.

Zerafine stared. "It's a pattern," she said. With only a few exceptions, the black sections defined a circle centered on a part of the main house. "What's this room?"

"That's the salon we ended up in."

"Then the center of the pattern is the room Morica Akennos came out of."

They looked at each other, grievances for the moment forgotten. "I very much doubt that's a kitchen," Gerrard said.

"But what is it?"

Gerrard tapped the paper. "The reason there are no apparitions on the estate?"

"No," Zerafine said. "Look. It's simply not possible that Talarannos has been spared. Alita has to be concealing the apparitions. All these blacked-out areas, those have got to be where they keep showing up. That's why she wouldn't let us see them. And Morica was working on something that made Alita very nervous when she thought I might learn what it was—something that happens to be at the center of that pattern. Something is going on there."

"That's a big leap. You're going to have to walk me through it. I'm just a big dumb ox."

"You are *not*," she began, putting her hand on his arm, then snatched it away as if the touch burned. They looked at each other, then Gerrard said "I'm sorry" just as Zerafine said "I didn't mean—

"

"I was angry, I said things I didn't mean, please forgive me," Gerrard said.

"No, I was rude and insensitive, I'm so sorry," Zerafine said.

They both fell silent again. It felt like an apology, and yet not. Zerafine was still going to the dinner. She knew he wouldn't stop thinking she was wrong. But it was enough to break through the wall between them, at least some of the way.

"You are not a big dumb ox. I know it's a leap, but it feels right. It makes all the pieces make sense." She began ticking things off on her fingers. "Something happens, or somebody does something, on the Talarannos estate to cause the apparitions. I'm certain of that one. It fits with the timing and with Alita closing her estate off. Speaking of which, what did you notice about the servants?"

"That there weren't any. I mean, any visible. I saw a lot of movement behind windows; we were being watched."

"So Alita's people are all in on it, or at least bound to silence."

"Loyalty or fear," Gerrard said. "Either works well for keeping a secret."

"True. Where was I?" She looked at her index finger. "Right. Talarannos causes the apparitions. Two," her middle finger, "the apparitions spread through the city. Want to bet if we mapped everything out, we'd see the same ripple effect?"

"Please don't tell me we're going to do that."

"Don't have to. I'd still bet on it. Three," ring finger, "Genedirou figures out a way to get rid of the apparitions. The people on the hills, not willing to sacrifice their comfort, have him do so. But Genedirou is a show-off and his banishments draw attention. Alita has to come up with a story that includes detesting Genedirou—"

"That part I'm sure is real."

"Agreed. She comes up with a story that keeps him away either because she doesn't want anyone to figure out that Talarannos is the source of the apparitions, or to hide whatever Morica's doing that's

139

probably also related to the apparitions."

Gerrard rubbed his beard again. "But if it all started with Talarannos, how do you explain the unnatural coincidence that all five of the ruling families are overrun with apparitions? Assuming Gordou follows the pattern."

Zerafine opened her mouth, then closed it again. "That I don't know. We know all the apparitions are connected, so could Alita have set off a chain reaction? Remember, we also had four spots in the lower city that were similarly overrun, so it's not just the estates. But then what do all nine places have in common that they'd be the ones affected? And it still doesn't answer the question of what event, what action, would be able to disrupt the city's spirit on this level. The only thing we can be sure of is that Castinidou and the heads of Vidannos and Akennos don't have any idea what's going on, because if they knew what Alita knows, they'd have been keeping the same secret."

Gerrard nodded. "So where does this leave us?"

"Stuck, again, unless we can get back into Talarannos and poke around the off-limits areas, or that secret room." Zerafine sighed. "Or we could approach Castinidou and see if there's a pattern to the apparitions at his place." Her stomach rumbled. "I'm ready for a meal," she said.

"You just ate an hour ago," Gerrard objected.

"A few nibbles, maybe. Barely enough to sustain me. You, you'd starve on a diet like that." Zerafine took a deep breath. "And after that, I want to go shopping."

"For what?"

Zerafine paused before answering. "A new dress," she said.

Gerrard seemed to turn to stone. She could see him turning over objections in his head. "All right," he finally said, but the quality of his silence after that defied her to speak to him further.

Chapter Seventeen

With Nacalia an enthusiastic helper and Gerrard a stone statue in the corner, Zerafine chose a black knee-length tunic over black pants: classic, but beautiful. Zerafine admired herself in the shop mirror while wondering what her motivations were. If Dakariou showed interest in more than just conversation, would she take him up on it? It had been a very long time since she'd slept with anyone. Despite what she'd said to Gerrard, she was aware that she *didn't* know Dakariou very well, and that kind of intimacy was, well, *intimate*. But he was handsome, and he made her feel desirable in a way it turned out she'd missed. *But* – her thoughts went around and around in this vein all the way home.

That evening, she dressed, put her hair up, and almost as an afterthought put on her gold earrings, giving her head a little toss so they'd jingle. Gerrard was in the sitting room, reading a scroll. "I thought you didn't like to read," she said.

He rustled the scroll at her. "*Laxtian,*" he said. "Epic Kionnaran poetry. There's a stall around the corner – I should say, *now* there's a stall around the corner, Nacalia says it wasn't there two days ago – that sells books from all over the known world. I haven't read this since I was a boy – figured I'd see how well it holds up."

They watched one another in silence, Zerafine uncomfortable, Gerrard uncommunicative. "Nacalia hired the chair," Zerafine said. "I'll be back later."

Gerrard's jaw was set in that hard line, but he shrugged. "If you have to do this, at least stay inside the chair. Don't let anyone see you. Even without the robe, you could be recognized."

"Gerrard, this doesn't – it's not like I'm leaving you," Zerafine began, but he gave her a puzzled look. "That's not what I'm worried about," he said.

"Good, because – good," she said. "Please don't worry about

me."

"Worrying about you is my privilege," he said, and went back to his scroll.

She left the house to find Nacalia waiting in the courtyard. "Are you coming back?" she asked in a small voice.

"Of course I'm coming back!" Zerafine exclaimed. "You keep Gerrard company and I'll see you soon." *It's just dinner,* she thought; *why is everyone overreacting?* But even she knew it was about more than dinner.

Dakariou's home was in one of the nicer neighborhoods at the base of Akennos hill; it was nicer even than Berenica's compound. It was an older, two-story building with an atrium rather than a courtyard, and Dakariou met her there.

"You're simply beautiful this evening," Dakariou said. "It's really a pity you have to wear the robes almost all the time. You deserve to be noticed for who you are."

"A *thelis* of Atenas is who I am," Zerafine told him, mock-seriously. "But I appreciate the compliment." She accepted his offer of a seat next to the fountain. The atrium was designed to look like a natural forest glade, and the fountain was a waterfall that emerged from a false rock wall at one side of the room. The water rippled and bubbled over rocks carefully placed to produce a pleasing sound. The air was cool and smelled of fresh water and green things.

"I hope your visit to the Talarannos estate was everything you hoped for?" asked Dakariou. He sat close to her, intimate but not intrusive.

"It was, but I thought we weren't going to talk politics tonight?" Zerafine teased him.

Dakariou laughed. "My pardon, madama. I'm afraid with me it's a hard habit to break."

"I've noticed that about you. How did you come to be such a political animal?"

"Well." Dakariou sat a little more upright. "That's a long story, but then I believe we have plenty of time." His eyes captured hers in silent inquiry; she had no idea what he saw in hers. "I wasn't from the wealthiest family, but my parents made every effort to see that my schooling was the very best. Even so, there's always a divide between the haves and the have-lesses, and everyone knows where it is. Here, allow me." A servant had entered the atrium bearing a tray with two tall glasses. Dakariou took both and offered one to her; it was a delicate sparkling wine that tickled her nose. "I had two choices: I could fight a battle every day of my life, or I could keep my head down and be someone's toady. I decided to take a third road. Information. Anything you wanted to know, any test you needed to pass, anyone you wanted to blackmail, I was the one to go to. And since that meant that I had everything I needed to blackmail others, I was given a certain amount of respect. I parlayed that into an entrée into politics via the son of someone who, while not on the Council, was close to those who were. And then I made myself indispensable again. Ten years later, and here I am as Castinidou's left hand, the one the right hand doesn't know about."

"That sounds very...cynical."

"Politics is cynical. They called me the Weasel, back at school." Zerafine choked on her wine. "Are you all right?"

"Just swallowed the wrong way, that's all." Gerrard would love hearing that. Assuming he was ever willing to speak to her again.

"Anyway, that's my sad story. Politician born and bred." Dakariou looked up as the servant approached again. "Shall we go in to dinner?"

Over the first course, snails in butter and roasted asparagus, Dakariou said, "And you, madama? How did you come to such an, may I say, *unlikely* career?"

"I believe we know each other well enough that you can dispense with the 'madama,' Dakariou."

"Very well. *Zerafine.*" His voice caressed her name and she felt a blush beginning. Perhaps his intentions were a little more obvious than she'd believed. "How does one become a *thelis* of Atenas?"

"The first requirement is to be born on the god's day. The last day of the year." She patted butter from her lips. She'd never had snails before and found that she liked them.

"So everyone born on that day is destined to become *theloi*?"

"No, but no one not born on that day can do so. Though many of those who don't choose ordination still become lay acolytes, or serve in the holy city. It's considered an unlucky birth date, so one might as well embrace it."

"And you, specifically?"

"I can't remember ever wanting to do anything else." A different servant cleared her empty plate and brought pork medallions in a dark wine sauce. A third servant topped off her wine glass. "I saw the *theloi* in their red robes, coming through town, and I said—that's what I want. So when I was twelve I left my family behind in Dardagne, my parents and my brother and sister, and went to the holy city of Atenar for training."

"I can't imagine knowing my path so certainly. When I was a boy I wanted to be a wrestler." He laughed, and Zerafine joined him. "But I changed my mind after starting school."

"We go to school as well, in Atenar," Zerafine said. "Reading, composition, mathematics, natural philosophy. And consolation."

"I've never understood why they call it that."

Zerafine organized her thoughts. "Ghosts seem frightening because they're so violent, so unpredictable," she said. "But they're just terrified, angry, lonely creatures that are fragments of who they were in life. We show them who they used to be and tell them that it's all right to be afraid, but that they can leave it behind. It's like comforting a child, often."

Dakariou shuddered. "You are far, far braver than I."

Zerafine smiled. "I'm not brave. I'm just not afraid. You can't fear, in front of them, or you lose control. *Theloi* have died from fear."

"I still honor you for it." He saluted her with his glass, and she returned the salute. Again, while his face was merry, even mocking, his eyes were disturbingly serious.

After dinner, they took their glasses into the sitting room. Dakariou either had excellent taste or a very good interior decorator. The room was comfortable, not very large, but managed to seem cozy rather than cramped. Zerafine waved away the offer of more wine. She felt she would need all her faculties to keep up with her host.

"Tell me what it's like, traveling all the time," Dakariou asked. He sat on a couch perpendicular to hers, again close enough to be intimate without making her feel uncomfortable. "I've never been out of Portena."

"It's not very exciting. You sleep in a lot of bad roadside inns and eat local cuisine, which usually translates to 'food you wouldn't eat unless you were desperate.'" Zerafine smiled. Did snails qualify? "On the other hand, you meet a lot of different people and see a lot of different cities. We go back to Atenar around once or twice a year, usually for High Holy Week—what you'd call the Last of the Old Year—and it's good to see friends again. You know, the kind of friends you like, but not well enough to spend a lot of time with."

Dakariou grinned at that. "I can think of some people I know who'd fit that category." He set his glass down on the floor. "And that *sentare* of yours, you've been partners how long?"

"Six years," Zerafine said. She felt uncomfortable discussing Gerrard with this man. "You can request a certain partner, or they pair you up and see how it goes—I had a couple of other partners for a month or two before I met Gerrard."

"He's with you all the time, I've noticed." Dakariou was disturbingly, heartpoundingly close.

"That's his job." Was he moving closer?

"I'm glad he's not here tonight," he whispered, and kissed her.

Reflexively, she kissed him back. His lips were warm and soft and oh, so experienced. She kissed him again, but something was wrong. Something—

Oh no.

Sweet goddess of light. I'm in love with Gerrard.

I am the stupidest person ever to walk the known earth.

She'd stiffened after the second kiss, and Dakariou pulled away and searched her face. "I've made a mistake," he said, a questioning note in his voice.

"No, I have," she said. "Dakariou, I am so sorry. I've led you on."

He pulled back a little, puzzled. "Zerafine, I don't want anything from you. I find you beautiful and desirable and I'd like to share your bed for a night or, if you're willing, more. But I know you'll be moving on eventually, and I don't expect this to go any further than that. I hope I didn't make you feel otherwise."

She shook her head ruefully, laughing even as her world rearranged itself so fast it was dizzying. "That's what I thought, too," she told him. "But it wouldn't be fair to either of us for me to sleep with you when I'm in love with someone else."

Dakariou looked at her for a moment, puzzled, then threw back his head and laughed. "It's that ox of a *sentare* of yours, isn't it?" he said. "I should have known better than to bring him up. The more fool me."

"Dakariou, I can't tell you how sorry I am. I swear to you, I only just realized—"

"Don't apologize. I'm not going to tell you I'm not disappointed. But I should have realized the two of you were too close, in love or no, for me to fit myself into a space between." He laughed again, this time at himself. "You won't despise me for wishing things were otherwise?"

"Of course not," Zerafine said. "I just wish I'd realized sooner."

"Don't hate me for wishing you hadn't realized at all." He took her hand and kissed it. "What are you going to do?"

Zerafine closed her eyes. "Nothing," she said. "He doesn't feel the same. If I told him, it would embarrass him so much, and how could we work together with that hanging over our heads?" She looked at Dakariou. "I don't know," she said.

"You could give him a little credit for being able to handle the blow," he said.

Zerafine shook her head. "You know how I said I was fearless? That's only with ghosts. I am a coward when it comes to my own life."

Dakariou stood, went to the dining room door, and spoke to a servant there. When he returned, he said, "I've asked them to summon a chair for you. This is just a guess, but I think you won't be staying the night."

"Dakariou, you are a wonderful man."

"Don't give me too much credit. I'll be crying in my cups come morning." But there was a twinkle in his eye that Zerafine was certain meant he wasn't taking his rejection too hard. She felt a moment's relief that was soon supplanted by a giant, looming dread of facing Gerrard again.

They chatted pleasantly on neutral topics until the chair came. To Zerafine, it seemed to take forever. When it finally arrived, and Dakariou had helped her into it, he said, "Can I see you tomorrow? Politically, not personally, I mean. I do want to hear what happened today at Alita's."

"Come by in the morning."

"I will." He kissed her hand again. "And, Zerafine? Don't let fear rule you." He smiled at her and closed the curtains around her. There was a jolt, and the bearers started down the long road back to home. And Gerrard.

Chapter Eighteen

Alone at last, Zerafine's thoughts and emotions crowded in until there was barely room left in the chair for her. In love with Gerrard. Her *sentare*. Her best friend. In hindsight, it was obvious — the way she felt safe with him, the long conversations that ended with both of them in tears from laughter, how they'd been able to spend six years together without getting sick of one another. Even now, even when they were fighting, he was still the person she wanted to see first in the morning and the last person she said good night to. Worrying about him leaving her — that wasn't fear, it was *jealousy*. And now that she allowed herself to, she thought of his height and the breadth of his shoulders and the way he shrugged and his wry smile, and realized how much she desired him, too.

Dakariou was both right and wrong. Gerrard had never looked at her as anything other than a companion, and her telling him that she felt otherwise wasn't going to change that. But she couldn't just keep silent and pretend nothing had changed. He knew her too well for that. She could either tell him, or let him find out himself, and the latter option was just cowardly.

The jolt of the chair being set down startled her. She'd been so lost in her own thoughts that the trip had seemed to take no time at all. She swung her legs around to get out, and was startled to see long arms reach through the curtains and grab her roughly by the wrists. Hard hands yanked her out of the chair and threw her to the rough ground.

Confused, she looked up, and cried out when a booted foot kicked her hard in the jaw. Terrified now, she tried to crawl away and was grabbed again, this time under the armpits, and hauled upright. She felt a curse begin to burn deep inside her chest. Hard hands held her, and someone thrust a wad of greasy cloth into her mouth. "Don't let her speak," a harsh voice said, and another voice said, "Shut up." Then someone punched her in the stomach, and she tried to hunch over the pain, but the hard hands kept her from falling. They hit her, and kicked her, until her world was nothing but red agony.

Someone screamed, very close by, a shrill noise that went on and on. The man holding her cursed. "Finish her the fast way," said the second voice, and someone pulled her close to his chest. She felt something cold slide into and out of her side, so cold it burned, and the man dropped her, and she landed hard on the ground. Footsteps receded into the distance. Without thinking, she pulled the cloth out of her mouth, and the god's curse boiled out of her, words in an alien language, burning like acid. More screams, from farther away. *Thank you, my Lord.* She tried to smile, but she couldn't feel her lips.

Someone was leaning over her, a man she didn't know. The nearby screaming had turned into sobs. "Get a healer," the man said. "Can you stand?" Zerafine wanted to tell him, *I can't get a healer and stand at the same time,* but her mouth wasn't working right. He hauled her upright, and she made a sound that would have been a scream if her throat had not been torn apart, so it came out a reedy hiss instead. Her side felt hot and wet, and her legs shook so much that had it not been for the stranger, she would have fallen again.

He brought her into a small house and laid her on a bed. It was lumpy and smelled a little of urine, not so much that it was objectionable, but she was having trouble seeing so it was a good thing her nose still worked. She stared at the pattern of cracks in the ceiling. One of them looked like naked Genedirou doing his ritual dance.

From somewhere nearby, an argument was going on.

"...saw their eyes, burned out of their sockets, Atenas's curse..."

"...that woman, the emissary..."

"...killed Alestiou..."

"...be better just to let her die...."

"I didn't kill Alestiou," she protested, but nothing came out. Tears came to her eyes. Was that going to follow her the rest of her life? It occurred to her to wonder just how long "the rest of her life" was going to be. It felt like an awful lot of blood was coming out of her side. She couldn't feel anything but cold fire there.

A louder voice, stronger. "I know who she is. I also know I a'nt goin' to let a woman die in m'bed if it's not Kalindi's will. So get out o' my way and go get the damn healer already!"

Good for you, sirrah, she thought. *Let's not let any women die in your bed.* Her stomach clenched, and she first retched, then vomited on the floor. So much for dinner. *Sorry again, Dakariou.*

The noise outside the room was growing. Did the stranger have all his neighbors over at once? She couldn't make out the argument anymore; everything seemed to be coming from a long way off. The stranger who'd half-carried her to the bed was beside her. He had a blanket or sheet or something and was pressing it into her side. She wanted to tell him not to bother, she was warm enough, but she realized her feet were actually very cold and she wished he'd put the blanket over them instead. The line drawing of Genedirou on the ceiling really was quite fascinating.

She heard someone enter the room and felt, rather than saw, the person push the stranger aside. "Let's take a look here," said a woman. With a great effort Zerafine turned her head to look at the new person, whose white hair was disheveled as if she'd just come from her bed. The woman moved the sheet aside and felt along the wound. Zerafine hissed again at the pain. "Sorry," said the woman, but she sounded sort of detached and far away, so it was hard to tell if she meant it.

"*Thelis,* can you hear me?" the woman asked. Zerafine nodded once. It was too hard to do more than that. "I have to ask you if your god has called you home. Do you understand me? Tell me if Atenas has called you home. Just a nod or a shake of the head."

Zerafine gave this question due consideration. She was injured enough that it could be considered a sign that her time in this world was over. On the other hand, she'd lasted this long and that knife wound probably should have killed her. If it hadn't.... With an effort, she made her head flop from side to side. The room spun.

She heard someone shouting her name. Why was everyone so far away? The woman said, "Get him out of here," and then, "My dear, this is going to hurt quite a lot," and then hands gripped her shoulders and feet and someone was shoving a stick wrapped in a rag into her mouth, and she tried to spit it out because it reminded her of being gagged, but the woman said "You'll want to bite on this" so she took it between her teeth and —

Up until now, she thought she knew what pain was. Now she arched her back and screamed voicelessly through her damaged throat, biting down on the stick so hard that she felt it snap inside its wrappings. Fire tore through her side and into her chest, her arms, her head. She fought to be free of the hands holding her, instinctively trying to get away from the pain that filled her. Then her vision spiraled into blackness, and she couldn't fight any longer.

She woke in a blissful pain-free state. The crack in the ceiling no longer looked like Genedirou; it was a cat climbing a tree. How much difference a change of perspective can make. Someone was sitting on the foot of the bed. She looked; it was Gerrard. He was staring at his two clasped hands as if waiting for them to reveal the secrets of the universe.

Her body told her it had a pressing demand. She moved to sit up, and Gerrard startled. "Don't get up," he said.

"I have to use the commode," she told him. Her voice sounded rough and her throat itched as she spoke.

He gave her his hand and assisted her to a chamber pot in the corner, then tactfully turned his back while she used it.

"Back in bed," he said, guiding her to it with his hand on the small of her back as if she were a child.

"I feel fine," she said, pulling away. His touch made her uncomfortable; she needed him to keep his distance, wanted him never to let her go.

"Healer's instructions, not mine," he said. She'd expected him to be angry with her for proving him right about going out alone.

Instead, his face was impassive. "We're waiting for a litter to take you home."

"I can't go yet. I have something I need to handle." Without waiting for his permission, she ducked out of the small room, staggering a little bit as her legs tried to give out on her. It opened directly onto the street. The paving stones were cracked and a thin line of dark fluid ran in the gutter, which was clogged with trash. How had she ended up in a neighborhood like this? The crowd of people she'd heard before was still gathered, talking in low voices. Their conversations trailed off as, one by one, they noticed her standing there.

"Which of you brought me here?" she asked.

A man came forward. He was grizzled, perhaps in his fifties, with a large nose and a scar across his cheek. "I did," he said. He had the kind of belligerent expression on his face that conceals fear.

Zerafine committed his face to memory. "I heard you and your friends talking, before the healer came," she said. Then she made her deepest bow, knee to the ground without regard for the filth, hands spread wide, the kind of bow a ruler might expect of his vassal.

"Thank you," she said. "You could have let me die, and as far as you knew you would have been justified. You chose otherwise. I am in your debt. Whatever you ask, if it's in my power and the god's will, I will do it for you."

Silence gripped the crowd. "I didn't kill Alestiou," she added. The silence felt like a void that needed to be filled.

The man said, "I only did what any right-thinkin' man would."

Zerafine said, "You did what a thousand others would not have."

The man scratched his head. "D'you think you could replace the bed what you bled on?" he asked. "It a'nt a good one, but it's mine."

Zerafine smiled at him, her heart light. "I'll have it to you before tomorrow night," she promised.

"What are you doing out of bed?" The white-haired healer pushed through the crowd, a bowl in her hands and righteous indignation on her face. "What is she doing out of bed? I told you to make her stay there," she said, addressing Gerrard.

"We've established that I can't make her do anything she doesn't want to do," he replied, his tone neutral, but Zerafine heard the rebuke and it burned inside her like a coal.

"Then you ought to try harder. Sit on her, if you must, you and that massive body of yours," she grumbled. She shooed Zerafine back into the room and made her lie down on what, Zerafine realized, was a bloody, gory mess. She definitely owed her savior a new bed.

"Sit up a little and drink this. Don't worry, it's not nasty." Zerafine sipped at the bowl and made a face. She'd hate to learn this woman's definition of "nasty." "You need to drink it all, but take your time. Young man, I expect you to make sure she doesn't exert herself overmuch. She'll want to at first, but a healing like that takes it out of you, and I'm too old to use any of my own energy. Her mouth didn't heal. Any idea why not?"

"The god's curse," Gerrard rumbled. The healer's mouth made an O of surprise.

"Well, I think it will get better on its own. She's already able to talk and I imagine most of this is superficial." The healer peeled Zerafine's upper lip back from her teeth, a difficult task considering Zerafine had just taken another sip of the vile liquid. "Lots of fluids, plenty of rest, sleep if you can, and call in at the Goddess's temple if you're not recovered in twenty-four hours." She patted Zerafine's cheek. "You were lucky. That was a nasty beating someone gave you, quite aside from the knife wound." Zerafine felt Gerrard tense beside her.

Nacalia peeked into the room. "Litter's here," she said. She didn't look at Zerafine at all. Gerrard helped Zerafine to lie down in the litter and then gave a command to the bearers to head out.

The litter was surprisingly comfortable, the jolts minimal.

Zerafine curled on her uninjured side—no, they were both uninjured now. It had been a miracle that she had survived. She remembered the hands grabbing her, hitting her, and she clenched her eyes shut, willing the images to go away. She drifted off to sleep, barely waking when the litter came to a stop. Someone— Gerrard—picked her up and carried her, cradled like a baby, to her own bed. She felt something brush her face, then she fell into a deep, painless sleep.

Chapter Nineteen

Zerafine woke once, in the early hours, feeling as though she'd been beaten. Then she remembered that she had. She curled into a tight ball, cried a little, and fell back asleep.

When she woke again, it was full daylight, and the aches had mostly subsided. Nacalia was asleep on her bed, curled up like a kitten. She woke when Zerafine moved, said "You're not allowed to get up yet," and ran out of the room. Zerafine, amused, propped herself on her elbows and waited. Nacalia returned with Gerrard in tow, half dressed, hair tousled. Zerafine caught her breath. She had seen him without his shirt on many times before, but from her new perspective, the sight of his bare chest, the ridged muscles of his stomach, made her dizzy with desire. Her heart thudded against her ribcage like a captured animal. Amazing that he couldn't hear it.

"How are you feeling?" he said.

"Sore. Achy all over. But this—" she pointed at her side—"doesn't hurt. It doesn't feel like much of anything, really." In pointing at her side, she realized she was still wearing her filthy, torn clothes from the night before. She couldn't believe how stupidly eager she'd been when she picked them out. Poor Dakariou. Poor her, for that matter.

"The healer said that a divine healing repairs the body at the cost of your vital energy," Gerrard said. "You're physically entirely healed, but you need to take it easy while your body refills those stores. Please don't argue with me about this. If you don't rest, you *will* collapse and you could even die." He sounded weary, resigned to her willfulness. She wanted so badly to throw herself at him, to reassure him that his opinion mattered more to her than anyone else's.

"I'll rest," she said, her voice sounding tiny in her ears. "But Dakariou is coming over this morning to talk about the Talarannos estate."

"Dakariou is *not* coming over," Gerrard said grimly. "I spoke with him last night and we're meeting at noon. He's going to tell me about the progress he's made finding out about the men who attacked you."

"When did you speak to him?"

"Five minutes after I dragged him out of his bed and asked him some very blunt questions about why he'd sent you off with four men who turned out to be assassins."

"That wasn't his fault."

"No, but I was looking for someone other than myself to blame." For a moment, pain shone through the cracks in Gerrard's impassivity. *He's not angry with me. He's angry with* himself.

"Will you tell me what he finds?"

"Of course." But he still looked grim.

Zerafine looked at Nacalia, standing in the doorway, listening avidly. "Nacalia. Go to your room. Gerrard and I have to have a private conversation. And, Nacalia? When I say 'your room' I mean your room, not the hallway, not the sitting area. If I have to chase you away, I'll hurt myself, and you don't want that, right?" Nacalia, her eyes wide, shook her head vigorously, and was off like the wind.

"Shut the door," Zerafine said, "and sit down." He obeyed, looking puzzled and a bit wary. "Now, you listen to me, you big ox. *This was not your fault.* Nobody even thought to assume that I was in mortal danger. No one thought not to trust the bearers. Not you, not Dakariou, not me. *No one* could have expected this. So stop blaming yourself. As someone wise once told me, either forget about it or learn from it."

Gerrard shook his head. "You have no idea," he said, "what it meant to me to watch you in agony because of something I didn't protect you from. It's what I *do*, Zerafine. If you're injured that badly, it should only be because I am lying in a dozen pieces on the ground beside you. We argue, we don't always agree, but I never dreamed I would let you down so completely."

"I don't—" she began, then didn't know how to continue. This wasn't something she could make better, and her first instinct—to grab him by the ears and kiss him—would be less than useful. "Gerrard, *sentare*, I forgive you," she said. "I forgive you. I want you to figure out how to forgive yourself."

He looked away. "It would help if you let me do my job," he said, and she could hear the edge of humor in his voice. Zerafine smiled and lay back.

"I promise," she said. "No more solitary dinners, no traveling with bearers unless you're with me, no meetings with the Council, nothing." *If I could, I would keep you with me always.*

"Oh!" she exclaimed, and Gerrard sat up straight in alarm. "I have to break my promise already!"

Gerrard looked at her with such despair that she added, "I have to take a bath."

He laughed. It was such a relief to hear him laugh. It was as if their argument had never happened.

He did have to help her fill the tub, but once he was gone, she sank into the warm water and watched it turn pink from the blood the healer hadn't scrubbed off. There was a spot the size of a parsis low on her left side, just above her pelvis, scar tissue that felt dead under her fingers. She shivered, once again remembering those hard hands on her, a kick to the stomach...the healing had rid her of all those injuries as well. She tried to think about the attack impartially and only succeeded in making herself sick nearly to the point of vomiting. Very well, she'd forget about it. A day of nothing but rest seemed like a good idea, even if it hadn't been healer-mandated.

Clean, scrubbed, and dried, she put on her oldest, softest gown and went into the sitting room while Gerrard took his turn in the bath. She was feeling a little wobbly, so she sat down and put her feet up. Aesoron emerged from the kitchen with a tray.

"It's good to see you doing so well, *thelis*," he said. He pulled another couch around to where it faced her and set the tray on it.

"I'm told you are to eat well, so Fidonia has prepared some of your favorites. Let us know if there's anything else we can do for you." He bowed low and retreated.

"Thank you," she called after him. She was starting to feel hungry, and the food did look good. There was a carafe of fruit juice and she drank thirstily, gulping down the cold liquid that soothed her still-sore throat. Everything was well-seasoned without being spicy, soft without being mushy—did Aesoron and Fidonia know everything without being told?

Nacalia peeked out of the hallway. "Can I come out now?" She looked nervous.

"Have you been in there all this time? Yes, you can come out. Come have some of this food."

Nacalia leaped onto the couch and buried her face in Zerafine's stomach. "I was so scared!" she wailed in a muffled voice.

Zerafine stroked her dark curls. "Nothing to be scared of," she said. "I'm fine now and it's not going to happen again."

"Those men hurt you so much, and I di'nt know what to do, I should've screamed sooner," she replied, still muffled. Zerafine went very still.

"Nacalia, are you saying you were *there*?" she asked, prying Nacalia's face away from her midsection to look at her directly.

Nacalia nodded. "*Sentare* had me follow you in case anything bad happened, which it *did*, but I di'nt know what to do. Then the man came and I was going to get the healer, but somebody else did, so I ran for *sentare*. He was mad," she added. "He di'nt yell at me though, just at the handsome man."

Dakariou, Zerafine thought. "Because you did everything right," she told the girl. "You know you probably saved my life? If you hadn't screamed, that man wouldn't have come."

Nacalia perked up. "I saved your life?"

"You did. I owe you a lot."

"Can I have the rest of your juice?"

"I think I owe you more than that."

"That's okay. I like juice plenty." She drained the carafe without using the glass. Aesoron appeared beside them with a full carafe and whisked the empty one away. He was *good*.

Gerrard came out, fully dressed—*what a shame*—and fastening his belt. "I'm leaving now to take care of the bed you promised your savior," he said, "and I probably won't be back until late, so don't stay up waiting. Nacalia will get you whatever you need." He took up his staff from where it leaned against the wall.

"Wait," Zerafine said. "You have to know *something* already."

Gerrard sat down next to her. "The god's curse was powerful," he said. "It killed them, so they must have meant to leave you dead. They—they must have hurt you badly, by the way it burned them from the inside out." He turned his head away for a moment, and Zerafine impulsively took his hand. His skin was warm and dry, the palm striped with calluses, and he closed his other hand over hers and gripped it for a moment. "I'm *fine* now," she said, and he released her. She pushed away memories of hard hands, a boot to the jaw.

"Dakariou seems confident that his sources could identify them, missing eyes or no," he went on. "They meant it to look like a typical robbery gone wrong. It was supposed to seem as if your bearers had wandered into a bad part of the city and then abandoned you when they were set upon. But there was no evidence of anyone there but you and your attackers, who were dressed as bearers themselves. There's no question this was premeditated. I'm meeting Dakariou at the transport company to find out what happened to the real team."

"Will you be able to find who was behind it?"

"I hope so," he said, but he didn't sound confident.

"We know who was behind it," she said.

"Us knowing isn't the same as proof. I can't walk into one of the wealthiest estates in Portena and start swinging."

"There has to be *something* we can do. Alita must have been truly desperate to try this."

"Alita has the resources to cover this up. It was sheer luck you survived."

"Perhaps Sintha's watching over me instead of Alita."

"Don't joke about it," he said. He stood up. "Rest. Eat. Sleep."

"You keep telling me that as if you don't think I'm listening."

"I know you hear what I'm saying. I don't trust that you'll listen." He looked as if he wanted to say more, then shook his head. "I'll see you later," he said.

After the door closed behind him, Nacalia said, "*Sentare* told me I could sit on you if you di'nt obey."

"I'll tickle you until you turn blue if you try."

"You wouldn't." But she retreated to the end of the couch, just out of reach. "I can bring you stuff."

"Why don't you—" Sending her to the book stall Gerrard had mentioned was probably a bad idea; who knew what she'd come back with? "Let's play that game you were playing with Gerrard the other day," she said instead.

They played several rounds of the game. Nacalia won all of them, Zerafine being distracted by her private thoughts. She had to tell him sometime. Sooner would be better. She couldn't tell him. She had to tell him. Someone came to the door with an enormous bouquet of flowers and a note from Dakariou, apologizing for his role in the attack—what role?—and wishing her a speedy recovery. It made her tear up for a moment. After a while, she told Nacalia she wanted to rest and that the girl could go out and amuse herself for a while. She lay on the couch, sleepless, trying out opening gambits.

Gerrard, we've known each other a long time —
Gerrard, I know this is going to be awkward —
It's only fair I should tell you —
You've always been my best friend, but now —
I hope you'll understand when I tell you —
I love you —

Eventually, in desperation, she sent Aesoron to the book stall.

He returned with a history of religion in Portena that mostly kept her thoughts occupied.

"The ancient people," she read,

lived in fear of the natural forces that shaped their lives. The gods heard their pleas and obeyed. (What god do you pray to if your heart is so heavy with love you can barely breathe?) *They cast wide their nets and brought down the powers of heaven and earth, wind and sky, water and fire, took them out of themselves and tamed them to their own purposes.* (I can barely tame myself. Someday, sometime, I'll slip up, and he'll look at me with bewilderment in those gray eyes and not even know me.) *Kalindi built her throne where their great victory was won, and all eyes turned upon her.*

She already knew this. She flipped ahead a few pages.

The eldest of them, Atenas, He Who Walks Alone, stood apart from the gods, and would not join their victory. They pleaded with Him that they might be One, but He turned His back on the gods and went His own way. But Atenas took compassion upon men, whose spirits would have been lost after death. For their sake, He made a place for them in His courts. Thus do the Twelve bless us in life, and the One judge us after death.

Atenas as savior. It was not a perspective she'd heard often outside the gates of Atenar. She laid the book down on its face, careful of its spine, and stared at the ceiling. No cracks to suggest humorous figures. She wondered how well received the book was in this bastion of Kalindi worship. No one in Portena was likely to take well to the idea that Atenas was the Goddess's superior in any way, even if only in age. She wondered who the author was.

Someone knocked at the front door, and it swung open without an invitation. Berenica entered. Zerafine sat up, too quickly, and her head swam for a moment. It seemed she really wasn't as well as she believed.

"I came to see how you were getting on," Berenica said. She gathered her red robe around her and sat on a couch opposite Zerafine. Her beautiful voice was cool, neutral. She glanced at the book next to Zerafine. "Interesting reading choice," she said.

"It was Aesoron's," Zerafine replied. "He has impeccable taste. I'm enjoying it very much."

"Thank you," said Berenica. "It's nice to be appreciated."

"*You* wrote this?" Zerafine exclaimed, then, "I'm sorry. I didn't mean to sound so astonished."

"It's not exactly what one expects from a *thelis*," Berenica admitted.

"But—and again I apologize for my incredulity—why?"

"There is so much fear of Our Lord," Berenica said. "So much misunderstanding. Preaching is useless. We teach people not to fear simply by doing our duty, consoling ghosts, helping people come to terms with their loved ones' deaths, or their own, and even then we risk being called murderers. As you know." Berenica rolled her sleeves away from her hands. "I saw an opportunity to reach people another way. Tell the old familiar stories, but tell them as we learn them, with Atenas playing a vital role in the works of the gods."

"Is it...popular? Did it accomplish your goal?"

Berenica smiled. "It's not being read by everyone, but people have begun to talk about it. Discuss it. I admit it's gratifying." The old Berenica surfaced, a gleam of pride in her eye.

"I think...it would never have occurred to me to take your approach. I suppose I thought of those stories as sacred because we don't talk of them to others. But that's not true."

"No, it isn't. I sent a few copies to Atenar and the *Marathelos* approved. Arland, on the other hand, started an ongoing correspondence battle about my interpretations of certain points of doctrine."

Zerafine laughed. "I can imagine he would."

Berenica smiled. "He's never been happy that this shrine holds some of the oldest sacred records of our sect. He wants them all safe where he can see them."

"I didn't know that! What records?"

"Nothing special. The creation story, the records of our earliest *theloi* and their journeys. The Unholy Wars. It's their age that makes them special, not their contents. There are hundreds of copies in Atenar."

"I'd love to see those records."

"Perhaps when you're well."

The conversation died off. Zerafine wondered at the change in Berenica's attitude. Perhaps all it took to win her over was to nearly die.

"I officiated at Alestiou's funeral this morning," Berenica said. "I heard you've been blamed for his death."

"He asked for Our Lord's blessing, and I gave it to him." She remembered the look of peace on the great man's face. "He was in so much pain."

"I owe you a debt for that," said Berenica. "It should have been I who gave it to him. I...have not treated you well. It's been difficult for me to do my duty, this last year, and I lashed out at you in guilt." Her voice was tense. Zerafine could imagine how much this admission cost the proud *tokthelis*.

"I was not kind to you," Zerafine said, and realized it was true. "I resented your treatment of me because I was so proud of my responsibility and wanted to be praised for it."

"It seems we've been guilty of the same sin," said Berenica, and a tiny smile touched her lips and was gone.

"Pride butting heads with pride," Zerafine sighed. "How exhausting."

"I agree." Berenica rose. "I'll leave you to rest now. Thank you for the visit."

"Thank *you*," said Zerafine, meaning it. "I'll come by in a few days to see those records, if it's all right with you."

"Of course," said Berenica, inclining her head. "Rest well." She left, closing the door quietly behind her.

Well. This was a day for surprises. Zerafine picked the book up and turned it over in her hands. Berenica an author. That was a new one. She'd misjudged the woman entirely.

Chapter Twenty

Nacalia came back and wanted to be entertained. They played a few more games until dinner. Gerrard still wasn't back. Zerafine was firmly but gently instructed that she was to take her meal on the couch. She'd started to hate the couch. After dinner, she read a little more. Berenica really was talented. She had put a new spin on old legends that kept Zerafine's interest despite her thorough familiarity with the sources.

Eventually, tired of waiting for Gerrard despite his instructions, she lay down on her bed and folded her arms across her stomach. She would tell him tonight. She couldn't bear the tension any longer; it had sat like a ball of acid in her stomach ever since Berenica's visit. He had to come home eventually, and she would tell him no matter how late it was. Then she would flee to her room and cry.

She'd begun drifting off when she heard the front door open and close. Her heart began pounding. *Wait until he goes into his room.* But he went into the bathing room instead. *Surely he isn't going to bathe at this time of night? What time is it, exactly?*

She heard the bathing room door close, then, farther away, his bedroom door. *Now, before you lose your nerve.* She slid out of bed and went down the hall, and knocked. "Gerrard?" she said. Her voice trembled.

"What are you doing still awake?" he said through the door.

"I want to talk to you." *Come on, open the door and let's get this over with.*

"Can it wait until morning?"

"No."

There was a pause. "You have to promise not to laugh."

Zerafine raised her eyebrows. "Why would I laugh at you?"

"Just promise."

"I promise."

x

164

A moment later, he opened the door and stood glaring down at her. He was dressed for sleep, shirtless and wearing his undershorts. She put her hands over her mouth.

He'd shaved his beard. A part of her mind registered the newly revealed smooth line of his jaw, his firm chin, but the rest of her was preoccupied with not laughing. The top part of his face was its usual sunburned red, the color it always turned in summertime. The lower half of his face, the part the beard had obscured, was as pale as his chest.

She choked on her laughter. His belligerent stance dared her to let it out. She couldn't help herself. Her hands couldn't keep it in.

"Thanks," he said bitterly, and moved to shut the door. She stepped into the doorway, blocking it.

"I'm not laughing at you," she said. "I'm just imagining what you must have felt—you have it shaved off, and then—"

His hand went to cover his face. He turned away and went to sit on the bed. She followed him, closing the door behind her. The chickens on the wall mocked her.

"Whatever possessed you to get rid of it?" she asked.

"I was trying to impress a woman," he said.

She stopped laughing. The ball of acid returned with a vengeance. So it didn't matter after all. "I hope she appreciates it," she said, trying for a light tone.

He glared at her briefly, then turned away again. "Right now she's laughing at me after she promised not to," he said.

It took her a moment to register his words. Her ears rang with them. All her carefully planned words vanished into the distance. Dimly, she realized that he was speaking again.

"I couldn't figure out why I hated Dakariou so much," he said. "I thought it was because he was using you to further whatever plans he had. It wasn't until he asked you to dinner, and you said yes, and he was looking at you the way a man looks at a woman he desires, and I thought, She's going to sleep with someone, and it's not going to be me. And I wanted it so desperately to be me." He blew out his breath explosively. "I thought I could get past it, because I owe you that much. But I love you, Zerafine. It's not possible for me to be around you and not think of being near you, of kissing you and holding you and...well. Please go. I can't face you now. I can't bear to see you look at me with disdain, or embarrassment, or worse, pity. I just can't."

She heard her own thoughts echo in his words. A dozen feelings raged inside her, but the one that came out on top was pure, beautiful relief. Without a word, she stood in front of him, slid her hand along his smooth cheek, and kissed him.

If kissing Dakariou had been pleasurable, kissing Gerrard was like a revelation. She pulled away and saw that she'd surprised him. Of course she had. His gray eyes were wide and his face was frozen in astonishment. She brushed her lips against his once more and murmured, "Don't make me do all the work, love."

Then his arms went around her waist and he was kissing her until she couldn't breathe. She pulled away just enough to gasp and heard him laugh a relieved, joyful laugh. He kissed her again, kissed the column of her throat, then went back to her lips. "You'd better not be doing this out of pity," he whispered, and she put her arms around the back of his neck and showed him just how little pity had to do with it.

They broke apart, after a long, long moment, and gazed at one another. They both started to laugh, Gerrard's booming deep chuckle harmonizing with Zerafine's higher peals of mirth. "I can't believe it," Zerafine said. "You—"

"You—"

"I was in agony all day, not knowing how to tell you."

"*You* were in agony? *I* thought you were going to die without knowing how I felt."

"I thought you were angry with me."

"I was dying of jealousy is what I was. When did you know? How long?"

"I figured it out when I kissed Dakariou."

"You did *what?*"

"Take a breath, my love. It was only once or twice. Long enough for me to realize I was kissing the wrong man."

"I knew he deserved more than the one punch I gave him."

"Why did you hit the poor man? He's got to be half your size."

"I told you. Jealousy and pure terror. Remember, at the time I thought you were dying."

"I'm really glad I didn't die."

"So am I." He pulled her close to him again and kissed her, just once, but long and sweet. She put her arms around his neck, ran her fingers down his bare spine. He smelled good, like wood smoke and the minty scent of whatever he washed his hair with and pure healthy male. "This is like a dream," he whispered in her ear.

"Better than a dream," she replied, and she kissed him again, this time with intent. She could feel heat rising in her, starting in her chest and ending somewhere between her thighs. "Help me take this off," she said, pulling at the hem of her gown.

"Are you well enough?"

She gave him a direct look. "I have been lying on that couch all day. I was lying on my bed until ten minutes ago. If I'm going to lie down again it will be on my terms, with you beside me."

He helped her peel her dress off over her head and remove her undergarments. His eyes gleamed at the sight of her, and she was treated to his wolfish grin. This time, the wolf had seen a little ewe lamb he wanted very much. He took off his undershorts, and it was her turn to grin with pleasure, just before laughing in delight at how pleased he was that she wanted him. He slid his hand over the curve of her breasts, her hips, and whispered, "So beautiful."

"So are you," she said, and then they were lying together on his bed. It wasn't very wide, but then they didn't need it to be.

Zerafine lay with her head on Gerrard's broad chest, with its short, coarse blond hairs, and listened to the beat of his heart slow to normal. "I love you," she said.

167

"And I you," he replied. "I'm still astonished that you're here in my bed."

"I'd be happy to remind you of how real I am."

"I'm going to need a minute."

"Just a minute? I'm impressed."

"I never guessed you would be this insatiable."

"I never had the right partner until now."

He brought his arms around her and squeezed, gently. "I will be your partner forever, in every way that counts," he told her.

She smiled into his chest. "Just think how much we'll save on accommodations," she said.

He laughed, a deeper rumble now that her ear was pressed against him. "I would like to think," he said, "that my company means somewhat more to you than that."

She lifted herself on her elbows, breaking his hold. "One bed," she said. "Think how narrow some of those beds are. And you'll be able to guard my body better than ever before."

"And what a lovely body it is," he said, seizing her and rolling her onto her back as she shrieked a laugh. "Let's take another look at it."

Later:

"I have a confession."

"What?"

"You know when I came into your room this morning with my shirt off? I took it off on purpose so you'd see how good I look naked and be filled with desire. Stop that. I swear, woman, how can this relationship go anywhere if it's founded on you laughing at me all the time?"

Even later:

"I'm sorry I was so stubborn about dinner with Dakariou."

"I'm sorry I called you a bully and proud."

"I'm sorry I didn't apologize sooner."

"I'm sorry I let my jealousy influence how I treated you."

"Did I tell you I love you?"

"You can never tell me enough."

Still later:

"Zerafine. Zerafine, sweetheart, wake up. It's a dream."

"They hurt me so much. I can't stop thinking about it. They wouldn't stop kicking me."

"Don't cry, love. It will never happen again, do you hear me? Never. I swear it."

"Promise?"

"My life on it."

They finally fell asleep, wrapped in each other's arms, and Zerafine didn't dream anymore that night. She woke to the sound of someone knocking on the door. She judged it was about an hour past sunrise. Reflexively, she sat up and wrapped the blanket around her chest, pulling it off Gerrard's shoulders. He came instantly awake, but didn't sit up.

The knocking came again. "Madama *thelis*?" said Aesoron. *Does that man know* everything? "There is a *thelos* from the temple of Sukman here to see you."

She looked at Gerrard. "Surely not Genedirou?" she said.

"Aesoron would have said," he replied. He rolled out of bed and tossed her gown at her. She made a face. "I'm going to look like a slob," she said.

"You're going to look like a woman awakened at an ungodly hour by someone she wasn't expecting," he said, pulling on his undershorts.

She waited until he was fully dressed before opening the door, feeling an unaccountable shyness at being seen coming out of his room. There was no reason to be ashamed, but their love was so new, she felt tender of it.

But Rovalt, waiting in the sitting room, didn't even notice. He stood, wringing his hands, unable to keep still. "Zerafine," he said. "I apologize for bothering you so early, but...." He swallowed hard. "Genedirou's dead."

Chapter Twenty-One

"Sit down, Rovalt," Zerafine said, sinking onto a couch and patting the seat next to her. He stumbled to her side and landed heavily on the couch. "What happened?"

"A banishment," Rovalt said. "Like a hundred others. They've taken longer, lately, but.... The apparition was a man. It was a big fat man. Genedirou stepped inside it. I've never seen him do that before." He shuddered. "The thing sort of collapsed on itself, it shrank until it was nothing, and Genedirou had a massive seizure. And then he was dead. I don't know what to do." He covered his face with his hands and shook. Zerafine put her arm around his shoulders.

"Rovalt, you have to tell me everything that's happened since the banishments became difficult," she said. "Those things could kill others."

"I know," he said. He raised his head. "Genedirou wouldn't talk about the details. He always said it wasn't my job to understand, just to serve. So I only know what I've observed. Every time, it takes — took — a little longer. And it looked like it was harder every time. Like he was having to work to get Sukman's attention. The apparitions, too...at first they'd just dissolve, but lately they would fold in on themselves, or shrivel up. It was as if they were fighting for their lives."

"But Genedirou was never hurt by any of them?"

"Not until today." He covered his face again and let out a sob. "I don't know what to do," he repeated, his voice muffled by his fingers.

"You have to carry on. Genedirou wouldn't have wanted the daily ceremonies to stop just because he was gone, right?" Zerafine felt a little uncomfortable, a *thelis* of one faith telling a *thelos* of another what to do, but Rovalt was clearly unhinged by his superior's death. She also felt guilty. If she'd been more patient with

171

Genedirou, more willing to subordinate herself to his pride, would they have been able to find a solution that didn't leave Genedirou dead?

"Did you arrange for the body to be sent to your sanctuary?" she continued. "I can send someone to Berenica's house if you haven't done that yet. And worshippers will need comforting. I know you can handle all that."

She wasn't as certain as she sounded, but Rovalt nodded. "I can do that." He wiped his eyes. "Will you find out why he died? And stop the apparitions from killing again?"

"You can leave that to me," she assured him, and led him to the door. When he was gone, she slumped against its dark solidity and shook her head. "This isn't good. I wish I'd been there to see it."

"You realize how callous that sounds," Gerrard said.

"I know. I don't mean it that way. But it would help if I knew what happened to the apparition to make it deadly. Even banishing Baz didn't do more than make my arm hurt for a short time." She plucked at her old gown. "I need to get dressed. And we need to talk to Castinidou."

But Castinidou wasn't available, not even to the official emissary. He was closeted with the rest of the Council, discussing how to handle the crisis. Though the banishment had been performed on private property, the tale of Genedirou's death spread at the speed of gossip and grew mightily in the telling. By the time they left the Capitol, their errand unfulfilled, Zerafine had heard rumors that the apparition had swallowed Genedirou whole—that it had turned into a wolf that bit his head off and spat it on the ground—that it had dissolved his bones to jelly so there was nothing left of him but a skin bag. As disturbing as the images were, Zerafine was relieved that she *hadn't* heard the far more disturbing rumor that apparitions had begun attacking people across the city. For now, the problem was contained.

"I don't want to hang around here waiting for Castinidou," Gerrard said. A hot wind blew through the plaza, chased by clouds that promised rain.

"Neither do I." She was still getting dirty looks from passersby, though most of them just kept their heads down against the wind. There were far fewer glares and warding gestures than on the day of Alestiou's death, but she didn't feel like exposing herself to their antagonism. Zerafine chewed her lower lip and thought. What else could they do? Return home to wait? Sit the hours out—and she had no doubt it would be many hours—inside the Rotunda? She had no desire to wait at all, but what else was there? Unless....A grin spread across her face. "I have a truly excellent and cunning idea," she said, and headed off across the plaza toward Talarannos hill.

"What are you—wait. Just stop there a minute. That's not an excellent and cunning idea, it's insane. If you muscle your way into Alita's estate, she can have you brought up on charges, emissary or no. Portena has some very strict ideas about property rights and unreasonable searches."

"I'm not going to force my way in. I'm going to ask them, nicely, to let me speak to Morica Akennos. And if they won't, then *you* can muscle my way in. Didn't you say just the other day that you rarely get to flex your muscles in my defense?"

"That was when I thought the worst thing we could face was a mob of uncoordinated rabble."

"Seriously, if they refuse, I'll go away quietly and we'll think of something else."

Gerrard reached up to scratch his beard and seemed mildly surprised to find bare skin. "All right. But I don't like the look in your eye."

"What look?"

"The one that says that you're not going to let them refuse."

She patted his cheek. "I can be very persuasive."

He captured her hand, kissed the tips of her fingers. "I remember," he said.

"Zerafine!"

She turned to see Dakariou running toward them, a satchel

bouncing awkwardly at his side. When he arrived, panting a little, she hissed in sympathy. He looked exhausted. He also had a truly spectacular black eye.

"I won't ask how you got that," she said, and glared at Gerrard, who managed to look impassive and smug at the same time. "I'm so sorry."

"Not your fault, madama," he said. "What your *sentare* undoubtedly *didn't* tell you is that he only got one blow in before I twisted his arms behind his ears and held him under the fountain until he calmed down." At her amazement, he added, "I said I didn't take up wrestling as a career. I never said I gave it up entirely. Grand Amateur Tournament winner, four years running." He eyed Gerrard. "That's an...interesting look for you, sirrah. I'm sure the color will even out nicely in a few days."

Gerrard now looked impassive and embarrassed. "An amateur wrestler got the better of a fully trained master longstaff fighter?" Zerafine said, teasing. "I may have to fire you."

"I didn't have the staff," Gerrard muttered. "I was in a hurry. Remember, you were dying."

She took his arm. "No wonder you were so upset."

Dakariou looked from one of them to the other. "And may I congratulate you both on working out your...little difficulty?" he said with an arch smile.

Zerafine looked at him in confusion. "I know I told you," she said, "but how did you know that Gerrard —"

"He figured it out that night," Gerrard rumbled. "Something about how I was behaving more like a man in mortal fear for his woman than a worried colleague."

"And you didn't tell him how I felt? Dakariou, how cruel!"

"It was your secret, my dear," Dakariou said. "Yours to keep, yours to share. I thought it best to let the two of you work it out yourselves. Besides, it all ended well, no?"

Zerafine had to admit he was right. She wouldn't give up that memory of Gerrard's quiet voice confessing the same feelings, the same fears that had gripped her that whole awful night and day. "Then I suppose I owe you my thanks," she said.

"Please don't. I haven't forgiven myself for letting you go into mortal danger. It's not rational, I know," he said, throwing up a hand to forestall her objection, "but there it is. I've tried to make up for my failings by finding out who hired those assassins. It wasn't an easy trail to follow. Two of the four men were known thugs for hire. My agents learned that the other two were, we think, professionals lately come to Portena. And may I say that I hope never to make you angry at me, Zerafine. What you did to those men...I've never seen anything so destructive."

"I didn't do it. Atenas did," Zerafine said, feeling her eyes go moist at the memory. "When one of His own is threatened, sometimes He intervenes with swift and proportionate justice. An insult to the god might be answered with, oh, temporary muteness or blindness, or an attempt to strike me might result in a broken arm. It's why we have *sentaren*, to deliver a less...punitive form of justice. Those men wanted me dead, so...." Gerrard put his arm around her. She hadn't added *And Gerrard wasn't there*; no sense reminding him of something painful that he already knew.

Dakariou looked respectful and, she thought, a little afraid. "At any rate, my agents were able to trace your attackers back to an intermediary," he said, "who in turn had been hired by a woman we only just located a few hours ago. That woman...she's refusing to talk, but the man she hired to do the recruiting says she wore Talarannos colors when he met with her. Not the official livery, but it's a start."

"So you can prove Alita was behind it?"

"'Proof' is a complicated thing," he said. "If we can get the woman to talk, and it's doubtful that we will, it's still her word against Alita's. So if you're looking for justice in the courts, you'd have a tough time of it. You'd have better luck under Atenas's justiciary—"

"Except that as a *thelis* of Atenas I can't receive judgment or act as judge on my own behalf."

"Yes. Exactly. So what you're left with is knowledge you can use to protect yourself against future attacks. I don't know if Alita will try anything so openly again, but you should be alert. If it were me, I'd use it to blackmail her, but I know that's not in your repertoire." He grinned.

"If I need the Weasel, I'll call on you," she said, and Gerrard snorted a laugh. Dakariou glanced at him. "You've certainly got a menagerie looking out for you. The Ox and the Weasel." Gerrard glared down at him; Dakariou was unmoved by his looming menace.

"I've got to run this errand for Castinidou now," he said. "The Council is, well...saying they're in an uproar would be understating it. You might want to stay out of their way for a bit," he added. "Some of them are criticizing your handling of the situation, saying that you've acted too slowly, that Genedirou wouldn't be dead if you'd been more diligent, that sort of thing. I'm sure you can imagine who's leading that faction."

"Alita's definitely with the Council at the moment?" Gerrard said.

"Ranting her little patrician heart out," Dakariou said.

"Good. Thank you for the news, Dakariou," Zerafine said. "I think we're about to solve the mystery. Don't tell the Council, though. I want to be certain of the answer."

Dakariou glanced over his shoulder at Talarannos hill, then back at her. An evil smile spread across his face. He took her hand and kissed it. "Good fortune to you, madama," he said, and walked away in the direction of Kalindi's temple.

"He's clever," Zerafine said, watching him go.

"He was taunting me," Gerrard growled.

She patted his arm. "If you didn't make it so easy for him, he would stop." Then, in a lower voice, she added, "If it helps, you might remember that the bed I slept in last night was not his."

Gerrard brightened. "That's true," he said with reminiscent

pleasure, and Zerafine laughed at him.

Chapter Twenty-Two

With Nacalia in the lead, they trod up the hill to the Talarannos estate for the second time in three days. At the gate, Zerafine pulled the cord and heard a bell ring, somewhere in the distance. They waited. Zerafine pulled the cord again, harder, though this didn't seem to make the bell ring any louder. Gerrard pounded the door with his longstaff. Finally the gate creaked open and a small, stout woman in Talarannos formal livery peered out. "Madama isn't home," she said in a voice that belonged to a much larger person.

"I know," Zerafine said. "I'm here to speak to Morica Akennos."

"She's not receiving visitors," the woman said, and made as if to close the gate.

"Wait," Zerafine said, and Gerrard inserted the end of his staff into the gap to prevent the gate from closing entirely. "May I ask your name?"

The woman looked suspicious. "Toria."

"Toria, *tokthelos* Genedirou was killed by an apparition this morning. You and everyone on this estate are in danger. Morica's experiments may make things worse. I need to speak with her to ensure the estate's safety." Only half of that was a lie. No, not so much a lie as a calculated guess, because her mouth tasted no bitterness.

Toria's small, round eyes darted between Zerafine, looking innocently earnest, and Gerrard, looking stolid. "Move your stick," she said, kicking it, and shut the gate.

Zerafine sighed. "I suppose—" she began, but then the gate swung open fully, and Toria motioned to them to come in.

"You better be right," she said darkly. "Atenas alone knows why I take such risks."

"You're a worshipper," said Zerafine, startled.

"My dad was a *thelos* 'fore he gave up the traveling life. I adore

Madama, we all do, but she's been toying with things she ought to have let lie." Toria glanced up at Gerrard. "My mam was dad's *sentare*," she added. "Damn near deadly with a longstaff, she was."

Zerafine smiled at her. "Thank you, Toria."

"Don't thank me, thank the god, because when Madama finds out I broke the rule I'm like to be out on my ass. But just this morning I was thinking it wasn't right, keeping this secret, and I believe you're a sign from the god that I'm doing the right thing."

Toria led them into the salon and knocked on the door. "Visitors for you, madama," she said.

"Who—wait a bit. I'm not ready." Moments later the door opened and Morica Akennos stood before them. She wore a leather apron and a sleeveless tunic. Her hair was even untidier than before and she had a smear of the white powder on her cheek. A pair of complicated lenses rode high on her forehead. She seemed unsurprised to see Zerafine and Gerrard. "Good, you're here," she said. "Come in." She walked away as if assuming they would follow; exchanging a mystified glance, Zerafine and Gerrard did.

The room was small and windowless, but well-lit by lanterns and a few of Kandra's spheres hovering at the ceiling. It was also brutally hot. The source of the heat was a forge that took up most of one wall. A table bearing the tools of the blacksmith's trade, hammer, tongs, files of all sizes, lay adjacent to the forge, and a barrel of what Zerafine took to be water or oil stood opposite. But pride of place belonged to a bizarre contraption of metal bars, some rough, some filed down, about three feet in diameter. A cage. And it was made entirely of *seicorum*. She'd never seen so much refined metal in one place in her life. Even Atenar kept its stores in raw ore. No wonder Gerrard had gotten such a good exchange rate.

Akelliou Rodennos paced back and forth in front of the forge. When he saw Zerafine, he threw up his hands and shouted, "Morica, why did you let *her* in here? She's going to ruin everything!"

"I told Alita she needed to come. She'll understand. She knows about spirit," Morica, focused on the cage, responded absently.

"It's *because* she'll understand that she's a danger," Akelliou retorted. He glanced at Zerafine, then at Gerrard. "She won't let you continue."

Morica turned her gaze on Zerafine, suddenly very intent on her. "You won't make me stop," she stated. "I've done good work. You won't undo it." She had her hand on the table and began tapping her fingers against it, one-two-three, one-two-three.

"I just want to understand more about what you're doing," Zerafine said. Morica was clearly unstable and saying the wrong thing might make her shut down completely. "Your...experiments...caused the apparitions?"

"It was a side effect," Morica said, still tapping. "Leaks. Cracks in the surface."

"*Stop telling her things,*" Akelliou hissed. He grabbed Morica's arm, but she shook him off. "But I want her to know," she said.

"Alita said not to tell anyone," Akelliou said.

"Alita doesn't understand. *She* does." She pulled the lenses down over her eyes. They were round and silvery and made her look like an insect, long limbs and all. "You can look at it," she told Zerafine, and pointed at the cage.

Zerafine furrowed her brow. Did she mean...? She sat cross-legged on the floor next to the cage and took three deep cleansing breaths, then opened her heart's eye.

She nearly fell over backwards. A gigantic knot of spirit threads nearly filled the cage, the filaments so close together that it looked like a solid mass. Hundreds, possibly thousands of threads emerged from the ball toward the floor, fading into near-invisibility before leaving the confines of the cage through the gaps in the *seicorum*. The effect was that of a vine, or a snake, lifted in the middle by a stick and allowed to hang down on both sides. Its surface was covered with dozens of deep cracks, as if the knot were made of mud that had dried and split under the scorching sun. As she watched, she saw threads emerge from one of the cracks and tangle themselves together, drifting away from their parent until they brushed against a *seicorum* bar. Then the knot dissolved and the threads fell back to be absorbed by the ball.

Zerafine reached out to touch it, then restrained herself. If a small one had killed Genedirou, who knew what an apparition this size could do to her? But—was it really an apparition? There had been no image associated with it, nothing to indicate the cage wasn't empty. "This is a piece of a bigger thing," she said, giving herself time to come up with the questions she actually wanted answers to. "The apparitions come from it."

"I figured out that it's all one piece," Morica said. "That was the key." She took a long rod from the table that to Zerafine's inner sense looked black, without the fuzzy edges most objects appeared to have from that perspective. She slid it between the gaps in the bars and Zerafine saw the knot recoil from it. *Seicorum* again. She let go of her meditative state and stood up.

"I tried to tell them to stop," Akelliou said, apparently forgetting that he wasn't speaking to Zerafine. "After they broke it, I told them it had gone too far. It's not my fault."

"What do you mean, broke it?" Gerrard said, looming over Akelliou. Akelliou cringed.

"It cracked when Morica started to cage it," he said. "Then the apparitions came from the cracks. Don't blame me. I didn't do anything."

Zerafine gave him a scornful look. "The apparitions are all over the city, but you only caged it here."

"It's all one piece," Morica said, tapping her fingers more insistently. "I had to isolate it so the other estates wouldn't be affected. *You* know. You were supposed to understand."

"I do understand," Zerafine said, and felt the lie turn to bitter acid in her mouth. She'd have to be more careful.

"What *I* don't understand," said Alita Talarannos, "is why you are here on my estate without my permission." She noiselessly closed the door behind her.

"You sent her. Didn't you send her? I told you I wanted to talk to her," said Morica. She wrapped her arms around herself and began to hum tunelessly.

"I told you it was too dangerous for her to see your work," Alita said gently. She put her arm around Morica's shoulders. "I wish you'd listened to me."

"I'm sorry I'm such a thorn in your side," Zerafine said, glaring at Alita so she'd know she wasn't sorry at all. "I imagine you're disappointed that you haven't been able to get rid of me permanently."

Alita glared back. "As I said, this is private property and I want you gone."

Akelliou said, "I tried to make her leave, Alita. I told Morica not to talk to her."

"Shut up, you pathetic whiner," Gerrard said.

"I wanted her to tell me how to make it do what I want," Morica complained.

Her words made something shift inside Zerafine's head. *How to make it do what I want.* As if it were a dog, or a horse in training. Impulsively, she said, "Did you know it was alive when you started, or did you only figure it out later?"

Alita stared at her. "It's not alive. It's just spirit. It flows through the city."

"I thought that, too," Zerafine replied. "How could it be alive if there was no body? But there's nothing that says a living creature can't be pure spirit. And just now I saw it recoil as if it was backing away from something painful, which it seems *seicorum* is to it. That it's a living creature that doesn't happen to have a physical body is far less ridiculous than that it's loose spirit or some kind of embodiment of the life of a city.

"Let me see if I have this right," she continued in the face of Alita's stunned silence. "You discovered this creature on your estate because it's somehow more solid here, or closer to the surface — the details don't matter. The point is that here, at this estate, you were

182

capable not only of perceiving it, but of capturing it. But you fractured it when you caged it, and it started...let's just say 'bleeding', shall we?"

"It's *not alive*," Alita said through clenched teeth.

"You know what? I was going to give you the benefit of the doubt about that, that you didn't realize it was alive, but now I think maybe you suspected otherwise. But, again, it doesn't really matter. The bleeding took the form of apparitions—I'm not totally sure about that, but who knows what enough concentrated spirit in one place might do? That explains Genedirou's banishments; he was putting a patch on the problem, but it wasn't a perfect seal and there were loose ends. But why didn't you let him work his ritual here? The apparitions must have been an annoyance."

"I needed them for the experiment," Morica said. "If I touched the source it fought back. I learned so much from them."

"Don't answer her questions, dear," Alita said. She regained her poise and began to speak, but Zerafine overrode her.

"Only one more question, Alita, and I'll be gone. Just one question. What was the point of all this?"

Alita said, "I don't have to answer—"

"It gives us power!" Akelliou blurted out. "All our estates, there's a source on each one. Luck, wealth, power, anything we want. It makes us better than others."

"Akelliou, why are you kissing up to the emissary?" Alita said, rounding on him.

"It's not fair that you're keeping it all to yourself!" he shouted. "You promised it would be me next, but you're just saving it all for yourself!"

"Oh, shut up, Akelliou," Alita said wearily. "As if I would ever have helped someone like you. I may hate your uncle, but he's three times the man you are."

"I would agree with that," Zerafine said. "Goodbye, Alita. Morica, I'm sorry."

"Sorry for what?" Alita said.

Zerafine shook her head. "She's a genius, Alita. And you've got her torturing an innocent creature. Do yourself a favor. Take all this apart."

"How is that a favor to me?" Alita sneered. "I'm not going to give up my power just because some upstart *thelis* from nowhere tries to ride her moral high horse over me."

"It's a favor to you," Zerafine said, "because if you don't, I will. And I will make sure everyone in your social circle knows what you tried to do. How long do you think your power will last when your peers find out you were trying to gain an unfair advantage over them?"

"I can make sure you never leave this estate," Alita said.

Zerafine laughed. "Now you're just embarrassing yourself. Unless you happen to have a few more assassins on tap." She turned away and let Gerrard precede her out the door. "Let's leave quickly. Just in case."

They found Nacalia outside at the front of the house, playing with a litter of kittens, Toria watching over her. "Does Alita know you let us in?" Zerafine asked.

"Not so far," Toria replied. "But I think she will."

"If she fires you, come to the shrine. We won't let you suffer for this."

"Thanks for that, madama."

Once on the road, Zerafine breathed easier. The wind had died down, and the clouds provided a welcome break from the sun's rays. She'd sounded much more certain than she was. For all she knew, Alita might have had fifty men in her household guard, and Zerafine had no doubt that she could have made good on her threat. "You could have defeated fifty men, right?" she asked Gerrard.

He gave her a surprised look. "No."

"Then I'm glad she didn't have fifty men waiting outside."

"I might have been able to handle twenty. Definitely ten."

"You inspire such confidence."

He grabbed her around the waist with one arm and lifted her

off her feet, and kissed her, startling a few other pedestrians. "I'm not entirely sure I can handle *you*," he said.

"Put me down, ox! Such unprofessional behavior."

"Sorry." He didn't look sorry. "So. It's an actual creature. And here I thought that was the impossible scenario."

"I wonder..." Zerafine began.

"Yes?"

"If it's a creature, and it's wounded, I wonder if the *theloi* of Kalindi might be able to do something about it. It certainly seems to have vital energy enough to permit a healing."

Gerrard scratched his chin. "Would they even be able to perceive it?"

"I don't know. It's worth asking, anyway."

"And we'd have to find a spot where they'd be able to reach it."

"We've got nine of them. Eight, since Alita's never going to let us back in."

"True. Do you think she's going to dismantle her contraption?"

"No. Maybe. I hope so. Who knows what could happen to the creature if this plan works? It might destroy her setup for her."

Gerrard nodded. "You want to talk to the *Marathelis* of Kalindi now?"

"Is it a woman, then? I never even thought to ask."

"Her name is Yelenita and Dakariou said she's a good choice to follow Alestiou. Strong-willed, a good administrator, maybe not as close to the Goddess as Alestiou was, but a good woman."

"I'm impressed. You managed to say all that without making the face you always make when you say Dakariou's name." He looked surprised, so she pursed her lips and furrowed her brow and said, "Like that."

He laughed. "I suppose I no longer feel threatened by him," he said.

Zerafine grabbed his tunic collar and pulled him down for a kiss. "Now who's being unprofessional," he murmured against her lips. She poked him in the stomach.

Chapter Twenty-Three

They climbed the temple steps--it turned out there were one hundred and sixteen of them—only to find that they could not see the *Marathelis*, because there was no *Marathelis* yet. More specifically, Yelenita's investiture would not be held until sunrise the following day, and until then, she was in seclusion to meditate and pray. In fact, the entire temple was closed in preparation for the momentous event. Waiting out a rainstorm in the temple portico, Zerafine drummed her fingers on her arm, then stopped, remembering Morica's agitation. Her heart was full of compassion for the woman.

"I'm all out of ideas," she confessed. "And I feel impatient at being balked. It's going to be nearly twenty-four hours before we can talk to Yelenita, and we can't even ask one of the *theloi* healers to help because they're all in seclusion too. Now what?"

"I know something we can do," Gerrard said, grinning at her.

"In the middle of the day? I think we'd get tired of doing that after only a few hours."

"I *was* talking about getting food," he said, his grin broadening. She blushed.

They ate at an outdoor restaurant, Nacalia bouncing in her excitement at sitting with the grown-ups, then let Nacalia lead them on a tour of the city. Zerafine's appreciation for its beauty grew. She knew it had its darker side. Too many parts of the city were old, decaying, their inhabitants scraping a living any way they could, but it was hard not to appreciate Hanakou's Palace, a remnant of a two-centuries'-past regime filled with beautiful statuary, or the wild gardens surrounding the temple of Ventus, god of fate. It would not be such a bad place to settle down in. The light wind made the city's oppressive heat finally bearable.

They returned home for dinner, and then Zerafine and Gerrard retired to Zerafine's room, where they found that there was at least one activity they didn't get tired of for a long time.

They returned to the temple of Kalindi at midmorning the next day, hoping to miss the great crowds thronging the plaza for the investiture. Their arrival was almost perfectly timed; they still had to fight the crowds, but most of the traffic had cleared. Despite the now constant wind and occasional rain showers, the plaza had been full that morning as most of Portena turned out for the ceremony. More crowded were the stairs to the temple, as thousands of worshippers clamored for the *Marathelis's* vicarious blessing, conveyed through brass tokens stamped with the stylized image of the sun.

The temple of Kalindi was as exquisite on the inside as it was impressive on the outside. The deep portico provided shade for supplicants—or would, on a day less overcast than this—and led directly to the offertory chamber, its floor a vast mosaic of green and gold tesserae, where in normal times worshippers brought items to be blessed, or came to receive blessings themselves, leaving behind a coin or two. Now it was thronged with people trying to reach one of the *theloi* who were handing out blessing tokens.

A *thelis* noticed Zerafine's red robe and hood and pushed through the crowd toward her. "Madama *thelis*, how can I help you? Have you come for the *Marathelis's* gift?" Her face showed moderate dismay that a *thelis* of Atenas might want the blessing of the Queen of Heaven's representative.

"No, madama *thelis*, I am here to speak with the *Marathelis*," Zerafine said.

The *thelis* shook her head. "I'm afraid that's impossible," she said. "These four days of preparation are arduous, and the *Marathelis* is resting. You'll have to come back tomorrow."

"I apologize for my insistence, but my business is quite urgent," Zerafine said. "As the representative of Atenar I am *invested*—" she gave the word emphasis to make a comparison with

Yelenita's investiture—"with the authority of the *Marathelos* of Atenas, and as such, I require that I be admitted to the *Marathelis's* presence. I promise I will not take much of her time, but I will not be denied."

The *thelis* looked stunned, and Zerafine had a moment's flash of guilt at bringing all that power to bear on the poor girl's head—she couldn't have been more than seventeen—that faded when she remembered why she was there. "I'll show you the way," the girl said in a tiny voice, and Zerafine had to quash another moment of guilt. She hoped the girl wouldn't be blamed for Zerafine's intrusion.

The *thelis* brought them through a tall door at the back of the chamber, which led onto a long, narrow hallway. More mosaics, these on the walls, showed scenes of Kalindi's victories over the forces of nature. At the end of the hall was a much smaller door. The *thelis* opened it for them and bowed them inside. The room was paneled to waist height in exotic woods and painted a deep blue above the paneling. Backless couches upholstered in gold silk were scattered throughout the room atop a wooden floor stained dark to match the paneling. A window opposite the door looked out on the city and Rodennos hill.

A woman stood looking out the window. "It's a beautiful view," she said. "I'm not yet accustomed to it." She was tall, as tall as Gerrard, and wore her long black hair clasped at her neck with a band bearing Kalindi's circle. Her simple gown was dyed dark green. She turned to look at them, and seemed first startled, then annoyed. Zerafine saw that her eyes were a dark brown and her face had begun to show lines on her forehead and the corners of her eyes. They were not welcoming eyes.

"*Marathelis*," Zerafine said. "I apologize for my unannounced arrival."

"*Thelis* emissary," Yelenita said. "Please be seated."

Zerafine chose a couch and Gerrard took his position behind her. Yelenita sat across from her. "I trust you have good reason for intruding on my solitude," she said.

The abruptness with which the woman leaped past common pleasantries startled Zerafine. "I—ah, I have a request that is quite extraordinary," she stammered, "but I hope that you can help."

"Make your request, and we'll see." The *Marathelis's* tone was neutral, but Zerafine was sure this woman was not the ally Alestiou would have been, and she felt a pang of loss. She launched into her story, explaining what she'd learned from the moment she'd entered the city until the discovery that they were dealing with a creature rather than the idealized spirit of the city. She paused, and the *Marathelis* interjected, "So if I understand the implications of your story, you would like our divine healers to attempt to heal this creature."

Mildly antagonistic she might be, but stupid she was not. "That's correct, *Marathelis*," Zerafine said. "But my understanding of how a divine healing works is limited. I depend on you to tell me if such an attempt is even possible."

"Have you—but of course, you received healing yourself. Lenara, the *thelis* who healed you, brought me the information," she added, when Zerafine looked puzzled. "Then you know that there are two ways we accomplish a healing. The first is to use the patient's own vital energy to fuel Kalindi's touch. The second is for the healer to use his or her own energy to do the same."

"I think the second way would be suicidal. This creature is huge. I don't think there are enough divine healers in the world to accomplish it."

"Perhaps." Yelenita's face twitched in a slight smile. "But I have my doubts about the first method as well." She leaned forward just a little, as if inviting Zerafine to share a secret. "You see, Kalindi's gift only works on creatures with self-awareness on a human level. Trees, insects, fish are all living creatures, but we cannot manipulate their vital energy. Suppose this creature has only enough awareness to respond to stimuli? It's possibly you may have jumped to conclusions too quickly."

Zerafine was determined not to lose her temper. Besides, Yelenita had a good point. Even so, she wished she could have walked into this room and met someone who would just do as she asked for once. "You're right. I have no way of knowing what kind of consciousness it has. But wouldn't it be worth finding out? Whatever it is, it's creating apparitions that now have the ability to kill, and it *is* clear that those apparitions come from the fractures in its...whatever it has instead of a body. If my guess is right, your healers are the solution."

Yelenita tilted her head and looked at Zerafine for a long moment. "All right," she said. "You will take one of my *theloi* and show them the creature. They will be able to tell me if your plan is worth trying." She stood up and went to the door. "If so, I will be happy to assist you."

"Happy" isn't the word for it, madama. "Thank you," Zerafine said, and followed the *Marathelis* down the long hallway and into the offertory chamber. If their initial passage had caused a stir, Yelenita's appearance caused all activity to come to a complete stop. The *Marathelis* didn't seem to notice or care. She glanced around the room, said, "Dianya," and beckoned to the young *thelis* who had brought them to see the *Marathelis.* Dianya came over at a nearly running gait.

"Dianya, please give the *thelis* of Atenas whatever she requires," she said, and left without another word. Dianya looked stunned and fearful. She made a hasty salute, which Zerafine returned.

"Let's walk," said Zerafine, "and I'll explain what we're going to do."

Dianya listened in silence, round-eyed, as Zerafine for the second time related the story of her investigation. "What you'll do is examine the creature and decide whether a divine healing would be able to affect it," she finished.

A gust of wind tugged at Dianya's tunic; she smoothed it automatically. "I'll do what I can," she said, "but I'm not a very experienced healer."

"I think just having the ability will be enough," Zerafine said. The same gust of wind, or its brother, blew the skirts of her robe so it billowed behind her.

Nacalia led them to the closest location where many apparitions had been seen, a crossroads just off the plaza. Gerrard fended off traffic so that Zerafine and Dianya could work. Zerafine centered herself and looked for the creature. The last time she'd been here, they had been looking for apparitions, so she had never looked at the place with her heart's eye. Now she could see the increasingly familiar tangle of threads glowing with white light, apparently rearing about a foot into the air from the center of the crossroads. It was invisible to the material eye, but traffic passed around it rather than through it, people even bumping into each other to avoid it.

"Can you see it?" Zerafine asked. Dianya shook her head. Zerafine took the young woman's hand and led her to the creature. People parted for her as readily as they did for it. Zerafine reached down her hand and brought it as close to the creature as she dared. It made her skin tingle. "Look where my hand is," she said.

Dianya clapped her hands palm-to-palm in front of her and threw her head back to face the sun, currently hidden behind clouds that increasingly looked like rain. "I can't see it," she said after a while. "I can see...something...but it's like a residue."

"Look again," Zerafine said, her heart dropping. "Right here." Rain started to patter down on the pavement, on her bare head. The air smelled of lightning.

Dianya knelt on the ground and bowed her head. "It looks like...dust...or maybe flakes of gold," she said. "There's nothing there I could heal, even if I used my own energy."

"You're sure?" Zerafine said, biting back *You said you weren't very experienced; maybe you're just wrong.*

The young woman nodded. "There just isn't anything there."

Zerafine sighed. "Thank you for your help. Would you give my respects to the *Marathelis?*"

As Dianya made her way through the crowds, Zerafine walked back to the curb, slowly, scuffing her sandals along the concrete pavers. "And we're left with nothing again," she said.

"Not nothing," Gerrard said. "You now know it has no vital energy." He got a funny look on his face. "It has no vital energy," he repeated.

"That means it's not alive," Zerafine said. She was pretty sure she had the same funny look on her face. "It's dead. It's a ghost."

"It's the biggest ghost ever," Gerrard said.

"But what kind of creature could be that big," Zerafine began, then felt everything she'd learned start to fall into place. The apparitions. The moving streets. The fractures on the creature's surface. "Sweet goddess of light," she breathed. "I have to talk to Berenica *right now.*" No more jumping to conclusions. There was just one more thing she had to know.

She kept getting ahead of Nacalia until Gerrard scooped the child up and ran with her, Nacalia pointing the way. Now Zerafine could see it when the streets rearranged themselves. This was very bad. The rain no longer fell vertically, but was blown nearly horizontal by the wind at their backs. Zerafine welcomed how it propelled them along. It took less than ten minutes for them to fetch up against Berenica's gate. Zerafine flung it open and hammered on the front door until Berenica's silent servant opened it; she nearly knocked him down in her haste to get inside.

Berenica sat in her front room reading a book. "Can I help you with something?" she asked, irritable but trying to be polite.

"You wrote that the gods tamed the powers of heaven and earth," she panted. "Was that literal or metaphorical?"

Berenica laid down her book. "I don't know what you mean," she said. "I had all my information from the records. Would you like to see them?"

"Yes. Please."

They went next door to the shrine. The rain was falling more heavily now, drenching them in the few minutes it took to get inside. Berenica went into the sanctuary and opened a drawer in the base of the altar. She drew out a book bound in tattered black leather. "It's been rebound, but it's still very old, and the pages are very fragile," she said, and laid it on the altar.

Even in her excited state, Zerafine opened the cover carefully. There was no title page. The first page was covered with neat and surprisingly legible printing in three columns. Zerafine ran her finger down the columns until, at the top of the third, she found what she was looking for.

"'The gods found a world ready for them,'" she read aloud, "'its people crying out in fear of Water and Earth, Wind and Sun. They broke them, bound them to their will, and took them from the world that men and women might have peace. Upon this place did Kalindi build her temple, and the whole world looked to her.' There has *always* been a temple to Kalindi in Portena. And Portena is the oldest city in the known world. This isn't about some mythic battle against the abstract forces of nature. The gods—the new gods—overthrew old ones to make a place for themselves." It was so obvious to her that she couldn't understand why they stared at her with incomprehension. "Don't you see?" she continued. "One of them is right here in Portena. It's not just a dead creature. It's a dead *god*."

Chapter Twenty-Four

"That's—" Gerrard began. He tried out several words in his mouth, rejected them all.

"Not just random capitals, but proper nouns. Names," mused Berenica. "I wouldn't have read it that way. Well, I obviously didn't."

"I was looking at it all wrong," Zerafine said. "I knew it was spirit because I could see it with my heart's eye, but I wasn't *thinking*. I was so caught up in the idea of a living creature with a body of spirit that I didn't think to wonder why I could see it so clearly. A spirit inside a body is a dim glow. A spirit without a body is bright. Stupid, stupid, *stupid*."

"But—a *god*?" Gerrard exclaimed, but Zerafine overrode him.

"Everything fits. Alita and Morica must have killed it in their first experiment. It wasn't fractured, it was *fragmented*. The gods— oh, I can't think straight, there's too much—"

"I understand," said Berenica. She tapped the page, then snatched her hand away as if remembering how fragile the book was. "The old gods were the embodiment of nature. We still have storms and mountains, but they clearly aren't sentient. I think the Pantheon took the old ones out of their 'bodies' and put them...where?"

"Into the cities," Zerafine continued. "The cities became their bodies." She began to pace from one end of the altar to the other. It was all coming together. "The streets moving, reconnecting, that was the ghost trying to get back into the only body it ever knew. And—oh, Atenas take me for a fool, the apparitions, they're its *memories*. They're leaking out of it like water from a rusted pipe."

"Zerafine, slow down," said Gerrard, grabbing her arm and interrupting her pacing. She looked up at him as though she'd forgotten who he was. "This old story, it's a pretty thin thread to hang all this supposition on."

194

"But she's right," said Berenica, her beautiful voice faint. "I have studied these records for years. Look at them in the right way, and they all point to the existence of older gods. Atenas Himself is supposed to be older than Kalindi; we take that to mean that He was the first of the Pantheon, but suppose He's even older than that?"

Gerrard shook his head. "I can't argue with you. It just seems impossible."

"But it's true," said Zerafine. Her excitement drained away, leaving her feeling empty and cold. No, the cold was coming from outside. A powerful gust of wind blew through the sanctuary, ripping through the book's pages as if reading them at high speed. Berenica gave an uncharacteristic squeak and threw herself over the book, protecting it with her body.

Zerafine pointed. "You think that's natural?" she said, raising her voice to be heard over the wind. "The ghost has grown in strength every day. I think it's finally strong enough to start pulling in the forces of nature to make itself a new body. That's where it came from, after all."

Berenica shut the book and put it away. When she stood up, her face was white and trembling. "I can't do it," she said. "I can't—I haven't performed a consolation in over a year. Someone died, and...I can't get past the fear. Ricenz and Darlen do the consolations now, but—"

"They're barely more than acolytes," Zerafine finished the sentence. She took Berenica's hand. "It's all right," she said. "I think it was always going to be me. I think it's what I came here for." She released Berenica's hand and turned to leave, then looked over her shoulder at the *tokthelis*. "You might pray for me," she said. Gerrard followed her.

Outside, the wind had abated enough that their words wouldn't blow away. Gerrard stood with his back to the wind so Zerafine could stand in the shelter of his body. Nacalia crouched behind her. "You can't do this," Gerrard said.

195

"I have to," said Zerafine.

Gerrard shook his head. "No, I mean it's not possible. You're not even big enough to get its attention. And all that spirit lashing around...it will kill you and not even notice."

"I don't think that's inevitable. Genedirou died because he didn't know what he was doing. I've faced spirits almost every day for the last six years."

"Small spirits. Ghosts. Not an out of control god who's probably been driven insane by Morica Akennos."

She put her hand on his arm. "If I do nothing, the city will be destroyed, and us with it. If I try, there's a chance I'll succeed. You know me too well to think I'd stand by and do nothing."

His eyes closed. "I can't protect you from this," he said, his voice wooden.

She reached out and drew him close. "No."

"And I can't stop you."

"Not without making me something other than I am."

"So what *can* I do?" He put his arms around her and hugged her back.

She smiled. "I may need you to hold me up."

He kissed the top of her head. "That, I think I'm good at."

Nacalia said, in a small voice, "What can *I* do, *thelis*?"

Zerafine took a deep breath. "You can take us to the plaza. I think, on this day especially, we won't get there without your help."

They had the street to themselves. People took refuge anywhere they could, huddled together against the rain and the freezing wind. Zerafine looked straight ahead, but she knew that hundreds of eyes were on her as they passed, unwavering. She had no attention to spare. She was fighting her fears: fear of inadequacy, fear of failure, fear of—no. Fear of death was unacceptable in a *thelis* of Atenas. But she knew that even two hundred and twenty-seven—no, make that twenty-eight—consolations of human ghosts were no preparation for what she was about to attempt.

The plaza, like the street, was empty. Scraps of paper and

roofing tiles flew through the air like harbingers of worse to come, as though the wind would soon be wild and strong enough to tear people from their hiding places and cast them in all directions. Zerafine knelt in front of Nacalia and put her hands on the girl's shoulders. "It's time for you to take shelter. I know the rest of the way."

Nacalia's tears were real ones. Zerafine had no idea how much she understood about what was about to happen, but she said, "Don't die, *thelis*," and Zerafine realized she understood all too well.

"I will try to come back," she promised, and hugged Nacalia, then gave her a little push in the direction of one of the temples. The temple of Ormus, she saw, and was inspired to tell Gerrard, "See that you buy out her contract and apprentice her there. If anyone was born to serve the god of travel, it's her."

"See to it yourself," Gerrard said. "I don't want to deal with that Karra woman again." His words were teasing, but his voice sounded hollow.

They proceeded to Kalindi's temple against a wind that seemed determined to prevent their arrival. Gerrard ultimately had to put his arm around Zerafine's shoulders to keep her from falling over. They climbed the one hundred and sixteen steps slowly and with great effort, the wind snatching at their breath as though alive and mischievous — or malevolent. It might actually be alive, or at least possessed of consciousness, at this point, Zerafine thought. At the top of the stairs, at the center of the paved semicircle laid out in front of the temple, Zerafine stopped to catch her breath. She looked out over the city with watering eyes, feeling almost as if she could see the wind outlined against the roofs. A brief shower caught her in the face, and she wiped her eyes with the sleeve of her robe.

"Here," she told Gerrard, and, "Don't let me fall." Gerrard moved behind her and grasped her firmly about the waist. His presence was a comfort, but not one she could indulge herself in reflecting on. "Wait," she said, and turned around and kissed him.

His hands slid around her waist further and he kissed her back, lightly, then hard and insistent. She felt more water slide down her cheek. "Don't go saying goodbye just yet," she teased him through her tears. "And don't forget that I love you."

He kissed her once more, and said, "Never."

She again turned her back on him and began to relax, breathing deeply and feeling the tension slide from her shoulders, her back, her legs. She opened her heart's eye and began to search the city. She could see, from this height, tiny sparks that marked the apparitions, the old god's memories—no longer stationary, but flying wildly through the streets leaving streaks of light. There was, however, a pattern to their movement. As she drew further back and broadened her gaze, something began to take shape below her.

It was only barely humanoid. Its limbs—too many limbs-- draped the streets and cradled the hills. She looked for the Talarannos estate and saw a brighter spark there, looked further and found the four sparks of the other estates. She blinked her heart's eye and the pattern came into focus: eyes, shoulders, navel. Down in the city, four sparks marked knees, toes, a hip. Very little of its spirit body remained intact, and even the face was the merest suggestion of an outline of a distorted head. The winds surrounded it, dove into it and raced out again screaming, a sound Zerafine realized she was hearing with her own ears as well as in her entranced state. She could see it move, see the streets shift as it tried to force its way back into the only body it had known for almost a thousand years.

Uncertainly, Zerafine drew a symbol and let it float away. It went only a few feet before disintegrating. She needed to be more confident, and, she thought, more daring. From deep within her belly she drew on reserves she had always suspected she had but had never needed to use. A single shape, golden like the sun—how fitting—emerged from her body and danced away toward the old god's head. A golden circle. Kalindi's circle.

It got far more of a reaction than she'd expected. As it brushed the creature's body, it shuddered, then convulsed. Streets moved so quickly that Zerafine thought the change might even have been visible in the waking world, and she heard human screams atop the wail of the winds. It had definitely felt that. It probably remembered the gods who had defeated it, stripped it of its power all those years ago. No wonder it was angry. She could feel its consciousness gathering, saw the apparitions swarm about its head. She tried another symbol, the lightning bolt of Kanu, god of storms, and it flicked its attention around and centered it on her. Its awareness felt like a weight, like the down comforters people used in the North that felt light when you drew them over you and then settled, bit by bit, until they were heavy and warm. This pressure, however, was neither warm nor comforting. It reminded her of being in Sukman's presence, as if two giant fingers were trying to crush her head and make her eyeballs pop out, as if an anvil were being lowered onto her neck a fraction of an inch at a time, trying to snap her spine. It was terrifying. She was afraid—

She dropped out of her trance state and cursed herself. She felt Gerrard's hands supporting her; he said, "What's wrong?" but she shook her head and re-centered herself. No fear.

Through her heart's eye she could see the old god gathering itself, growing nearer. She began drawing other symbols now, less potent ones, searching for the ones that would remind the old god who it had been. She only realized that this was a bad idea, that reminding this ghost that it had once been a master of the skies might make things worse, when the first of its memories reached her, and she saw—

—*fire and smoke and cries of pain* —

— *dancing in a circle, the stars wheeling above* —

— *thunderstorms in the mountains* —

—and she pulled free, watched the memories without being engulfed by them. There were so many, so many, back to the days when it had been the wind, flying free, to the days of the war with the new gods, and its terror at being bound, and that last memory

199

gave her the key. She felt its sadness, and fear, and she wept for...him. Not it, but him. Compassion filled her to overflowing. She reached out and spoke to him.

"Come home," she whispered, or shouted — it was all the same here. "There is no more place for you here. Come home. Let Atenas bring you home."

She felt its anger turn to confusion and then fear. Its memories whirled out of control again; she drew symbols of peace and comfort as fast as her mind could shape them. "You're afraid now," she said. "But you don't have to be." She cautiously began drawing its memories together. It was so *big*. She firmly kept thoughts of failure locked away.

It shuddered, breaking apart all her careful construction, and wailed a piteous cry that she knew only she could hear. It longed and it feared in equal measure. It was too afraid, and too powerful, for her to contain with her inadequate knowledge. The realization that no one else could do better was scant comfort. She reached out to him, and felt the spirit cling to her like a child clings to its mother.

In that moment she knew with perfect clarity what she had to do. Her heart cried out against it. But there was only one other way for this creature to enter Atenas's realm, and only one person who could open the way for him.

Setting aside her anguish, she grasped the old god to her. "Come to me," she said, and opened her heart's eye as wide as it would go. She felt him stir and flow into her, through her, and the pressure increased until she could barely endure it. She felt her heart burst and her veins fill with ice, but she kept her grip on him, her lungs freezing up, her eyes frosting over, her heart's eye wide open. It hurt more than Kalindi's healing had, and she would have cried out if she'd had any air left in her lungs. *Open, damn you*, she screamed inside her failing brain, and at last the silver arch appeared before her, and gripping her burden with the last of her strength, she tumbled through it.

Chapter Twenty-Five

She must have blacked out for a second, because she opened her eyes and saw no remnant of the daylight world, no silver arch. Instead, grayness surrounded her. If there were walls, they might have been ten feet away or a thousand. The surface beneath her feet was gray and smooth, with a little give to it. No light shone above; a gray radiance hung in the air around her. The pain was gone.

At her feet sat a naked child, perhaps two years old. It was not an attractive child. The boy (as she saw when she squatted next to him) had patches of mousy brown hair growing randomly on his head. His eyes crossed so much he appeared to be permanently looking at the tip of his nose, and there were patches of red rash on his cheeks. She raised his head and saw, swimming within the depths of his black eyes, golden symbols shifting and merging. She tugged on his hand, encouraging him to stand. The boy rose up slightly and then sank down as if his legs wouldn't support him.

Zerafine looked around again. She realized that she was naked herself. That, at least, she had expected. What she had also expected, but did not see, was some indication of where to go. She stood up and rotated slowly in a complete circle: nothing. She took one step and lights blossomed around her foot, curving away as if outlining a path. More lights came on and stretched away in all directions. She stood at the hub of a dozen possible paths, all identical. Against the gray background, she saw words drift like phantoms: CHOOSE A PATH AND FIND ITS END.

Instructions, yes, but how to choose? Twelve paths might mean the twelve gods, but no symbols showed which path belonged to which deity. And Zerafine would need a thirteenth choice, herself. On the other hand, those instructions....

Zerafine stomped her left food into the spongy ground. "This end," she said into the void.

About fifty feet away, the second of the three arches into

Atenas's realm reared up in a place where moments ago there had been nothing. "Come on," she told the boy, tugging his hand again. He didn't move, didn't give any sign that he understood her words. She bent over, hauled on his armpits, and lifted the child to sit astride her hip. His limbs were short and spindly. This wasn't going to be comfortable for either of them, but she wasn't about to leave him behind. He made no effort to support himself, though he did wrap his legs as far around her waist as he could. Her bare feet stuck unpleasantly to the ground as she trudged toward the arch. She circled it once, examining it: a flat ribbon of silvery, matte-finished metal that arched perhaps fifteen feet over her head, ten feet wide at the base. She hitched the boy higher up on her hip and stepped through.

Her foot came down on a rough, black surface that felt like unfinished wood but had no visible grain. Momentum carried her two more steps, then she turned to look behind her; again, the arch was gone. She set the child down for a moment and drew a deep breath. On all sides, mists shifted like black draperies in a wind that Zerafine couldn't feel. This would be the great judgment hall of Atenas, but where was everyone? It was supposed to be thronged with those who would testify for and against a soul, but failing that, it should certainly have held the Lord of Death's throne, its back rising beyond vision into the heights of the sky, its feet extending deep beneath the surface of the earth. Or what passed for sky and earth, in this place; it was a thing scholars had debated for centuries.

But it was empty.

The boy looked up at her. A thin line of spittle ran from the corner of his mouth down his chin. Instinctively Zerafine wiped it away, then shook her fingers because she had nothing to wipe them on. "We can stay here or we can move on, sirrah, and I see no reason to do either," she said. He reached out and took her hand, then pointed his face in a direction somewhat to their left. His eyes had come uncrossed and were nearly gold from the symbols thronging them.

"Very well," Zerafine said, and hoisted her burden again. She set off in the direction he indicated, his head lifted alertly even though he still, aside from maintaining a death grip on her hand, showed no awareness of her presence. She ducked through a wall of billowing mists and heard the laughter of children; another, and voices spoke in a language she didn't understand. The boy's attention never wavered, and she wondered how much he was aware of anything else in his surroundings.

She realized, after a moment, that someone paced beside her, a few yards off and always beyond a curtain of mist. "Don't turn," he said. His voice was a mellow tenor. "Don't stop moving."

"Why not? Am I in danger?" she asked. Her voice shook.

"You left danger behind at the first arch," the stranger said. "But you have not yet reached your destination. Turn aside, and you will not find the path again for some time."

"Where am I going?"

"Where all men and women go, in the end. To be judged."

"Why doesn't he—" she bounced the boy in her arms a little— "look the way he did before?"

"Could you have carried him if he did?"

"I don't understand why I have to carry him at all."

"You resent it, then."

"No! I chose this path. I just wish—"

"Yes, Zerafine?"

She stopped. She turned to face the stranger, ignoring the boy's wordless keen. "My Lord Atenas," she said, "I wish You would not speak in riddles now that we are in Your realm."

The Lord of Death smiled. He was tall and wide, his black skin darker than night, and when he stood still it was like looking into the abyss to meet his gaze. When he moved, light slid across the curves of his body and pooled in the hollow of his throat, in the creases of his eyelids. He wore his red robe open over bare flesh and his hood flung back across his shoulders, leaving his bald head uncovered. He took her free hand and, with a flicker, they had moved to stand beside his throne, or his throne had come to them. Dim figures moved in the mists behind the god's throne. Atenas was now twenty, thirty feet tall, and his voice boomed from far above her head. "Sit down," he said, and whether or not it was a command, Zerafine sat in the backless chair that appeared next to her. There was no seat for the boy, so she took him on her lap. He wiggled his bony bottom against her thighs and seemed to lose interest in his surroundings once again.

"You have come to Me before your time, Zerafine," said Atenas. He took his seat on His throne and laid both His enormous hands flat on His knees, and added, "And you come in company."

"He couldn't find the way here," Zerafine explained, "and this was the only way I knew to make sure he received justice."

"Your compassion is noted. However, your efforts are wasted. There is no place for him here."

Zerafine gaped. "No place? We are taught that everyone has a place in Your halls if only they can find the way to them."

"Every human," Atenas corrected. "He is not human. He is god."

"Then all the more reason for You to accept him home! He's one of You!"

Atenas was silent.

"My Lord," Zerafine cried, "I have served You my whole life. I gave up my life and everything in it to bring this terrified spirit to you. I deserve an explanation."

Far above, one eye gleamed. "Deserve? Brave words."

"I am not brave. Merely unafraid."

Atenas leaned over until his vast face was less than a foot from hers. "Not afraid that I might take your afterlife away because of your insolence?"

She stared him down. "My Lord is just as well as merciful. There would be no justice in that. And no mercy to deny me an understanding of why my life's ending has been wasted."

Atenas sat back and then stood before her, once more only

slightly larger than human size. He reached out as if to touch the boy's head, then drew back. "My brothers and I came into being when the world was young," he said. "It was a wild, glorious place. Mountains danced with the sea, and the wind carried both in his arms. Glorious. We were life itself. And then—other life arose. Human life. Beautiful, fragile life. It lived, and then it died, and had I not taken pity it would have been lost forever. So I made a place for it in My realm. But my brothers...were not so gentle.

"It was not their fault," Atenas added quickly, and there was a note of pain in his words. "They could not understand this new, delicate life. Other forces, however, did." Atenas turned away and faced his throne. "Forces that arose because of humans, in response to humans. There was war. We lost. New gods arose and there was no room for the old ones anymore. The...Pantheon...could do nothing to me." He chuckled, and Zerafine shuddered at the menace in it. "My brothers, though..." He turned back around and knelt on the floor before Zerafine—no, before the boy in her arms. "My poor brothers."

"Do you know what still gives Me pain, after all these centuries?" he said. "The new gods were right. Humanity could not survive in a world where seas raged out of their beds and mountains walked on their roots like giants. But I could not bear to see them destroyed by the new gods. So I swore an oath." Atenas stood up. "I swore that, were they destroyed, I would not accept My brothers' spirits into My realm. Their unquiet ghosts would tear the world into its four quarters and wreak havoc upon the rest. It was not a truce, but it was enough."

"So the gods took the old ones from their bodies and locked them away," Zerafine said.

"Buried deep and under their watchful godlike eyes," Atenas agreed. "And My oath stands."

"But—the gods didn't kill Your brother!" Zerafine said. "It was an accident. A stupid, *human* accident."

"I cannot break my word," Atenas said. "It would mean war,

again, and your people will not survive it."

"They're going to be destroyed anyway, if You make his spirit go back," Zerafine shouted, "because we have nothing that can contain a ghost the size of a city. The record says You turned Your back on the new gods and Your face toward humanity! You may be fulfilling the demands of justice in turning this ghost away, but it is neither just nor merciful to make humanity pay the price! Why is there no other way?"

"Because the Lord Atenas is unwilling to pursue it," said a voice like a thousand chiming bells. A woman emerged from the veils surrounding Atenas's throne. Where he was black as ebon, she was flowing honey, her skin and hair and eyes a thousand shades of what in the living world could only be called gold. Her robe of emerald green and lapis blue fell open over a lushly rounded body. She laid her hand on the god's shoulder. "Atenas, hear me, I beg you," she said.

"Kalindi. Speak." His gaze rested on Zerafine.

"It has been a thousand years or more since we were at war. Even gods can change."

"Change enough to give up a dream of conquest?"

Kalindi laughed, a sound even more bell-like than her speaking voice. "Atenas, there is nothing left to conquer. Your brothers have slept peacefully these many years and their presence has blessed Our cities. We were wrong to force You to make that choice, and wrong not to see that We both wanted the same things. If I swear to You that We will not destroy your brothers, will You allow this one to return home? And the others, in their time?"

Zerafine became conscious that she was holding her breath and that she held the boy's hand crushed in hers. "Will that serve both justice and mercy, My servant?" Atenas asked her.

"Surely that's for You to judge, My Lord," she whispered.

"This is not a case in which I trust My judgment. My desires are in conflict with My oath. I must leave it to you."

Zerafine, stunned, could not breathe for a moment. "Why me?"

she asked, her voice faint.

"Because you can see more clearly than I, in this matter. Because you came before Me with no desire other than to see justice done. Because you felt compassion enough to let My brother destroy you, for his sake. I cannot see where justice is in all of this. So you must."

Zerafine looked into His fathomless eyes. She imagined what He must have seen, through the centuries, what He must have felt to see the last of His family lost to him. "Justice should not be mocked by mercy," she said. "But neither should mercy be denied for the sake of justice. Let Your new oath take the place of the old. Bring Your brother home."

Atenas turned to look at the golden goddess, then reached out to touch the boy's head. "I swear it," He said.

A blast of arctic air threw Zerafine backward off her stool. A wild wind threaded with silver and blue blew around the throne, tore the mists to shreds and flashed star-like between the two gods. Atenas raised his hand to caress the wind and left it raised in salute as the old god spun away laughing and out of sight through the silver arch that had appeared beside the throne.

Zerafine struggled to her feet and was assisted by a large, black hand. It felt like ordinary skin, if a trifle cooler than human normal. "My thanks," Atenas said.

"I am Your servant," Zerafine said.

"You are the only servant of whom I have asked so much," said the god. "You have earned your place in My realm. But I think I owe you more than that. Ask, and I will do it for you."

Zerafine's heart pounded. "There is only one thing I want, Lord."

"Name it."

"I want—" funny how her spirit could get as dry-mouthed as her body—"I want to live out my time in the human world. I want to finish everything I left undone."

Atenas gave her a sad, compassionate look. "That is beyond My power, My servant. Your body was damaged badly in your spirit's journey here, and a further two days have passed since you left it. I could return you to your body, but you would not thank Me for it."

Zerafine struggled not to cry. "I understand," she whispered. *Goodbye, Gerrard.*

Kalindi cleared her throat. Even that sounded like bells, tiny flittering ones. "You are not the only one whose power extends into the human world, Atenas," she said.

Kalindi. The divine healer. "Would you—" Zerafine asked, unable to finish.

She gazed at Zerafine solemnly. "*He* will have to ask me for it," she said. "I have already put myself in his power today. He must abase himself in return."

Atenas looked grim. Then he knelt on one knee, crossed his arms over his chest, and bowed his head. "*Please,*" he said. Zerafine was too embarrassed to know where to look. That a god should lower himself on her behalf! It was...

...actually, Kalindi was smiling, and Atenas had tilted his head up just a little bit to wink at her. The Queen of Heaven burst out laughing. "Ah, stop it, my love, the girl won't know what to think," she said, caressing Atenas's bald head. He took both her hands and rose to kiss her golden lips. "Remember," he said, taking in Zerafine's confounded expression, "even gods can change."

Then he leaned over and pressed his lips against her forehead.

Chapter Twenty-Six

She woke lying in darkness that smelled of cloth and dry air, and knew immediately that her body was dead; no heartbeat, no breath, no blood rushing in her ears. In the next instant she felt herself filled with a tender warmth that washed through her, dizzying her so that for a moment she felt like a creature of pure spirit. Then it passed, leaving her slightly chilled and with a tingling sensation in...yes, surely that was skin and not spirit. She sat up and felt rapidly up and down the length of her body, across her head and her face, reassuring herself that she did still have a body and it wasn't that of a rotting corpse. Her body was wearing a thin, sleeveless, ankle-length tunic that felt like silk, and the surface beneath her buttocks was rough stone. For a brief, panic-filled moment she thought she had already been interred, but then sense reasserted itself; she was lying on the altar in the shrine for the required three days before burial.

She slid off the altar and felt her way to the wall, then groped around until her fingers brushed wood. Was there no handle on this side? No, there it was. She wrenched at it—maybe she was feeling a little panicky after all—and felt it give, then pulled hard until it slid, ponderously, toward her.

The antechamber was lit with the traditional torches, but she could see, high above, light coming in through the ventilation shaft. Gerrard leaned against the wall, deeply asleep, his longstaff lying across his lap as if it had fallen from his hand. He would have been here the whole two days, guarding her body in death as in life, but even he had to sleep sometime. He was unshaven and the torches made the dark circles under his eyes more pronounced. He must have been exhausted to fall so solidly asleep that the sound of the door opening hadn't roused him. He looked wonderful. She studied him, wondering how she could wake him without terrifying him. In the end, realizing that was impossible, she prodded his leg with her toe and said, "Wake up."

He went from sleep to alertness in a breath, but awkwardly, scrambling to stand and grab his staff in the same motion. Then he saw her and his mouth went slack. He looked at the sanctuary door, still ajar, back at her, then rubbed his eyes with his free hand and stared at her again. His lips moved soundlessly.

"I came back," she said, and smiled. Then fear touched his eyes, and she said, "That sounded far less ominous in my head."

He dropped his staff on the floor with a clatter. He reached out to touch her arm, felt his way up to her shoulder, brushed her cheek, ran his fingers over her face as if he were a blind man. Zerafine closed her eyes and smiled again. "I promise, it's really me," she told him. "And you're not going to *believe* what happened while I was there." She opened her eyes. There was so much pain and longing on his face that she began to cry. "Gerrard, sweetheart, say something," she pleaded.

He reached out and drew her into his arms, crushing her in his embrace, saying her name over and over again until great wracking sobs shook his whole body and he couldn't speak anymore. She put her arms around him and cried out all the fear and pain she'd felt, all the tension and the overwhelming presence of her god and the demand He had made of her. She cried until she felt she could never cry again. She felt Gerrard stroking her hair, wiped her eyes and her nose on his shirt and lifted her face to his. "I can't breathe," she said.

He loosened his grip just a little. "Don't ask me to let go entirely," he said, and she shook her head and tightened her own arms around him so he would know she had no intention of going anywhere. He brushed his lips across her forehead. "Two days," he said. "You were dead for two days. I had to carry your broken body through the streets of Portena to the shrine. It was—Nacalia was disobedient, again, or I wouldn't have made it back. I could barely see." He kissed her forehead again, wound his fingers in her hair. "Please don't ever do that again."

"I don't think it will be necessary," she said, and kissed his mouth. His lips tasted like tears. He kissed her in return, first gently, then with a sort of desperation that broke her heart even as it filled her with joy.

They broke apart, after a while. "I'm sorry," he said after a moment in which they simply looked at one another, "I'm still a little overwhelmed by all of this. How could you even return? Why aren't you still there?"

Zerafine smiled. Her heart felt whisper-light. "I told you, you're not going to believe what happened," she said. "You'll want to sit down." Nestled into his lap — the thin silk of her tunic gave her no protection against the chilly marble of the floor — she poured out the whole story. He held his breath when she told him of her judgment, gave a short bark of laughter when she described Atenas bowing before Kalindi, then sat silent when she was finished.

"So if any of the other gods die, they'll be able to find their own way to Atenas's courts," he finally said.

She leaned her cheek against his chest. "Yes. No human intervention necessary."

"And you stood in judgment in Atenas's court and changed a thousand-year-old oath sworn by a god."

"That's the part that leaves me breathless with wonder. Atenas deferred judgment to *me*. Who else in all of history can say that? I can't tell you how humbling it was."

Gerrard said, in a quiet voice, "I don't know if I'm worthy of you anymore."

Her head snapped up, and she was halfway to an outraged protest when she saw his mouth quiver with a suppressed smile. "You — you are just — " Their conversation paused for a moment in favor of more pleasant activities involving lips and tongues and hands.

Later, Gerrard said, "And Atenas and Kalindi...."

"Are in love. Or whatever it is gods have in its place. It was — shocking, actually."

"It could shake the foundations of two faiths. Are you going to tell anyone?"

"I don't think anyone will believe it. And, really, what would it change? But yes, I'm going to tell the *Marathelos* and ask his advice. And then I'm going to tell Arland and watch his eyes pop out of his head."

Gerrard laughed. "I was going to say that would be cruel," he said, "but it occurred to me that you'd give him a whole new field of study and he would love you forever."

Zerafine laid her head on Gerrard's shoulder. "Just so long as *you* love me forever," she said.

He slid his thumb along her cheekbone. "Forever and past forever." His hand fell to her lap. "What happens now?"

Zerafine thought about it. "First thing is to resurrect me," she said. "That's going to be interesting. I hope I don't give people as much of a shock as I gave you. Did Berenica already send word to Atenar?"

"I don't think so. It's been a harrowing two days."

"That's something, anyway. Then the next thing we do is have Berenica marry us. I think I can say with some certainty that Atenas will accept our oath."

"You're amazingly confident that I'll accept your proposal. What was your backup plan?"

"I was going to tempt you with my body, but you'd probably settle for a good dinner." She squealed with delighted laughter as her *sentare* tickled her, then kissed her again, slow and sweet, like a promise.

"I'm going to take that as a 'yes'," she said, a little breathlessly. "After that...I guess we get back on the road. Visit Atenar, and then move on."

Gerrard gave her a serious look. "Zerafine, you went to Atenas's courts and returned. You can't expect to go back to being an ordinary traveling *thelis*."

"Why not? What should I do instead?"

Gerrard frowned, caught without a ready answer. "It just seems like you've done something so big that you'll never be able to top it. How can you go back to traveling the roads and consoling those little ghosts and sitting in judgment in tiny towns that barely appreciate you?"

"You mean, will it satisfy me? Yes, Gerrard, a thousand times yes. Atenas chose me because I only did what I always do. Are those little ghosts any less worthy of peace than a god? And now that I know what it's like on the other side...how can I turn aside from that path?"

Gerrard blew out his breath. "What a relief," he said. "I was afraid you were going to ask me to give up the staff and settle down somewhere. I love you, but I'm not ready for that."

"Neither am I." She pushed herself up and gave Gerrard her hand, a token gesture because she could never have pulled his weight up by herself. "Shall we see if we can frighten Berenica?"

He laughed, and led her from the shrine into the golden sunlight.

Glossary and Pronunciation Guide

Aesoron: AY-so-ron

Akelliou: ah-KEL-ee-oh

Alestiou: ah-LES-tee-oh

Alita: ah-LEE-tah

Berenica: ber-EN-ih-cah

Castinidou: cas-TIN-ah-doh

Dakariou: dah-KAR-ee-oh

Gerrard: ger-RARD

Gordou: GOR-doh

Marathelos/thelis: Archpriest or -priestess, chief representative of a god; MAR-a-thee-los

Morica: MOR-ih-cah

Nacalia: nah-CAH-lee-ah

seicorum: ore manufactured by an unquiet ghost; say-COR-um

sentare: bodyguard of the *theloi* of Atenas; sen-TAH-ray

Talarannos: tal-ah-RAN-os

thelis/thelos/theloi: priest; THEE-lis, THEE-los, THEE-loi ('th' as in 'think')

tokthelos/thelis: high priest or priestess, leader of a community of *theloi*; TOK-thee-los

Yelenita: yel-eh-NEE-tah

Zerafine: ZAIR-ah-FEEN

The Pantheon

The gods of the Pantheon represent dualities and therefore come in pairs. Most believe these pairs have a good and an evil god, but it is more accurate to say they represent balance between forces.

Kalindi, Goddess of the sun: chief god of the Pantheon. The divine healer. Symbol: sun, circle

Kandra, Goddess of moon: goddess of fertility and thieves, among other things. Symbols: star, moon

Hanu, God of the sea and sky: responsible for the bounty of the earth. Symbol: upward-pointing triangle

Kanu, God of storms: destructive side of his twin brother (they are identical, and the myth is that you don't know which you're dealing with until it's too late). Symbol: downward-pointing triangle

Sintha, Goddess of luck: represents good things unlooked for. Symbols: linked squares (idealized dice)

Ventus, God of fate: represents the uncaring whim of luck gone bad. Symbol: the blind eye

Ormus, God of travel and change. Symbol: crossed sticks or X

Arieta, Goddess of the hearth: worshipped by those who care for the household (male or female). Symbol: the circled square (the home surrounded by a sphere of protection)

Endelion, God of the forge: represents fire controlled for man's use. Symbol: hammer

Ailausa, Goddess of fire: represents fire untamed. Closest to a god of destruction this Pantheon has. Symbol: curved teardrop shape (stylized flame)

Marenda, Goddess of creativity and the arts. Symbol: U (vessel to be filled) balanced in M (symbol of humanity)

Sukman, God of madness: represents creativity that absorbs and destroys the artist, the mind gone wrong. Symbol: spiral

Atenas, God of Death: He alone in the Pantheon has no twin counterpart. He is depicted in red cowl and robes with His face hidden. He is prayed to by everyone at some time, mostly in entreaty that He will pass them by. His Priests dress like him; they are called on to ease the pain of the dying (Atenas's blessing), banish ghosts, and act as impartial judges because they cannot lie. They are often asked to predict when someone will die and always refuse to do so. They also try to teach people that Death is a part of life, to counter the perception of their god being frightening or evil. No symbol; death is everywhere.

ABOUT THE AUTHOR

Melissa McShane lives in the shelter of the mountains out West with her husband, four children, and three very needy cats. She wrote reviews and critical essays for many years before turning to fiction, which is much more fun than anyone ought to be allowed to have. You can visit her at her website www.mmcshane.com for more information on upcoming releases.

www.ingramcontent.com/pod-product-compliance
Lightning Source LLC
Chambersburg PA
CBHW051436170626
46809CB00006B/2496